W9-AAI-552

THE OTHER SIDE

"I WAS ENTHRALLED. MAGGIE IS SENSUAL, SENSI-
TIVE, INTELLIGENT, UTTERLY FEMININE—AND
AFRAID SHE IS GOING MAD. A GRIPPING, SCARY
STORY, THE BEST HORROR STORY I HAVE EVER
READ.
—Robert Daley,
author of *Prince of the City*

THE OTHER SIDE

"A ROLLER COASTER RIDE TO TERROR!"
—Michael Palmer,
author of *The Sisterhood*

THE OTHER SIDE

"WE ALL HAVE MOMENTS OF SHEER TERROR,
MOMENTS WHEN WE DOUBT WHAT WE *KNOW*
WE ARE SEEING. AS I READ *THE OTHER SIDE*
EACH OF THOSE MOMENTS CAME CHILLINGLY
BACK TO ME."
—John Saul

Now, turn the page for a frightening glimpse of . . .

THE OTHER SIDE

IT WAS IN THE BARN THAT SHE
FINALLY FOUND HER SON. . . .

"Mommy!" he burst out of the straw and scrambled toward her, flinging himself so fiercely into her arms that they rolled in the straw, the dust.

"Oh, Jebbie, are you all right?" The puffs of his rapid breathing stirred her hair and she knew his face was slick with tears.

"Who were you talking to, Jeb?"

He stiffened and held on to her so tightly that it hurt. Against her shoulder she could feel his thudding heart like a trapped bird.

"Who, Jebbie? I heard you whispering to someone."

He wailed, "I didn't do it. Didn't."

"What, the whispering?"

"No!"

"But the torn clothes in my closet? My hand?"

"Didn't!" he cried.

"I don't understand, Jebbie," she said softly. "I was there. I saw you. You stuck the scissors into my hand. You and nobody else, Jeb."

The tears gushed from his luminous eyes, sliding along his downy cheeks.

"Not me, Mommy, not *me*!" Jebbie howled as though he were being split in half. . . .

THE OTHER SIDE

The Other Side

Diana Henstell

BANTAM BOOKS

TORONTO · NEW YORK · LONDON · SYDNEY

THE OTHER SIDE

A Bantam Book / February 1984

The last two lines of the poem "Siege" and the last two lines of the sonnet "Pity me not because the light of day" by Edna St. Vincent Millay on page 49 from *Collected Poems*, Harper & Row. Copyright 1923, 1951 by Edna St. Vincent Millay and Norma Millay Ellis.

ISBN 0-553-23638-0

Published simultaneously in the United States and Canada

Bantam Books are published by Bantam Books, Inc. Its trademark, consisting of the words "Bantam Books" and the portrayal of a rooster, is Registered in U.S. Patent and Trademark Office and in other countries. Marca Registrada. Bantam Books, Inc., 666 Fifth Avenue, New York, New York 10103.

PRINTED IN THE UNITED STATES OF AMERICA

H   0 9 8 7 6 5 4 3 2

DEDICATED TO
my father, Philip Henstell, M.D.
with love, admiration, and gratitude

Special thanks to my editor Linda Grey and my agent Jane Rotrosen Berkey without whose active encouragement, support, and insights I couldn't have done it. Also, loving thanks to my son, Joshua, who inspired me, and to my daughter, Abigail, who—as she always does—sustained me.

The Other Side

Prologue

A thin curl of smoke, fine, like a baby's hair, coiled and twisted, undulated slowly up the mirror. It swayed softly against the glass, clung to it, lightly caressing it. For the longest moment it hesitated as though it had a mind of its own, then fanned up quickly, a curtain rising.

Maggie stirred restlessly in sleep, the reluctant captive of fading, shimmering dreams. Alone in the big bed she searched unconsciously for David, her hand groping beneath the sheet and blanket, tracking across the cool surface of the pillow. Suddenly she shuddered, falling through space, the empty space of sleep, and sat up abruptly.

"David?" she called, rubbing her fists against her eyes.

Outside, a chill wind blew across the naked treetops of Central Park, splaying light rain and rattling the windows in their frames.

"David?"

Then she remembered: David wasn't there. He had gone off—where? Yes, Boulder—a contract, a merger, a legal something that couldn't wait. Or was that last month? Phoenix? Cleveland? Her thoughts were cloudy; her head so heavy it might break off the stalk of her neck. But she tried to remember as the interchangeable cities rushed through her mind like leaves in the wind.

Chilled with loneliness, she hugged herself and shuffled through the montage of images that had brought her up from sleep, but already the outer edges were burning away in the pale streetlight that filtered through the windows. And then, propped up against the headboard, her knees to her chest, she thought she smelled smoke, faint and acrid, as though a cigarette had been left to smolder in a refuse-filled ashtray. But only David smoked, and David wasn't there. David was in a hotel room in a city whose name she wasn't certain of.

I'm imagining things, she decided, thinking how David always claimed she had the most vivid, technicolor fantasies. Always crafting something out of nothing, like an alchemist with base elements. She lay down and rolled over on her side, and lying in the dark, she stared out the uncurtained windows at the thin rivulets of water tracing intricate arteries on the glass. But lying down, she became aware that the smell of smoke was stronger, real now and not a fragment of the dream that had shimmered and broken.

She threw back the covers and moved quietly out into the hall and saw in the mirror—the mirror on the foyer wall, the mirror six feet from top to bottom, ornate with its heavy, gilded frame—the winding, twisting, dancing smoke. It was a very old mirror, in Maggie's family since her grandparents' time, and had hung for years in the old summer place, even though her mother and grandmother were unreasonably disposed against it. Certainly it was ugly with its entwining vine leaves and anonymous flowers and a snake whose scales were delicately carved. At either side blind cupids wept in sorrow. Only Maggie found it so monstrous as to have charm.

It glittered with an unholy shine, angled toward the back hall, and eerily reflected the swirling dervishes of smoke.

Maggie screamed and ran along the hall into the smoke clinging like ground fog, swallowing her feet, her knees, stroking the smooth insides of her thighs. There was a fire blazing at the back of the apartment behind the closed doors where her children slept. She could hear its obscene crackling like dry twigs snapping underfoot as she ran, her bare feet stumbling, sliding on the polished, hardwood floor. And the sound bounced loose, came untethered in her head as she felt the heat through the doors, felt it beating its fiery wings at the other end of the apartment like a trapped beast. It howled in its fury to break free, to eat its way through the heavy doors and consume her.

The worst of it seemed to be in the girls' room, the farthest room back, but she couldn't tell. She was dizzy with the smoke, coughing and choking, shrouded in the white swirling maze.

"Wake up! Wake up!" She pounded on the door, the wood hot to the touch, and slapped the flat of her hand against it, then curled her fist and beat until the skin cracked.

But the door was solid, and the knob—stinging, searing—wouldn't turn. Maggie wept with the pain, then kicked at the door, as though it was animate, as though it had feeling.

"Tracy! Kathy! Please—Oh, please—!" Maggie shouted, feet and fists assaulting the smoldering wood, her whole body a battering ram against the immobile door.

"Mommy... help... Mommy...."

She could imagine the two little girls entwined in their bedsheets, flailing at the smoke as they screamed out to her, the heat scorching the membranes of their throats, sealing the breath in their bodies. She could almost feel the iron bands tightening about their chests as the flames slowly danced from the curtains to the carpet, ate through the doll house and incinerated its minute occupants, raced across the shelves of books curling the pages, licked up the furry flanks of stuffed animals sleeping at the bottom of each twin bed, and greedily swallowed the dragging sheets as they trailed the floor until one horrendous wave of fire battered the room like a tidal wave.

Their awful cries rang in Maggie's ears: "Mommy . . . help . . . Mommy"—then the screams, like sharp knives in her brain. In panic she rushed for Jeb's room, throwing herself in a frenzy against the door that, ajar, sprang open. She fell from the force of her terror and crawled like a wounded animal across the carpet on her hands and knees.

The smoke was everywhere. It was impossible to see; enveloped in a whiteness as thick as cotton. Her eyes burned, tears cascaded down her cheeks. Accidentally, she crashed headfirst into Jeb's bed, and without thinking, by instinct, she reached up and yanked at him, pulling him still sleeping to the floor.

"Jeb! Jebbie, get up." She shook him, his body loose as feathers in her hands. "Hurry! A fire . . . your sisters. . . ."

The whole hall was dancing in flames, streams of fire racing maniacally up the walls, curling the paper, eating into the wood. The heat singed the hairs on her arms and pushing, shoving the four-year-old dead weight in her arms, she outran the fire as it reached out trying to snare the edge of her nightgown.

Somehow Maggie reached the foyer, a wild woman against the glass of the mirror, her hair electric with fright, streaks of soot painted on her cheekbones. She tugged at the chains and bolts of the apartment door, the fire door of heavy steel.

Jeb hung clutched against her breasts, his body pressed into hers, his body once again part of hers. He struggled to bury himself in her flesh.

He opened his mouth to squawl like a baby, to cry as he hadn't done for a long, long time, but there was someone watching. Someone could see him. Someone was looking back. Jiggling frantically in his mother's arms now, his mouth wide with an incipient shriek of terror, he saw the boy.

In his fright, Jeb could only barely grasp the resemblance. He knew him... him.... Yes, himself. It was himself in the mirror just opposite, his face peering wide-eyed over his mother's shoulder. He was looking at himself in the mirror, not another but him, with the same blond hair and the identical candy-striped pajamas. Only something was wrong with himself, wasn't as Jeb knew instinctively even in his terror *he* should be.

He, Jeb, stunned with panic, choking from the smoke, about to howl until he lost whatever clear breath remained in his lungs, was staring at himself and back at himself, only one of them was smiling, and one of them wasn't in his own front hall in his mother's arms, but somewhere else, somewhere *he* had never seen before. Himself was in another place with little pink flowers on the wall and dark carpeting and no smoke... waiting. He was waiting with outstretched hands there, in that different place, for Jeb.

All at once the door miraculously sprang open, and they raced into the hall with a rush, into the air, which they gulped until their ears rang.

"Mommy...."

Maggie was screaming, incoherent, pounding at the elevator door, yelling into the emptiness below for someone, anyone.

"The girls! Oh my God, the girls. Please someone, help... the girls... the girls back there... being eaten alive... the girls!"

Jeb's arms were locked around her neck, his legs had her waist in a death grip, strangling the air from her lungs. Maggie dug her nails into his skin, trying to dislodge him as his voice shrilled without words in her ear, his breath hot as the fire against her neck.

She had to get back, had to plunge into the smoke again, throw herself against the wall of fire. "Let go!" she cried, and with more force than she knew she had, she pulled him away. He fell to the floor, curled in on himself and shrilled his unending shriek as Maggie raced for the outer door, for the girls, for her babies, her daughters, whose pitiful cries she could hear over the whooshing of the flames, flying like the fire itself through her veins.

"Mommmmmmmmmmmiiieeee . . ."

And as she reached out for the door, had it within an inch of her outstretched fingertips, could almost feel its hot, slippery metal, could imagine now and forever the push to swing it inward, it finally and for always, closed shut with a terrible slam.

1

"Are you sure she's ready to come home?" David Brace asked.

Jack Klein shrugged, tapped his pipe against the already overflowing ashtray on his cluttered desk, and smiled to himself. For better or worse, he thought, there always comes this particular moment. The moment of panic, was what he privately called it, when the healthy question if the once sick are sick no longer. It was, he knew, natural, and arose from fear.

He looked across the big, sunny room from which he could see the gardens of Greenwood, and the white-jacketed attendants shepherding their charges like ghostly dancers. If it weren't a matter of uniforms and a wild array of "civilian" dress, one would have a difficult time distinguishing the keepers from the kept. The problem was that "abnormal" often—no, he thought, most times—appeared frighteningly normal. Which brought him full circle to David Brace's question.

"If you're asking whether Maggie is well, the answer is yes, as well, possibly, as she's ever going to be."

"What does that mean, Dr. Klein?" Jack heard the sharp note in the other man's voice and saw the flash of annoyance skitter across his face. Once again he regretted the husband's refusal to seek treatment with his wife. Not that Maggie had much choice. She had totally collapsed, gone out of her mind as the world would put it, with grief and

17

guilt. The latter, Klein thought, in no small measure because her husband thought her guilty, of stupidity and of neglect. Right or wrong it had made it more difficult to put back the shattered pieces of Maggie Brace.

"Maggie," he snapped down emphatically on his pipe stem, "is fine."

"But what does fine mean in the real world?"

David Brace was by every definition, a successful man. Not wealthy but well-to-do, a shade over comfortable. A corporate lawyer from a Main Line Philadelphia family who'd had the security of Choate and Princeton behind him before he made his own very distinct mark on the world, David had the arrogance that came from a worldly strength and an inner sense of certainty, a way of viewing the world that left no corner for ambiguities. Logic. Black and white. He was as precise as a computer. Even his occasional flashes of humor seemed more intentional than spontaneous. No chance he'd ever slip, or question his perceptions, Klein thought. So how can I explain to him what it really means to return from nether land of insanity?

And Maggie had been mad, hurtling through space, wrecked and broken, like a car that had been totaled in a crash. To come back had taken hard work, an act of faith, and some current live and strong that Maggie Brace had never let go of even in the midst of her despair.

"I'm very proud of Maggie, David, and you should be too. Many other women—men also—would never have recovered from such a tragedy. She's tough, your wife, with a great well of inner strength. But if you're asking, 'Is she one hundred percent better, guaranteed?'—exactly, in other words, as she was before the fire—the answer is no. She's gone into a darkness you can't understand, and I can only vaguely imagine; and she has returned, willingly I grant you, but she'll never forget that the darkness is there and that for a long time she was lost in it."

He could see that David was annoyed with his meta-phor. He sighed. "I told you before, she'll have to contin-ue her twice weekly sessions with me. A maintenance program. Reinforcement. And she'll be nervous, worried, ill at ease sometimes. Maybe even frightened. She might continue dreaming of the fire from time to time, though I doubt it. But I'm certain she's heard the last of the voices, your daughters' voices screaming for her. All in all, Maggie will take a great deal of understanding, patience, and nurturing." Klein paused. "And love, David." He could see the way David stiffened and, even this far away, how the pulse in his temple spasmed.

"I see." David turned his back to stare out the window. Klein wondered if he saw at all. He hoped he did, and hoped he had some compassion. But he was afraid that David Brace saw what he wanted to see, prescribed reality to fit his own inner workings.

"What about Jeb?" David asked, turning back to face Klein, his unsmiling face creased for the first time with true concern. There was no question that he cared for his son and—Klein guessed with no evidence but instinct bred from long years of observation—for his wife.

"What about him?"

"He hasn't seen Maggie in over a year. He's even stopped asking for her. And when I told him she was coming home today, he didn't seem to care particularly. He's changed."

"That, David, is your fault." Klein drummed his fingers on the desk with impatience. "I suggested repeatedly, and Maggie begged these last few months, that you bring Jeb here to see her."

"I told you I wouldn't bring my son to an asylum!" David said with real distress. "It was out of the question. You just don't take a child to a place like this; you protect him all you can. You give him the normal, not the sick."

"Greenwood isn't an asylum; it's a sanatorium, and if that continues to be your attitude, there might be more problems ahead for Maggie than either of us can foresee." The sanctimonious bastard, Klein thought, with an anger he could just barely control, and decided finally, after all these months, that he didn't really like David Brace much. That admission lifted a weight from his mind, and he could smile. Thinking, Klein, you old phony—though he wasn't old or phony—he said, "Ah, David, com'on." He slid into his ingratiating, little-boy routine, which complemented the boyish face beneath shocks of curly gray hair. "Maggie's going home with you, and she's okay, she truly is. And everything is going to be fine. You just wait and see if it isn't."

Maggie shifted nervously on the straight-backed chair in the visitors' lounge and hoped she wasn't wrinkling the gaily patterned red dress that David had brought her to wear home. Her palms were wet, and she could feel pools of sweat gathering beneath her arms and sliding in thin trickles down her ribs. Even though it was cool for early June, she was too warm. Since the fire, she seemed to flare with a hot flush more often than not, as though the flames were still inside, beating their way out through the pores of her skin. But she couldn't say that to Klein, who would never believe she wasn't mad if she said there was a conflagration gnawing her liver, her stomach, her heart and shooting its way along her arteries and veins. So she asked instead, midlife crisis? And he had laughed, pointing out that she was only thirty-four, young still. That got them off on another track, though not one that was much less dangerous, because she thought he meant young enough to have another child. No, he said afterward, not that, but young enough just to enjoy life and not give up—as she had given up, up and over into the darkness of her mind where she free fell until Klein had coaxed her back to firm ground.

What were they talking about?

You, dummy, what do you think?

They were talking about Maggie, the crazy lady who had let her daughters go up in smoke. No, she forced herself to intone like a litany, it was an accident, and even if the door hadn't slammed, I would never have gotten through the flames to save them. I would have died for them. And I did save Jebbie. I did ... I *did* ... synchronized to the beating of her heart.

Jebbie, her baby, her littlest, now her only. She hadn't seen him for thirteen months, one week, and three days. She had counted off the time one long afternoon when she was finally able to think of her children without anxiety and fear and guilt and the deluge of tears that threatened to drown her. He must be so much bigger now, six years old two weeks ago. Maggie had wanted to be home for his birthday, but for some reason Klein had not been ready to let her go. Or was it David? Did David really want her home? Maggie was as frightened of being alone with David as she was of seeing Jeb.

What did David and she have to say to one another now? And how could they knit together the unraveled ends of their life that she had let come undone? She tried to fantasize what it was all going to be, but could only envision David's face, looming over her accusingly.

Too much ... too much. . . .

She was shaking her head from side to side. The long, reddish brown hair stroked her cheekbones and curled about her neck. One of the day nurses peered into the room at her.

Careful, Maggie, careful. Catching the woman's eye, she smiled broadly, and the nurse, a blank but sympathetic portrait in white, nodded back.

Don't twitch, don't turn, don't do anything suspicious, anything to make them think you're different from them.

Maggie knew she had to appear more normal than normal. Act conservatively, think Republican, be polite, and crook her little finger when she drank her tea. None of which was all that difficult, she knew, since she had never been adventurous; imaginative, maybe, but not someone you'd pick out of a crowd.

But Maggie underestimated how others saw her. To even the most casual observer she was simply beautiful. There wasn't another word adequate for her tall, lanky good looks. Smoky-green eyes set wide apart in an oval face with pale, china doll skin. A straight nose that barely tilted at the end and a wide mouth that seemed shaped for laughter.

Only Maggie didn't laugh much these days, though she had promised Klein and promised herself that that would change.

She had made other promises too, had promised to pick up the dropped strands of her life, and her marriage, as though these were Steuben glasses dropped and shattered, now repaired with only fine, delicate cracks. She had promised she *was* going to be a good wife to David and a good mother to Jeb.

She seemed so vulnerable sitting there, Klein thought protectively, as he and David saw her framed through the doorway, like a Vermeer caught in that moment of repose. Though Klein knew she wasn't resting, was uneasy as hell with the sands of anxiety shifting and sliding in her mind, threatening, always threatening, to tilt her off balance.

Maggie sat up straighter when she saw them and made all those patting, touching motions that women do when they're nervous, and finally rose to her feet. But she didn't move any closer to David, waiting for her husband to go to her. Which he did, with only the briefest hesitation, and bent down, his hand on her shoulder, and brushed her upturned cheek with his lips.

They were, Klein approved, a handsome couple. David dark and brooding, almost Byronic, which shows how little looks really mean, Klein thought, since there wasn't a trace of anything poetic or romantic in his makeup. There wasn't, as far as Klein had been able to discern, a single soft spot in David Brace's armor. He was tough and analytical. He would certainly have gotten his daughters out of the fire; no way, would he have allowed any door to slam shut behind him. And if, after all, he too had lost them, he definitely would have pulled up his socks and gone on about his life without ever looking back.

How had Maggie gotten on with him; how would she fare with him now?

"Are you ready?" David asked.

"Yes. My bag's out by the front desk."

"All right, then let's go," he said taking her arm. She might have been a stranger, or an aged relative to be shepherded, protected.

"Do you have your prescription, Maggie?" Klein asked, walking beside them down the long hall to the front of the building.

"In my pocketbook."

"Don't forget, one three times a day with meals and one at bedtime."

"No, I won't forget. And I'll be here every Monday and Thursday at one o'clock," she said, smiling, trying not to look as afraid as she felt so that Klein would have no regrets about letting her go, no second thoughts.

When they left, Klein stood on the front steps and watched them drive off in David's Mercedes, feeling a shade bereft, for like many of the nurses and doctors he was fond of Maggie, touched by her beauty, saddened by her tragedy, and perhaps just a little in love with her.

Dear God, he said to himself, crossing his fingers though he believed in neither God nor luck, let her make it, don't let anything more go wrong for her.

2

They had little to say on the way home: a few desultory sentences that began and ended nowhere, safe comments about the weather, the scenery. Not quite strangers, but less than friends. No one would have suspected that they were married. They had lost that aura of intimacy husbands and wives have, even when they sit in silence and stare off into space like goldfish in a tank.

Maggie was anxious, churning inside with a sour swirling that brought bile up to her mouth and left a ringing in her ears. She had admitted to no one—not Klein, certainly not David, and not even herself—that the world "inside" had come to be more familiar, more reassuring and unthreatening than the world "outside." "Outside" was where she had to face things—not only the treacherous eddies of her own shaky mind, but responsibilities, and people, and flaring uncertainties like fire.

"Do you want the radio on?"

"No . . . no, it's fine like this."

He hadn't looked at her once since he'd come to get her, his awareness of her sliding over her like water on glass. Maggie wanted to scream so that David would be forced to see, to look at her directly and . . . and then what?

What would I do if he stared right into my eyes and saw down the long chute to where something, possibly madness, sits uneasily, and I don't want that.

"David?"

"Yes?"

"Nothing," she said, and watched the Connecticut turnpike streak by like a travelogue on high speed.

She didn't know what to say to him, nor, she suspected, did he know what to say to her. Her mind flinched from the memory of that terrible moment when he'd faced her across the hospital waiting room and howled with anger. And with pain? Did he hurt anywhere from what had happened? *Not like me. David doesn't hurt like me, but then I don't hurt like anyone else. I went out of my mind, left the whole damned inside of my skull vacant because I couldn't come to terms with reality.*

"Do you want me to turn the air conditioning off?"

"No, why?" she asked.

"You're shaking."

She couldn't say it was nerves. Crazy people—or rather reformed crazy people—weren't supposed to have nerves. They had to be models of strength and appear more sane than the sane. Never anxious, always serene; occasionally annoyed, but never, never angry; and not given to fantasies or wild imaginings like seeing the tortured face of a child in the dark cloud that floated just ahead.

"Well, maybe it is a little chilly," she said, and clasped her quivering hands together in her lap.

David reached down and turned the blower to low, then settled back as the Mercedes glided over the miles of highway. Maggie could hear the tires singing and tried to think of Jeb and home.

Home. How funny that Four Oaks was now home. She hadn't been there since the summer she was fifteen, when her parents had decided that they were bored, and had abandoned Connecticut for the Cape. But they had never sold the house, only rented it out, to other summer strangers. Four Oaks had been in Maggie's family much too long to ever let it go completely. After her parents' deaths, David had suggested putting it on the market, but Maggie, too, had been hesitant about giving it up.

"Why did you decide to come to Four Oaks, David?" she asked, realizing suddenly that she'd never asked before. "Why didn't you stay with Jebbie in the city?"

"It seemed the right thing to do at the time," he said sharply. "I mean," he softened his voice, "I wanted a complete change for both of us, Jeb and me. Besides, it's not all that far from Greenwood."

In case I go off again and dance across the lawn in my nightgown, chasing fireflies. Easier to call Klein and have him come and get me with his butterfly net.

They pulled off at exit seven, down the ramp, and right for four miles into Brighton.

"Brighton's so far for you to drive every day," she said.

He shrugged. "It's not too bad. Only a fraction over an hour door to door. I try to avoid the peak traffic times."

Route Nine went right through the heart of Brighton, with its village green, white steepled Presbyterian church, and Hogan's Inn whose dining room rated three stars in every travel guide. It was such a pretty little town, such a classic picture-postcard scene, that it made Maggie ache. It couldn't be real, but it was, and it hadn't obviously changed, except that there was a boutique where the five and dime used to be, a bookstore on the corner of Main, and a lot of cars. An outdoor cafe squatted where Main turned into Elm and Route Nine continued, and yes, she saw there was now a pizza shop just next to the gas station. Jeb would be pleased about that.

Jeb. Would he remember her? Would she, when it came to that, remember him? She had missed his entire fifth year. Six-year-olds were completely different from four-year-olds. And even though in the pictures David brought her from time to time, he looked the same, Maggie was as frightened of Jeb as she was of David. But what, she wondered, was she frightened of, or whom? And whom did she trust now with more than ragged wariness, except Klein? Klein she thought of as a hand dangling over the abyss, a hand that had pulled her, kicking and screaming to safety, out of the gaping maw that had almost engulfed her. Klein believed her.

David twisted and turned off the main road and into a series of secondary arteries that only a native would know. Maggie was sure, however, that even now, so many years since she had done it, she could maneuver the turns with her eyes closed, until they came to the mailbox. The same mailbox. And then they veered left and went down the dirt road for a quarter of a mile until suddenly Four Oaks appeared.

The house, buttressed by four towering oaks, seemed a compilation of children's blocks. It jutted, thrust, and lurched, and in its towering ugliness acquired a rather sedate imperiousness, as though it realized in the very fiber of its porches and doors and window frames that it was—due to the haphazard additions slapped on its flesh over the years—unique. In spite of white paint and bright green shutters, it was forbidding. The trees in the foreground threw a pall over it, turning its sheen gray, as though it had been rinsed with dirty water. Behind it, the woods encroached. Maggie hadn't remembered it so dark and haunting looking.

"Well," David said, circling to the left and pulling the Mercedes into the garage, "here we are." For the first time Maggie heard a note of uneasiness in his voice. She stared at him in surprise and before she realized what she was doing, she reached out and took his hand.

David tried to keep his face impassive, clenched his teeth to stop the involuntary spasm of his lower lip—a sign since childhood that he wasn't under his usual rigid control— and ordered his thoughts to cease swirling frantically like leaves in the wind. But he wasn't ready for this: the upturned face that he had loved for such a very long time, and that was now so filled with pleading. No, he wasn't ready at all. He had hoped that Klein would keep her just a little longer so that he could come to terms with the myriad emotions—love, hate, resentment, disappointment, fear—which he felt for Maggie. She was the same and yet a stranger, and he couldn't say with any certainty where she'd fit back into his scheme of things, into the fabric of his life out of which she had cut a wide and jagged hole, if she would fit back in at all.

She tightened her grip on his hand, holding onto him for dear life, and he stifled his resentment as he pulled her toward him, encircling her with his arms.

"Don't be nervous," he said, and yet was anxious himself. He stroked her hair, and thought of making love to her, not sure if he wanted to. The desire was there, but her fragility frightened him. What if she broke apart under his hands?

"I'm scared," she said; "it's been so long."

He had that wonderful freshly ironed smell, and with her cheek against the smoothness of his shirt she could hear his heart. In the silence she could rest in his arms forever, even with Jeb out there waiting. It was the first time in all these months that David had really touched her except for the most perfunctory brush of lips to cheeks or hand to arm.

She nestled closer to him, burying herself against him and thought: I'm home . . . all right . . . safe. . . .

The air buzzed. If you listened carefully, you could hear crickets rubbing their legs, one against the other, ants scruffing in the dirt as they hurried in and out of the hills, leaves that crackled as their branches swung ominously. And, if you tried very, very hard you could even hear the slight snap of wings as the birds flew high overhead in the clouds. There was a lot to hear and see if you were patient, if you held your breath—not until your ears sang, but just till that moment before—and then let it out so slowly it didn't even flutter the blades of grass just in front of your mouth. That was the trick—the waiting. Jeb hadn't always known anything could happen if he just let it. Like the beetle. If he hadn't been still as dead, it would have run off. But the silly thing didn't even know Jeb was there, waiting for it, like the sky waited for the moon to come up. It was going to walk right up to his nose, right up his nose, dumb beetle that it was.

It was a good-sized beetle, with a hard, reddish-brown shell, and it zipped across the grass like a wind-up toy. Bigger than his thumb. Did it have legs like the caterpillar in his catching jar, legs he had pulled off one by one before he enclosed the bug and waited with a shiver for it to die? The question was, should he pop the bottle down over it, then scoop it up and clamp a lid on top and pour rubbing alcohol through the slit his knife had made and watch it drown? Or should he light a twist of paper and drop it in the jar and watch the beetle burn? The last time he had done that, it popped. This beetle was bigger. A bigger pop.

He angled the jar, and the stupid beetle walked right inside like a guest coming to dinner. He didn't even have to swoop at it and pounce. As he tipped over the jar, the insect slid to the bottom, its feet frantically working on the glass for a grip. It tumbled over and over and landed on its shell. Yes, there were tiny little legs, pedaling back and forth, as if the bug thought it could walk on air. The match it was. Anything that stupid deserved to pop like a fire-cracker going off.

Jeb jiggled the jar sideways; the beetle flipped over, and finding itself right side up, stood still, but then paddled round and round in a circle, bumping its blunt little pin-sized head against the sides. Close up, eyeball to eyeball, it was an ugly thing.

Ugly thing... ugly things should die.

Do beetles hurt? Do caterpillars? Do butterflies when their wings are pulled off and pins are stuck through their middles? And flies when they turn to ash?

Frogs must when their legs and arms are cut away and they bleed and make that funny noise, not quite like a croak but not a scream either. Frogs are the best, and after that, beetles when they pop.

This one was just ready. The little bit of newspaper, twisted and curled just right, its end set flaming with a match, was thrust into the jar. The beetle ran like hell was after it, but the fire outraced it. The flame blew up the paper and brought it down on the hard shell that turned yellow and orange and red... and POP. And all the insides were swallowed up, the shell too.

The light dimmed. A gray curtain fell across the lattice, throwing the secret place into shadow. Jeb looked up and saw a face, crisscrossed by the strips of wood. An eye here, half an eye there. No nose really. A red mouth smiling. There was warm breath bubbling out of that. He could feel it through the open spaces.

"Jeb, Jebbie... it's me."

He scuttled backwards toward the darkness and the underbelly of the house. He could go far until he hit solid wood that went down and became, inside, the basement. The way into that was the sloping cellar door and the steps going down, but that was all in the back, at the other side. Still, he could go far enough in so she couldn't see him, or see only the vaguest outlines of him.

"Honey, com'on out."

"Jeb, you come out of there this minute." That was the

Daddy person and his was a different voice, was louder, harsher than the Mommy person.

He knew all right it was the Mommy person, and knew he had to get away from her. The opening through the lattice to the secret place was at the other side of the porch behind the trellis with its climbing roses. They didn't know it was there, that slight gap where the wooden frame had cracked and could be pushed aside. He crawled crablike along the base of the house, away from the voices and the Mommy person. He wasn't sure why he wanted to escape her, to get away, but he had to. Besides, it was time. He had been outside a long time now, too long.

"Jebbie, where are you?"

They had lost him in the shadows. Their voices grew fainter. He crawled as fast as he could, the light at the other end just ahead.

"Where did he go?"

"I don't know. Just leave him alone. He'll be out soon enough."

Just then he reached the far side and hooked his fingers into the lattice and pushed. It sprang free and he scrambled through the slight gap. He couldn't quite catch his breath, great sobs welling up in his throat. He wasn't scared, no, never that. He didn't know how to be scared except at make believe. But he had to hurry, there wasn't much time. It seemed so dark out, even though he was standing in full sunlight.

Hurry . . . hurry. . . .

He could still hear them as he ran for the back door, bolted inside and stumbled into *her*. He didn't like *her* at all, especially now as she grabbed him by the arms and said, "Just a minute, young man, where are you making off to? And covered with dirt, too!"

"Let go!" He shoved her away, her fat stomach yielding and soft as dough. Her lips parted in surprise. He broke free and ran down the hall just as there was the sound of feet on the back porch, only a second before the screen opened and then glided shut with the slight wheeze it always gave when it wasn't pushed hard enough.

"This is Sarah," David said, ushering Maggie into the kitchen, "we couldn't get along without her."

Yes, Sarah. David had told her about Sarah, about being lucky to find her, to get her to come up from Norwalk where her last job had been. Sarah was wonderful—yes, she remembered, Sarah was wonderful—and she kept them all together. Would she keep Maggie together too?

But right now she couldn't concentrate on *that;* she only wanted Jeb. Where was he, her baby, her Jebbie with his smiling face like a flower upturned to the sun? Her child, her perfect child. Maggie hurt from wanting to put her arms around her son.

Turning her back on the heavyset, older woman dressed in white—too much like a nurse, that—Maggie crossed through the doorway into the long hall down which they had just come. Standing in the archway to the living room, she stared into the gloom and might have been fifteen again so little had changed. It was the same bulky furniture that had been there since her grandparents' time, all mauves and browns. The heavy velvet draperies that, her mother used to say, did nothing but gather dust, had been replaced by sheer lisle curtains, but even these did little to disspell the shadows of the old house.

Someone came up behind her in the hall. "David?" she said, turning, but it was a woman, still, staring. With a start, Maggie realized that she was gazing at her own reflection in the mirror just opposite. It was her mirror, the one that had been in the New York apartment, but it looked so right just there, reflecting the room behind her, that it might never have been moved. Yes, she thought, remembering that it had been there before, just there at that precise place in the long, narrow hall. Years before, her mother had given it to Maggie because it was so grotesque with its fruits and flowers, gilded vines and snake. Yet the sheer weight of it counterpointed the sleek, modern chrome and glass furniture that Maggie had acquired.

"Maggie," David called from the kitchen, but she ignored him and went right down the hall to the room her father had called his study. She opened the door and saw that this room was much the same. There was her grandfather's desk, a solid mass of wood, which she knew concealed drawers within drawers, and the floor-to-ceiling bookshelves with their leather-bound volumes. Hadn't anyone who lived here in between made changes? Even the easy chair and upright bronze floor lamp were in the precise corner where her father would sit and read.

Still no Jeb. David called again, and Maggie went back down the hall, stopping at the dining room where the huge oak table sat like a liner in its berth. But the chairs were different, she noticed with relief. The old ones had been straight, plain and bone-jarring for anyone without a rigid spine. These were new, with comfortable-looking cane seats.

"Where's Jeb?" she asked, once again in the kitchen with its modern appliances and canary yellow walls. Above the sink was a shelf of healthy plants. The curtains had been polka dots, and they ruffled in the slight breeze that came through the opened windows. It was a pleasant, homey room that stirred no memories. But that woman. Maggie looked at her for the first time.

Sarah was squat, fat as though swelled by yeast, with steel-gray hair swept up and knotted atop her head. Her face, however, was angular and bony, with hollows where the hills of her cheeks should have been, and light, washed-out gray eyes that stared from the depths. She could have been anywhere from forty to sixty, and no smile pushed up her narrow, palid lips.

"I want to see Jeb," Maggie said, shaking at her own insistence. "And what was he doing under the front porch? It could be dangerous in there."

David sighed and pulled out a chair from the round table and sat down. "Sarah, get me a cup of coffee, please. Maggie, did you have any lunch before we left?"

"I have a nice shrimp salad in the fridge and some iced tea made," Sarah said.

"Fine. Forget the coffee then. Iced tea would be better. Maggie, come sit down." David got up and pulled out another chair, guiding her to it and sitting her down, as though she were a child.

"Where is Jeb?" She couldn't wait. Her hands sweated with longing.

"He'll turn up soon enough." Sarah filled up her glass just to the rim, so Maggie knew when she lifted it the tea would spill over and down the sides. "I keep a firm watch on him, but I don't believe in smothering," she said, watching Maggie with narrowed eyes.

Maggie, kneading at her hands below the table where no one could see, thought, she's been his mother this last year, not me.

"You'll have to give him time to readjust," David said, and looked the other way. He might never have put his arms around her in the car, nor ruffled her hair with his breath.

"You did tell him, didn't you, David?" Maggie asked, leaning forward and catching at his sleeve. "You didn't just decide to spring me on him?"

"Of course not," he replied angrily. "But this is yet another change for Jeb. You'll have to be patient with him."

Maggie sat back and saw Sarah gazing at David

sympathetically. "Are you saying that Jeb doesn't want to see me? That he isn't," she hesitated, "pleased that I've come home?"

She was disconcerted. It hadn't occurred to her that Jeb wouldn't be happy, delighted once again to crawl into her lap and put his arms about her neck and burrow his face into the hollow of her shoulder.

"We're all different, Maggie—you, me, Jeb," David said with that tone of finality she recognized, and which meant: I don't choose to discuss it now. But would he ever want to talk about it, and what did it mean? She *knew* she was different; God knows, she knew that. It was as though plastic surgery had been done on her soul. And because of that, she knew *something* had happened to David, because all this long year she had felt his disapproval for her "weakness" like a cold wind blowing against her skin. And furthermore, she understood that what had happened had to have had some effect on Jeb. But different? That meant that they weren't who they had been before, not just her but all three of them.

She sat quietly, not unaware that David watched her over the rim of his glass with a mixture of anger and apprehension, and that Sarah, a sour look on her face, glided noiselessly, for all her bulk, about the kitchen, regarding her with the same kind of wariness Maggie had grown accustomed to in Greenwood.

"I understand," Maggie said, not certain that she did, but instinctively knowing it was what she ought to say, that any more insistence on her part was dangerous. But her palms itched to stroke Jeb's face and hair; her arms ached to clutch him to her and to swallow his warmth.

Just then, as though he could sense her longing, Jeb appeared in the doorway. Maggie's heart lurched, and she thought she would faint from the sheer joy of seeing him at last.

He hadn't changed, or not much anyway. But she didn't get a chance to take him apart feature by feature and revel in the sheer sight of him, for before she could even speak or catch her breath, he launched himself at her—just as he had before, whenever she'd been away—and cried, "Mommy!" And then there he was, squirming all over her, arms and legs, and pink downy cheeks that were just turning that golden brown that only he could get, and blond hair that seemed even lighter.

They laughed and hugged and the chair almost gave way under them. He filled her lap to overflowing, and he whistled in her ear because his words came tumbling out of him one after the other, too fast to make sense; and she was crying quietly at the same time as she was hugging him, and laughing and smiling.

It was too much. It was happiness. She hadn't thought she would even recognize the feeling again.

3

It was like getting her sea legs again after having been too long ashore; becoming accustomed to the pitch and toss of normal life. June melted into July, days of runny, endless sunshine, and Maggie thought of herself as waking up after a long and troubled sleep.

David came and went like any other suburban husband, sometimes not returning to Four Oaks until long after dark. Often, in the drowsy warmth of their double bed, Maggie would hear his tread on the stairs, chart his passage in the undercurrent of her dreams, and half feel his body as he eased his way next to her. Occasionally they would touch, his hands fluting along her rib cage, traveling across her stomach beneath the sheerness of her nightgown, and then slipping down to stroke upward against her bare legs, finding his way at last inside her. He'd caress and circle and rouse her until in her own rhythmic way—dreaming, dreaming—she'd rise to meet him, her eyes shuttered against the dark.

"Oh, David . . ."

Where was the love of it?

She hadn't known at all what to expect as she had waited in Greenwood for this new life rolling toward her, but now, once in it, this tentativeness of David's, this hesitancy, bewildered her. She searched in the backwash of memory for passion, but her recollections were hazy, unreliable,

and she couldn't ask David: Are you still in love with me?
Am I still in love with you?

Time, she could hear Klein saying, it will all take time.

Everyone of them needed time to adjust, even Jeb, who
was, she couldn't doubt it, growing up. Maggie often
longed for his six-month, year, three-year selves that lurked
buried, and she treasured those moments when he'd come
and hove into the curve of her arm. But those moments
were fewer than she remembered and lasted less than a
minute or two before he'd squirm away.

He had acquired a veneer of self-sufficiency in the long
months she'd been gone. But it was only a veneer. Some
days he would dress himself without any adult fingers to
get the buttons in the right holes or the zipper up without
catching the tail of a shirt. Other mornings she'd discover
him at breakfast in a plaid shirt and checked pants, with
socks that didn't match, a T-shirt on backwards. Again,
there were meals where his table manners were excellent,
where he could—his face tight with concentration—cut up
his meat into neat precise squares; and meals at which he
slopped food all over the plate, couldn't get the spaghetti
anywhere but in his lap, and was just a shade away from
being surly and impolite.

She smiled thinking how loveable he could be sometimes, remembering the woodland bouquet he had brought
her one late afternoon to be set in a jelly jar at the table—
buttercups and daisies and puffballs.

And yet there were moments when he backed away
from her, when he resisted every suggestion she made.
Times when—if she coaxed him into playing a game—he'd
be awkward and clumsy, forgetting the rules. Then he'd
run off, as if she were threatening him, but where did he
go?

Sitting in the sunny kitchen, she asked Sarah who

shrugged and said, "Out. Under the porch most times. His secret place he calls it."

"But what does he do there? And those jars! I think he kills bugs in those jars. He never used to do that before," Maggie said, troubled.

Sarah tensed, as though attacked. "He is a child with a big imagination," she said, then she turned and poured herself a cup of coffee from the pot that was always on low on the back burner. She sat down opposite Maggie and regarded her remorselessly. "I expect," she said in a voice tinged with frost, "that he does a lot of things he never did before. I expect like Mr. Brace said, he's different *now*. Not that I really can say, not knowing the boy before."

Maggie was wary with this strange woman in white who parried and thrust at her and watched as if she thought to see Maggie go spinning off into space. It was a look that Maggie knew from Greenwood. "I suppose," she said cautiously, parroting David, "it's a stage he's going through."

"Suppose so," Sarah said and reached for a cigarette in the voluminous pocket of her apron. She lit it with a long kitchen match and settled in. Her very ease made Maggie nervous, counterpointing her own inactivity.

Sarah, indeed watching her, thought: she's trying to dredge sympathy out of me with a scoop shovel. So be it. And thought as she had many times since Maggie had come home, there's not enough sympathy under heaven and earth for *that* one. Not that she, Sarah, felt as the father did. Without them ever having discussed it—which wouldn't have been right—she knew that David was like a kettle on high boil, resenting, loving, uncertain.

That Maggie was crazy, she didn't doubt, for hadn't she, Maggie, been locked up for a long time, and wouldn't she have to be crazy with her two girls burning up. Not that Sarah could put her finger on exactly what it was that defined Maggie as crazy, just that madness was the appropriate response to what had occurred. She would have, she knew, been affronted if Maggie had been sane.

Not that it mattered in the slightest if Maggie was mad, as long as it didn't affect the boy, didn't upset him in any real, concrete ways. Just let her be crazy quietly, Sarah thought, and puffed on her cigarette.

"We should be doing more things together," Maggie was saying, drawing circles on the tablecloth with her fingertips. "But he's so—so—independent."

"He is that," Sarah said, smoke flowing from her mouth, and considered Jeb. There he is and there he isn't. As far as she was concerned he was "a poor child," who was "troubled" because of the "terrible thing" that had happened to him. All of which made Sarah sometimes want to hug him and sometimes want to swat his behind.

The two women eyed one another across the table. "Maybe I'll take him into town, and we'll just go around and maybe have lunch. Yes," Maggie said, and hurriedly stood up, as though if she didn't move fast, the idea would skitter away from her. Snatching the car keys from a hook by the back door, feeling buoyant with purpose, she went off to the yard to find Jeb.

It was so quiet outside that sounds had to be strained after—the fluttering of birds as they winged over the lawn, the ruffling of the grass beneath the wind's breath, the whispering of unseen presences. It was so quiet that for a moment Maggie's ears hurt, and she called out, "Jeb? Jebbie, where are you?" the words flying back in her face.

There was no answer, no magical appearance of one small boy. The junior-sized shiny blue, two-wheeler that had been Jeb's sixth birthday present, and on which he was wobblingly learning to keep his balance, leaned against the back porch. A big, red ball sat in the middle of the grass like a blood blister. Maggie walked around to the front of the house, to the drive where she saw a tin bucket filled with pebbles and a plastic measuring cup half full of water.

She peered under the front porch. The dimness was like murky water where both shadows and substances retained the same gray, grainy quality, as though everything was covered in cobwebs, filmy curtains that would be sticky to the touch. He wasn't there, in his secret place, with just the rows of jars and what looked like his old baby quilt with its pattern of bunnies and flowers and pink balloons—Kathy's and Tracy's before him. She tried to see further into the depths beneath the porch where the light diminished, but couldn't.

"Jebbie? Are you in there?" There was no answer.

She went along the front and tugged at the loose corner of the lattice. There are so many hidden places, darknesses where memories, where secrets gather dust, she thought, that I should leave this one alone. What do I know of my own son, anyway? What is it like to be six with two dead sisters and a mother who's . . . who left for somewhere, she amended, where nobody could follow.

Holding her breath, she squeezed behind the lattice and, dropping to her knees, went under the porch. It was a tight fit for her with the porch beams just inches from her head. The wood was encrusted with years of dirt, which drifted down in tiny motes and fell on her hair. Underneath, the ground was studded with small rocks that dug into her bare knees.

All the discards of accumulated generations had been stowed in the crawl space under the porch. Weathered boards hoary with age and spongy with rot. A shovel so rusted that its edges were eaten away. A broken ladder with severed steps. There was a piece of the lattice that had once been replaced and now lay propped up against the original front of the house, its paint peeled in long, jagged streaks.

It was silent and chilly as winter. The long, narrow emptiness widened slightly at the far end toward which Maggie crawled laboriously, to Jeb's secret place. The light lay flat against the cutout triangles, and even these were bisected by striations of darkness, the bushes sending out skeletal arms. A few tendrils had worked their way through the lattice, vined about it and curled out again, knitting the house into the earth.

The corner that Jeb had staked out was neat, the ground covered by the quilt, the jars lining the wall. A hidey hole, surprisingly cozy. Maggie smiled, settling back cross-legged. Yes, a hidey hole, not unlike the one she'd had at his age behind a big, high-backed chair in her parents' New York apartment, a free zone that, because the lamp was in the foreground, was gray and removed, a spot where she had been invisible.

Nothing wrong with this, she thought, nothing that I didn't do myself as a child, or probably David also.

She heard the front door snap, and the thud, thud of Sarah's footsteps, and then the crack as she banged the mop on the railing and a slow drift of lint showered to the ground. There was something at once safe yet forbidding in the secret place, hearing life, seeing the snatches of it, shards that had to be fitted one into the other with all their minute, hairline cracks.

The jars against the wall—the original front of the house before the porch had been added even before her grandparents had bought Four Oaks—were fat, and almost all the same size, from mayonnaise or peanut butter, Maggie thought, or maybe pickles, clean of labels but grimy now with fingerprints. All their tops were screwed on, and they were empty except for one with a sprinkling of ashes clinging to the sides, and one which had a dark lump of something that, in the dimness, Maggie couldn't identify. Curious, she held the jar to a patch of light and revolved it slowly until, like one of the Rorschach ink blots that Klein would test her on, it solidified into a shape, a recognizable picture that jolted her like a cattle prod. A tiny, greasy eye no bigger than a BB, stared sightlessly up at her. Where the other eye should have been was a charred hole. She was looking at a dead frog. A frog with its head half severed and a burned-out eye. What she now realized must be blood, frog's blood, pooled black as tar about the obscene, dead thing.

She dropped the jar and it fell to her lap, stuck between her crossed legs, the frog and its parts rolling along the glass sides. Jumping in shock, she cracked her head on the porch floor, sending off shooting stars behind her eyes.

The jar bumped to the ground, and Maggie scuttled backwards, flopping herself over on her hands and knees, feeling the cold slimy skin, the clammy trickle of frog's blood along her legs. Neither skin nor blood had actually touched her, but she could imagine it so vividly her flesh crawled.

Crabwise she raced to the opening, feeling the weight of the house pressing above her, the hidey hole not safe now with that ton of wood and iron pipes and heavy, laboring furniture about to collapse on her back.

Her fingers grasped the lattice. She had started to shove it out when through one diamond-shaped opening she saw at the edge of the lawn—no more than fifteen-feet wide at this side of the house—Jeb standing, his back to a copse of blueberry bushes with their green, not yet ripe fruit and scratchy branches. He was as clear as a precise photograph, and even though the distance should have shrunk him, reduced him downward to a manageable image, he seemed to loom bigger than any six-year-old had the right to be, though he was, she understood, no bigger than the bushes that arched behind him, no bigger than he was in real life. She just thought he was.

He was watching her. Yet hidden away as she was, he couldn't possibly see her. One foot was raised, just inches off the grass, whispering above the blades, as if she had caught him in midstep and time hung suspended about him. It didn't seem possible that he could stand that way indefinitely, that he wouldn't topple over. He doesn't have a back to him, she thought wildly. If I turn him around, all the veins and arteries, the spine with its bony ridges, will be exposed.

And then his foot slapped the earth, and he was off, running out of her field of vision, away from her; though again, she told herself, he couldn't see her, that she had been lost in the shadows behind the lattice, an invisible person.

She pushed at the wood, and the lattice swung out silently, and then she was in the sunlight, sweat trickling over her face, along her neck and between her breasts. She looked down at her pale green shorts and white T-shirt, splotched with dirt, her legs cut in tiny patches, spots of blood on her knees.

She ran into the house, the screen nipping at her bare feet, but there was no one in the kitchen. Overhead the vacuum cleaner whined.

"Jeb?"

She searched the downstairs, looking under tables, behind doors. She checked the coat closet and the pantry, and not finding him anywhere, she was starting up the steps, panic lodged midway in her throat, when she heard the front door slam.

He was standing in front of the mirror, not moving, solemnly regarding his reflection, as though seeing his image for the first time. His palms were flattened against the glass and his breath threw up an aureole of mist. Maggie thought she heard him humming.

After the longest moment during which she was certain

she had ceased breathing, he turned and smiled, her radiant Jebbie filled with light.

"What are you doing?" she asked.

"Playing with my friend," he said.

"Your friend?"

"You know, Mommy, my friend. See." He pointed to the mirror as she came up behind him. "My friend who lives in the mirror."

Now you see me, now you don't, Maggie thought, blinking at her own reflection. And down below her, just at waist level, Jeb smiling. He looked like Tracy at that moment, Tracy at six, and her heart lurched. She reached out, winding her arms around him, pulling him away from the mirror to her.

Why couldn't she learn not to conjure ghosts. Shivering in the warm, still hallway, her eyes filled with tears, and she wanted to cry out: I have to stop seeing children who don't exist, children who are dead and gone, no matter how, no matter whose fault it was. I have to stop hearing their screams—yet her ears rang with them—or see their terrible.... She closed her eyes against her reflection, against Jeb's image with its acetate overlays of memories, Tracy's face. Kathy's too. Nothing, no thing exists that's not real, she told herself.

Jeb was fidgeting beneath her hands, and her eyes flew open and again she saw herself towering above him, again saw the two of them, but now his eyes were hers, and the curve of his cheek definitely David's. He was just Jebbie now. Her Jebbie.

Slowly the earth stilled under her feet, and she smiled.

"Oh, that friend," she laughed, freeing him and pointing at the other Jeb. And then she reached for him again, but softly, and they hugged and spun around, their reflections spinning with them in a kaleidoscope of color, of motion.

They fell to the floor, dizzy, and giggled, tickling one

another. When she caught her breath, she nuzzled his neck and said, "Com'on. Let's have us a day out. Let's have some fun. Lunch at that new pizza place in town?"

"Sure, Mom." He laughed, jumping up, and taking her hand, he pulled her up from the floor.

There were too many cars, all bumper to bumper, moving inches at a time, and all, it seemed, honking their horns and spilling rock music through their opened windows, that made the whole town shake on its underpinnings. No, Brighton was not the same, not the sleepy little Connecticut village that had shutter-stopped in the backwash of time. People were everywhere, tourists in jeans and t-shirts, polyester bermuda shorts, and even here and there bathing suits. My God, Maggie wondered, where had they all come from.

The sturdy elms still bordered the green, but now all across the grass were people—on blankets, hooked into transistor radios and cassette players, throwing colorful frisbies that now and then arched out into traffic. Edgy, Maggie cut across Main to the newsstand, clutching Jeb's tiny hand in her own.

"Let me just pick up a newspaper, Honey, and then we'll go on home," she said. She had already bought him pizza, a frozen yogurt, and a red balloon, which was securely tied to his wrist and bobbed up and down like a buoy with each step they took.

She gave him a little tug, and they hurried across the intersection on the green light. Her head was starting to ache, just above the corner of the right eye, and a flutter of anxiety shot through her stomach. Had she taken her Valium after breakfast? It was all so blurry, the morning, and just when she had determined to pull things together, to have a routine, to be herself again (by which, of course, she meant the pre-Greenwood, pre-fire Maggie). First, there had been the coming out of sleep, of bad dreams—the kind that she thought, no matter what Klein said, would never stop—to David's touch, and then Jeb and the strange things she had found under the porch.

The tiny newsstand was thick with people. Jeb stared wide-eyed at the naked redhead sprawled across the cover of *Hustler*, and Maggie pushed her way to the counter and asked for a *Times*.

"All out. Try the bookstore on the corner."

The street seemed to have filled up even more as the late lunch crowd filtered from the two barewood and plant-hung restaurants on the block, and from old MacMulty's bar and grill at the other end of the square. Maggie and Jeb were tossed along like bobbins on the surf. The sun beat down, and the air, still as glass, was stifling. Jeb rolled back the sleeves of the shirt, which Maggie realized guiltily was too heavy, and she opened another button on her blouse. The swell of her breasts was beaded with sweat. The thump in her temples began like faint thunder.

As she swung open the door to the bookstore, a tingle of tiny bells sang melodiously and a gust of air-conditioned air swept over them. Maggie pushed Jeb toward a counter of children's books and angled to the side of the store where she saw a neat row of magazines and newspapers. It was a pleasant shop, properly hushed, an oasis after the turmoil of the street. Maggie snagged the last copy of the *Times*, but was reluctant to leave just yet. The pounding in her head slowed to a mild throbbing, her stomach steadied. She browsed, watching Jeb at the corner of her vision, the red balloon rising and falling as he turned the pages of a picture book. Jeb was so proud of his reading.

"Are you looking for something special?"

Maggie jumped. She had been glancing quietly at a book of poetry, letting the lines spring out.

> *This I do, being mad:*
> *Gather baubles about me*

She slammed the book shut and saw she'd been reading Millay. "No thank you, just browsing," she said.

"Do you like Millay?" the woman asked.

Maggie looked at the other woman for the first time and saw that she was short, darkly tanned, with a crop of curly black hair that shagged her skull, and intense eyes so deeply blue they were almost black. She wore a bright, colorful Indian shirt cut low so that heavy breasts were bared almost to the nipples. There was something electric about her, a static edge that kept her shifting as she blocked the aisle preventing Maggie from getting by.

"Millay?" she said, forgetting for a moment whose poetry she had just been reading. "Oh, I don't know. The only one I really remember goes—" She frowned, narrowing her eyes, trying to retrieve the lines. "Oh, yes:

> *Pity me that the heart is slow to learn*
> *What the swift mind beholds at every turn.*"

—Maggie recited, smiling.

The woman smiled back, and the angles of her face suddenly softened, coalesced into a subtle beauty.

"Actually," Maggie said, relaxing, "I just came in for a paper, but it's so nice here after all of that," she waved her hand toward the front windows where the steady streams of people swam like gaudy fish behind the glass, "that I didn't want to leave."

"I know what you mean. It's real wicked in Brighton in the summer. You wonder what they're all up to and why they're not swimming or powering their motorboats on one of the lakes on a day like this. Not that I'm complaining, you know. All the traffic is good for business. But in the winter, well, you should see this place then. You could hear a pin drop between here and Elm."

"I expect I will know, since we'll be here when they're all gone."

"A resident!" she laughed and stuck out her hand. "Welcome, I'm Lee McCann, and I own all of this." She gave a shrug, shaking her curls.

"Maggie Brace," she said, and felt her hand gripped just a bit too tightly before she managed to get it back.

One eyebrow arched slightly, and then in a flash, as though a storm had passed, Lee smiled widely and cried, "You must be David Brace's wife!"

Maggie was surprised. She hadn't thought David knew anyone in Brighton. "Yes, I am."

"Your husband is one of my best customers. I think he kept me solvent all through last winter. My, that man is a great book buyer," she said as though it was somehow sexy to buy books.

"David does like to read when he has time, and he likes to give books as gifts." She remembered the parcels he had brought to Greenwood, the books he had imagined would give her some focus for her errant thoughts. Books and flowers. Even early in their marriage he had given her books and flowers. Something for the inside and something for the outside, he used to say.

She turned and saw that Jeb was watching them. "Well," she said, "I guess we better be going."

"Is that your son?"

"Yes, Jeb. He's six."

Lee called out, "Hey, red balloon man, you want a lollipop?" The balloon dipped and hopped its way down the aisle in reply, as Jeb followed her to the cash register where, from a wicker basket beside it, she offered him his choice. He deliberated, torn between a lemon and an orange until Lee suggested he keep both—one for now, one for later.

"Later" led to Lee inviting Maggie for iced tea on the tiny patio that jutted into the courtyard at the rear of her store, and Maggie, pleased, agreed. It was such a *normal* occurrence, something she had done a thousand times— sitting quietly and sharing a drink, or a lunch with a woman friend—that she'd forgotten how long it had been, how her friends had drifted away, disappeared into their own lives, which seemed to have no connection to hers anymore.

In the beginning they had all been sympathetic, horror-stricken, eager at the same time to help and yet keep some distance between themselves and her palpable tragedy. They tried—Janet, Maria, even Jenny whom she knew only from parents' meetings at school—but as Maggie swam farther and father out into sea of her own despair, they had drifted away. Only Janet had come to see her at Greenwood, or at least David once told her she had. Maggie didn't remember; like so much else, she had forgotten that.

She would have liked to call Janet, had thought about it more than once, but put it off again and again. She feared they'd make one another uncomfortable, and it wouldn't be the way it was now, here with this stranger who wasn't a friend but could be. Why not? It wasn't impossible now that she had regained her moorings to have a friend. In fact, they all should, she and David and Jeb. It struck her for the first time how much they had isolated themselves, as though they were pariahs because the girls had died.

They didn't say anything of importance, she and Lee, but sat comfortably drinking iced tea that one of the clerks dispatched, had brought back from the luncheonette. Maggie talked about the Brighton she once knew and what it had been like before the tourists had discovered it. Lee said she was envious, since she'd been here only three years, having come down from Boston after her divorce.

Maggie liked her, liked the barely contained energy that made her bob up and down three or four times to check on the clerks in the store, and that had her crossing and recrossing jean-encased legs, which Maggie could see were long and slender, as she sat slouched in her director's chair. Maggie could feel the energy beating out of Lee's pores. It was such a change to be with someone who ached with life, someone who didn't mitigate his urgency around her for fear of jarring her loose from a precarious perch, someone who didn't know she was only newly reanchored on the right side of sanity.

Finally, the sun tilted, casting shadows, and the tiny boutique across the cobbled courtyard shuttered its doors.

"We have to get home," Maggie said reluctantly, "but we'll be back. And let me buy that book for Jeb. He's read it so many times that he probably thinks he owns it already."

Jeb wouldn't let Lee wrap up *Where the Wild Things Are* and clutched it to his shirt, the balloon, leaking air, just level with his nose. Maggie laughed and waved goodbye to her friend. She hustled Jeb back to the municipal parking lot where the Dodge had sprouted a ticket from being two hours past the meter. But even that didn't dent her good humor. It had been much too wonderful a day, just like the day she had started out to have, the kind of day that other women shrugged off without a thought.

In the car, just as they were leaving the lot, the balloon popped. The surprise made Maggie slam on the brakes, but then she and Jeb laughed. She unhooked the remnants from his wrist and deposited them in the trash bag attached to the dash before she started off again. Jeb let out a sigh and began to read the Sendak for the tenth time. They rode in a sweet silence, as the red and orange sunset capped the horizon and swam across the sky.

"Was it a beast that stole Kathy and Tracy?" Jeb asked.

A streak of pain shot into Maggie's heart, as though she'd been stabbed, the blade slicing through pulp and bone. "What?"

"A beast thing. Did a beast thing eat them up?"

"There're no such things as beasts, honey," she said. The windshield had darkened. Maggie wasn't sure if night had come on so fast that she'd been caught unaware or if the blood that was suddenly pounding in her head was fogging her vision. She flicked on the low beams and tried to control her shaking. Her hands gripped the wheel so hard her arms and shoulders screamed with the strain.

"If it wasn't a beast thing, how'd you lose them?" And before she could answer, he asked, "Are you going to lose me like that too?"

Maggie's teeth were chattering, and she struggled to speak. She turned to say, don't do this to me. You know what happened. David told you . . . I told you. . . . I remember telling you . . . holding you in my arms and telling you and crying. . . . Don't!

Jeb's eyes glittered in the last spark of dying light. Only his eyes shone out of the dusk. A tire caught the shoulders of the road and the car shook. Terrified, Maggie pulled back on the wheel, and they spun out into the middle, then settled, riding the white line. "It was a fire, Jebbie," she said, crying so much she could barely see.

"You should have found them, Mommy. You shouldn't have lost them," he said in a cold voice that wasn't a child's at all—a voice that resounded, words echoing, bouncing in the confines of the car long after they reached Four Oaks and he was out the door and she sat alone and tried to stop her shaking.

4

Maggie took to driving around the countryside. There was nothing for her to do at Four Oaks. Sarah ran the house with a professionalism that was beyond Maggie. David was absent more often than not, and Jeb. . . . She tried not to think of Jeb and thought of him too much. She thought of him under the porch trapping insects and killing them; of him before that mirror having intense, whispered conversations with his own reflection, as though it was only the reverse of himself that he trusted enough to be intimate with. He could, if pressured, do things with her—as if she were the child who had to be humored and he the parent who had to do the humoring—and so, occasionally, they did go swimming at the lake five miles away, or play miniature golf at the course outside town, but mostly he wanted to be alone. She looked for other children with whom he could play, but he wouldn't be caught. And truthfully, other mothers would make her uneasy with their implied accusation—if they knew—that she was dangerous. It wasn't as it was with Lee, who didn't make her edgy, perhaps because of her childless state. Twice Maggie had gone into town to see her, and once Lee had come to Four Oaks for lunch.

Mostly, however, Maggie's days were filled with driving, an aimless wandering that soothed her and didn't make her think. No, she tried hard not to think of anything as she pulled the Dodge closer to the shoulder, a horse van coming up on her left. It was a half van, and she watched the horse calmly staring back at her, until the van veered down one of the farm roads and disappeared. She guessed she was still in Connecticut but might have drifted over the border into Massachusetts. It didn't matter. She drove just to drive, to have something to do, and if she was heading for somewhere as much as running away from something, she supposed that the somewhere would one day come up at her like a stop sign, and then she'd *know*.

Off in the distance were gabled farm houses, sturdy paddocks, and acres of rolling hills. It was rich, comfortable New England countryside. Though she didn't recognize any part of it, and hadn't for an hour or more, over the years she had been many times to houses just like those that lay hidden from view, each sequestered in its own particular, private world. She was lost, both geographically and internally. Traveling the country roads she was, she knew, hoping to find her way as much to somewhere inside as out.

She crossed over a rickety wooded bridge straight off a calendar. Below the riverbed was summer dry with just a thin trickle of water slipping over the rocks. The sunlight danced and darted, striking sparks, and with the windows rolled down, the air blew her hair in a long, streaming curtain.

At the other side of the bridge, the road narrowed even further, and the bushes that banked it scratched at the Dodge. It had happened on one of her wandering days that the lane, not really a road, had just petered out, stopped in the middle of nowhere, a scabrous and mean-looking field jutting ahead, as if the farmer or roadmaker had come so far and just given up.

She thought it might be happening again, that she'd have to reverse as she had that other time, what turned out to be a longish distance. She had surprised herself that she'd done it rather than just sitting there trapped in the Dodge at the end of the road. That act, that minor act of survival, was so miraculous to Maggie that she'd talked about it all one session to Klein. For the first time she'd seen his confidence in her well-being slide.

He seemed unsettled. Why, she wanted to ask him, are you so dubious about what was for me a gigantic act of will instead of rejoicing? Surely, she wanted to insist, the fact that I didn't sit there turning to dust and made the effort to go back, is a significant indication of health. But even to Klein, there were questions she didn't put, statements she failed to make. At the last minute she had pulled back and laughed, realizing that this man held the keys to her freedom. If she didn't appear supranormal, if she wasn't just a slightly bored housewife whiling away her hours wondering what to do—what concretely she meant to do—with the rest of her life, he might lock her up again. It came as a shock, though she was cunning enough not to show it, that she didn't truly trust Klein either.

"I meant, I could have just sat there in that hot car and napped, like a lazy cat," she laughed. "And you should have seen me, backing out! An inch either way would have put me in the ditch. Then David . . , oh, he'd have been furious."

Klein visibly relaxed, settling back and smiling at her. "Are you so afraid of David's anger?" he asked, and she knew they were on safe ground again.

But this road did go somewhere. It sloped and curled finally into a small ghost of a town that clung to the shoulders, making a slight hump in the middle of the narrow valley, as though it had been dropped from the back of a truck. It wasn't much of a place, not scenic at all, just a curve of weathered clapboard houses fronting the road, a sagging, paint-peeling gas station with two rusty pumps, and a field behind, cluttered with derelict cars whose doors hung, when they had them; and a general store that wasn't built for the tourist trade.

Maggie angled the Dodge close to the steps that led up to the porch of the store and got out. She stood motionless, listening. The air was leaden, without a sliver of breeze to cut it. Her shoulders ached from driving so long, and without the wind blowing on her, she began to sweat. She flexed her arms, swinging her purse, and glanced up at the sky. The sun was low. Soon she'd have to start back. David never liked her to come in after dark. And he always knew. Sarah told him, Maggie was sure, just what she did and when. Maggie didn't blame her, didn't even resent her for it. After all, wasn't she a hand grenade with the pin pulled? It was only a matter of time before she detonated and destroyed them all. Or at least they believed that. She wasn't certain for all the shifting currents in her head.

I am—she recited so she could believe it—as sane as anyone in a world where insanity is the norm. I have had a breakdown because of a terrible tragedy in my life. *But I am better now.* I am only slightly nervous. I have problems that must be worked out and for which I am receiving help. I am not mad!

Defiantly, she looked around, as though she'd been accused, and said aloud: "I do not imagine things."

But there was no one about, no one questioning, no one listening.

I must be mad to talk to myself, to defend myself to myself.

And if she weren't crazy, then Jeb wouldn't be killing bugs and talking to himself for hours at a time.

The thought that David was right to be suspicious, and that Sarah was right to agree, depressed her. Neither of them had spent a year floating in a black hole. Her head ached with the pounding indecision. She'd get a Coke and wash her face if they had water, and then figure out on her map just where she was. It was time to go back. She felt a hook pulling in between her shoulder blades.

The inside of the store was a jumble. Shelves went from floor to ceiling, piled high with canned goods, boxes, sacks of flour, salt, coffee, as if someone were stocking up for the end of the world. Barrels commanded much of the floor space, and pots and pans swung on long ropes from the ceiling. Dust was everywhere, thick curtains of it, and grime coated the two narrow windows. Even the air seemed to shimmer with dust, making it hard to see.

There was a huge, rust-flecked ice chest in the corner, but when she touched it with her hand it was warm, and when she lifted the lid, it was empty, giving off a stale, unpleasant odor. She turned and called, "Hello," but no one answered. The vacant, dirty store was beginning to make her uneasy, and she went out onto the shaky porch, looking up and down the street. It was so quiet, so unpeopled, as if the last bomb in the last war had been dropped and the nuclear fallout had drifted through the last cloud while she was out driving the barren country roads. She gingerly stepped down the stairs and out onto the dusty street still without seeing anyone, until she came to believe that they really were all gone, all of everybody, not only Kathy and Tracy, as if somehow she had lost *them* all.

She retraced the street to her car, feeling the muscles in her back and neck stiffen as if she were being watched, as if someone besides David, besides Klein, besides Sarah, were charting her every move, and said to herself: Maggie, don't be foolish, no one cares about you that much, no stranger certainly. But having lived so long in her mind, living too much there now, her imagination was riotous, so that when she reached the Dodge and looked up toward the door of the ramshackle store and saw something rolling across the porch toward her, saw the wall of human flesh in its mountainous humps, she screamed and yanked at the car door. Before she knew it the tires were spitting gravel as she hit sixty from a dead stop, the engine screeching pain. She didn't know where she was going, or where a main road was, but it didn't matter. She was unbearably terrified of what she realized, even in the midst of the panic, was only a fat old man who hung over the porch like a descending moon threatening to fall, to tumble over on her, crushing her into dust.

From dust . . . from ashes. . . .

The rolls of fat on his arms, on his naked stomach hanging in a wide expanse between the top of his pants and the uplifted bottom of his T-shirt that outlined pendulous breasts, all that flesh was spotted with brown and pink patches of skin, birthmarks, and he was leprous, diseased. She would catch it from him . . . catch death from him.

Part of her mind said, he is scary, he is something terrible that should be hidden away. And the other part of her mind said, it's really crazy to be afraid of something only human.

The last paper had been signed, the last "i" dotted, "t" crossed. Every hand had been shaken, every back patted, every face wreathed in a smile. A thirty-million-dollar merger. Six months of work gratifyingly brought to a profitable close. Then why, David wondered, didn't he feel a sense of accomplishment, didn't he derive a soar of pleasure that would feather in his groin like the first stirrings of sexual desire? Usually, he felt that when he had done something, not well—he did everything well—but better than anyone else; done something, in fact, that no one else could have done and from which he had made a great deal of money. Oh, it mattered, it all mattered, and he'd been pleased when McGrath, chairman of Noval Chemicals, congratulated him and offered him a Havana, which David took but didn't smoke, but he didn't care enough.

Nothing was ever as *they* promised you, or as you promised yourself, he thought as he wrenched himself out of the canvas deck chair in which he had been sprawled, gave a slight nod toward the sun falling into the lake at the edge of the lawn, and entered the house through the sliding glass doors. He shook the glass in his hand, and the ice cubes clicked against one another like billiard balls. The scotch had gone so fast that the ice hadn't melted. Another drink in a day that would end with him having one drink too many, something that was happening too often now, as if the liquor really did have a palpable effect on the churning inside of him instead of just giving him a heavy head and a night of drugged sleep.

As he crossed the high-ceilinged living room to the bar at the left of the stone fireplace, Lee came out of the kitchen carrying a cheese board on which rested a wedge of brie, crackers, a knife.

"I don't like it, not at all," he said, pouring the scotch halfway up the glass.

"What, brie? I thought it was your favorite," she said, walking by him, out onto the deck. She put the board down on the small redwood table and sat in the chair next to the one he'd just left.

"Don't be thick," he said, following her. "You know what I mean." He leaned against the railing, his back to the sunset, and put the cool glass with its amber scotch and fresh ice against his cheek.

She pointed to the sun and the shifting light and said, "How can you not watch that? It's a miracle. Every night it goes down; every morning it comes up." She wouldn't look at him, resolutely staring ahead, her long, thin legs stretched before her.

"It's not a miracle. It's a fact of the natural order of things," he said.

"And it's not in the natural order of things that the lover should talk to the wife, even if the wife speaks first." It came out flat, a statement not a question. She turned her head and, steepling her hands in front of her face so that only her dark eyes were visible, she looked up at him.

She was much smaller than Maggie, and not as beautiful, not really beautiful at all, but in the dying light she seemed to glow, lit from within, as if the force of her anger made her vibrant. She was angry all right, he would have known without even looking into her eyes which shone, or hearing her voice with an edge hard as the ice in his glass. Her hands came down to her lap to curl like two hostile animals into fists. He thought she'd probably like to hit him, and irrationally that stirred him more than anything, and he wanted to drag her kicking and screaming into her bedroom with the skylight in it and under the stars stick his cock into her until she yelped in pleasure.

He turned his back on her to the sun, three-quarters gone, and watched the last portion sucked into the tree-tops, the splay of pink light on the water dying to deep violet, and felt his own life sinking out there on the lake, all his desires going down into darkness. How had everything gone so wrong, as if, after being a favored child, the gods had decided, enough is enough. The fire that had burned up his daughters had in its way incinerated Maggie, him, and their marriage. Only Jeb seemed unscathed. And now, the licks of flames were inching toward Lee, toward him and Lee. Well, why not? There shouldn't have been a Lee and him to begin with. Only now there was, and he didn't know what to do about it, didn't even know what he felt about it. Hell, maybe Klein was right, he needed help, not only for Maggie's sake but for his own. He felt the burdens of the night on his shoulders and wanted not to think anymore, not to feel, to be succored into a drunken sleep from which like the phoenix he'd rise up renewed. And all this wasn't like him. Nothing he seemed to think or feel or even do—mergers notwithstanding—was like him anymore.

"You can't be friends with Maggie, Lee. Be reasonable," he said. Which was true, it wasn't reasonable because it made him uncomfortable, made him feel even more guilty than he did already, and that was guilty enough. "She's uncertain, vulnerable," he continued. "Christ, if she ever knew about us—oh, Christ, who knows what she'd do."

"You think she's still crazy, but she doesn't seem crazy to me."

"I don't think she's crazy," David protested, his voice echoing out over the water.

Lee leaped out of the chair and exploded, "Then tell her. Tell her about us. Tell her you love me like you say you do. Tell her you want a divorce. *Tell her!*"

"I don't know . . . I love you. I love Maggie, too. I don't know," he cried as she hammered at him with her fists, beating against his chest. He dropped the glass, which thudded to the deck and rolled off the edge as he grabbed her wrists and held her away from him. She shook and buckled, and her fury made her so dangerously alive that instantaneously he hardened, almost breathless from the urgency. He whipped her around, capturing her in his arms as he lifted and carried her against him to the bedroom where he flung her down, dropping on top of her and pulling, pressing his way into her flesh.

It was only later when he left her sleeping that he wondered what was going to happen to them. He did love her, beyond wanting her that was, but did he love her more than he loved Maggie? And if he did, did he really want to leave Maggie for her? And if he eventually discovered where the truth lay hidden, would Maggie survive—crazy or sane, for no matter what he said he wasn't certain. Would any of them survive with all that pain and guilt?

Maggie had gotten really lost, driving for hours, at last coming to ground well up in Massachusetts where she finally saw signs to the turnpike. It was already dark, long dark, when she turned into the drive and, pulling up to the house, caught David in the glare of the headlights. The Mercedes was parked outside the garage, and he was leaning across it, as though caressing it, as if it were a lover from whom he was reluctant to part.

"Where the hell have you been?" he yelled at her when she got out of the car, slamming the door. "I was just going to call the troopers."

She was still shaking, her shoulder muscles in spasm, the arms sore from gripping the wheel in an attempt to control the tremors. Now, unmoored, she could barely speak. She clasped her hands in front of her like a child.

"Lost," she said, her teeth chattering, though it was a warm night, "I was lost."

David went up to her, his anger melting all at once, and she let him lead her blindly into the house, let him push and prod her, moving dumbly. She wanted to cry, I'm a person not an animal, and I'm scared, but the words were locked in her throat. She bit down on her bottom lip and saw before her as they entered the house the fat man rolling out of the light into the darkness to claim her. She gave a short shriek before she realized that it was Sarah standing in the kitchen, the light splayed out behind her. David gripped her arm more forcefully and walked her into the study. He switched on the standing lamp beside her father's old chair and sat her down.

"Now," he said, "where have you been?"

She tried to tell him, but it came out all jumbled, and even to her ears it sounded silly, a hysterical, not quite right woman's ravings.

"I don't believe it," David said, leaning over and taking her chin in his hand so that she had to look up at him. "You're imagining again, Maggie," he added, kinder now.

She shook her head from side to side like a metronone as he spoke.

"Where were you, Maggie?"

"I told you." Oh, she was so tired. She could barely keep her eyes open. All she wanted to do was go to bed and pull the covers up and sleep for hours and hours and hours.

"You *told* me something that smells like a scene from a grade-B movie."

"Well, it's true!" she cried, her eyes filling with tears. "I don't care what you think!"

Behind him she saw Jeb's face at the window, the nose pressed flat against the glass, the lips elongated. For a moment she had difficulty recognizing him. "Jeb," she said, pointing.

"What?"

She half rose in her chair. "Jeb. What's he doing outside so late? He should be in bed asleep." Her stomach turned over, her heart beat faster.

"He is in bed, asleep," David said.

"No!" But just then the boy drew back, and when David faced the window, it was blank with just the sheen of his reflection and hers.

"There's nobody out there," he said exasperated. "There's never anybody anywhere, Maggie. You see things in your own mind and think they're real."

Oh God, she thought, he sounds so sensible. But she had seen the old man, seem him falling toward her like a full moon descending. She *was* going to be crushed under his weight. *She knew it!*

And now Jeb had been looking in the window, spying on them.

"Do you want me to put dinner on the table?" Sarah asked from the doorway.

"Why did you let Jeb go outside so late?" Maggie cried. "He's only a little boy. He could get hurt."

Sarah looked bewildered. "He's in bed, Mrs. Brace, asleep. For hours now."

"No!"

They both stared at her, then David abruptly turned, his face flushed with anger, and left the room. They could hear him go up the steps. Sarah waited just for a moment, then shrugged, and returned to the kitchen.

The world is not, Maggie promised herself—paraphrasing what Klein once told her—a screen upon which I throw the wild imaginings of my mind. The world has its own weight and reality. And yet Jeb's little face appeared once more at the other side of the window. Maggie jumped up and caught a glimpse of him when he jerked back, as though on a pulley, and ran across the lawn. He was wearing pajamas and his feet were bare.

"David!" she screamed, flattening herself against the window, cupping her hands to see out, the dark night running in on her. There! A small white spectator, his face a smudge, there was Jeb far off in an inky sea of blackness. Then slowly he moved toward her, lifting his feet as if they were dead weights, his arms swinging along his sides. He was a toy soldier, all his parts made of wood, marching into the night. "Stop! Stop" she cried, for some reason she couldn't begin to explain, and beat at the glass with her hands, slapped at it, and as if to hold him back, but he came on, inexorably.

"Enough, Maggie!" David was at her, pulling her arm,

spinning her around. She shrieked. He was a two-headed beast, a monster with too many arms and legs all of which were flailing at her, assaulting her, clutching, arms going for her neck, hands grasping her throat.

"Maggie!"

He was carrying Jeb, and Jeb was reaching for her, crawling from David's arms to hers, flinging himself around her, face flushed from sleep, his mouth open wide, his eyes enlarged with shock. "Mommy, Mommy!" His heart thundered against her, and she thought she was going to faint, but David held her up. The three of them entangled together.

"You caught him. See, I told you he was outside. "Why—" But is wasn't possible, her thoughts screeched, still seeing Jeb on the lawn, his face superimposed on the face of Jeb in her arms.

"Maggie," David said sharply, "I just took Jeb out of his bed where he was sound asleep, to bring him down and show you. He couldn't have been outside looking in the window."

Maggie stared at him. She knew what she had seen. Yet, she knew David was right.

5

Klein was optimistic. The dreams, he promised, would dissipate like mist. Yes, insubstantial wisps might slither through her sleep from time to time, but, all in all, her subconscious had been swept clean. Only a perfunctory dusting would be needed now and then. That was what Klein had said. That was what he had *promised*, and in his certainty made her an accessory.

Maggie, startled up from sleep, felt guilty; dreaming dreams Klein had guaranteed she'd never have again, was a betrayal. Slick with sweat, as though from a nocturnal fever, she wiped her face and neck with the sheet and tried to slam a conscious door on that long corridor, that smoke-filled hall down which, sleeping, dreaming, she'd run, the slap, slap of bare soles echoing in counterpoint against the unseen, burning crackling. She could smell the acrid odor even now. Her heart pounding, she lay back against the pillow and tried to clear her thoughts as Klein had instructed her, focusing on the midpoint between her eyes in the red and black darkness of her skull.

At her left, David slept, his head turned toward her on the pillow, his breathing ruffling the damp hairs on her upper arm. Her fingers crept crabwise and touched his shoulder. Maggie wished, just once, he'd wake when she panicked and lull her back down into sleep. It never seriously occurred to her to rouse him. As close as he was, he seemed in the outer distance, farther away, in fact, than in that much bigger bed they once shared.

She asked Klein. "Why is it," she had said, bending forward in her urgency, feeling miles away from him in the open space of his large office, "that he's so withdrawn?"

But Klein wasn't convinced. "Is he?" he probed, curlicues of smoke arcing above his head.

"You mean I am imagining it?"

"Are you?"

Klein tapped his pipe—crack, crack—against the large ceramic ash tray. Maggie listened to voices, and then a high pitched scream, like the shrill C of a reed instrument. In her head or outside of it? She couldn't be sure, For Greenwood was the house of the mad, and mad often made strange, inhuman sounds.

"Are you, Maggie?" he asked again, not moving. If there was a voice out there, he gave no sign. But Klein too was often impervious to terror.

She turned in bed and tried to remember what David looked like with his eyes opened. They had been married such a long time, but so many of those years with their corrugated memories were a muddle. Was there, for instance, always that glaze of suspicion from David, or had it come with her breakdown? (It was all her breakdown to her; the death of her daughters and her madness leaking into one another, cause not differentiated from result.)

"Well," she had said in defense to Klein, "we never talk to one another."

"Never?" he asked, raising an eyebrow. He wasn't one for generalities.

"Oh, not never. But only about things," she said sitting back. She knew Klein believed—even with his arcane lexicon of symbols—that "things" weren't descriptive enough.

"What kinds of things?"

"You know. The weather, what we're eating, the house. I

don't know where he goes anymore, or what he does, who he sees. When he leaves in the morning it's as though he disappears and then miraculously he comes back. But there's a hole there, where he's been."

A shaft of moonlight slipped into the darkened bedroom and fell across the bed. The lines in David's sleeping face were more pronounced, and suddenly he seemed very old, older than his father or her own father had been when he died. Would Klein understand that? Why should he when he didn't understand the other, about David vanishing. Sometimes Maggie thought she was married to a shadow and sometimes to an indomitable presence that hung over her.

But it was the watching that bothered her most of all. Wherever she turned, whatever she did, when David was there he watched her. Not with love—she remembered that particular look of burning, of love so commingled and knotted with lust there was no separating them—but with apprehension. What, she wanted to scream at him, are you expecting me to do? Stab you with a steak knife? Set Four Oaks on fire so the blaze lights up the sky? Stiffly dance like a puppet and sing nonsense songs? What?

"Only I never ask him," she admitted to Klein.

"Why not?"

Her head went down, her hands clung together. "Because I'm afraid of what he'd say."

Klein was not so easily swept up in her fears. "There's nothing so awful it's not better known. And besides, he might just be worrying, Maggie. He might care so much that he's sick with worry."

She wasn't sure Klein believed that, all too aware that he didn't think highly of David, that he wasn't taken in by the charm or the power. But it was such a simple, such an ordinary suggestion that she herself had never thought of

it before, and wondered about it now. Could David love
her so much that he worried about her?

He groaned softly in sleep and shifted his shoulder from
under her hand, as if she were a bothersome fly he was
shaking off. She moved away to the far side of the bed.

There was another reason David might be constantly
watching her, a reason she grappled with now in the dark.
Because I deserve to be watched. Because I'm unreliable.
Because I could do it again.

Do what? Lose Jebbie and drown.

Noooo—Shaking from the howling inside, she went
rigid, tamping it down, stiffling it, burying it so far that
even Klein the archaeologist couldn't unearth it.

A wind blew up and scraped the flanks of the house,
which creaked and sighed like an old ship on unsettled
waters. A rushing sound filled Maggie's head, and she
heard whisperings, the faint voices of the past, of the long
gone who had slept there before, of her father and mother
and her grandparents before them. Their sighs rippled
through her and navigated in her blood, and strangely
enough the ghostly whimperings were comforting. Her
legs relaxed, her arms were loose again, and the metal
band that circled her chest released.

She keeled to sanity and thought: enough of this. I
won't lie here and think the worst. If I move, if I do
something, then I won't dream. And if I don't dream, I
can't have bad dreams. The logic was unassailable, so that
she swung her long legs over the side of the bed and stood
up. She'd go down to the kitchen and make some warm
milk, and while she sat drinking it she'd read the new
Vogue. In the warm yellow light of the nighttime kitchen
that would be such a normal thing to do that the cause—
her need to run from the thoughts inside her head—could
be forgotten. Nobody, not David, not Klein, not even
suspicious Sarah with her speculative eye, could fault her

for drinking warm milk and reading *Vogue*. They were accountable acts that lots of sane women did every night.

She groped for her robe, tossed over the back of the chair, and moved quietly so that she wouldn't wake David. There might be nothing wrong with roaming in the middle of the night, 3:07 A.M. on the digital clock beside the bed, but that didn't mean that she wanted to explain herself either. She had, after all, learned one thing at Greenwood: stealth.

Tugging the robe around her, she knotted the belt and crept out into the hall, the bare floor boards cool beneath her feet. The house was awash in silence. She glided by Jeb's room, the door half cracked, and didn't stifle her impulse to go in and watch him sleep, to reach down and smooth away the shock of hair that always fell across his brow.

She knew there was something wrong the moment she slipped through the door. The night-light beside the dresser was out, and the room was tossed with quaking shadows. She moved to the side of the bed and listened. But there was no sound, no shallow puff of breath. Dimly she made out the jumble of pillows, the twisted sheet and blanket, the twin, gnawed stuffed bears that had sentineled him most nights of his life. But no Jeb, no small body curled fetuslike, pajama legs riding high to the knees.

A shuttered moment and then a huge fist of terror punched her in the heart.

Lost . . . lost . . . lost him. . . . She turned and stumbled in her panic, catching the hem of her robe, and hit the bedpost with her knee. The pain was a thing apart, scarcely noticed, out there somewhere in some other woman's leg.

Don't, don't do this to me, she almost cried aloud, but had no sense of whom she was beseeching. Out in the hall again she wavered: to wake David or not. What if, part of her asked, it was nothing more than a wandering child, a night child, gone to the bathroom or down for milk himself?

But he wasn't in the bathroom. She switched on the light, and the glare bounced off the porcelain. Listening, she heard nothing but the steady drip of the tap.

Back in the hall the house suddenly seemed a foreign place, hard and unyielding. There was no sound, as though her hearing had gone. She stopped at the narrow flight of steps that led up to the third floor where Sarah slept. In the shadowy recess she could just make out the door on the landing closed tightly. Nothing there, no Jeb. She hurried further along the hall to the two unused bedrooms. At the first, she turned the knob slowly, and the seldom-used hinges creaked as the door opened. But no one was there, not in the single, neatly made bed nor underneath the bed, nor in the empty closet. No small child hiding in the second bedroom either. She caught herself turning in the mirror over the dresser, a tall, angular woman whose hair seemed to stand on edge, whose eyes were wide and staring, huge pits in a face of bone. For a moment she stood, captured, stunned and then thought: He's downstairs; he's at that mirror.

She was only halfway down the steps when she realized with a sudden shock of revelation that it was in that very mirror, Jeb's mirror where he spent hours with his *friend*, that she had first seen the smoke. How had she forgotten that? She could almost see it again leveling at her feet, her ankles, rising in a cloud of memory. The smell burned in her nostrils.

No more smoke, no more flames, no more fire: Klein had promised.

But Klein was wrong.

Maggie stumbled on the last few steps, her bare feeting slipping out from under her. She grabbed at the railing and went down, twisting her leg, sliding on the slippery edge of the silk nightgown and came to rest on the bottom step. To the left she could see the kitchen in darkness, no little boy sitting at the table in a puddle of light.

To the right the long hall began just beyond the wall. Maggie crept forward and leaning against the wall pulled herself up. She gulped air and tried to control the terrible shaking of her arms and legs. Her ankle was sore, but when she put her weight on it, it held.

Her fingers gripped the edge of the wall. If it weren't for the pressure beneath her hand and the feel of the hard wood under her feet, she'd think she was dreaming because Klein *was* wrong: She could still smell the burning.

She listened now, unable to move, the flicker of memories that were supposed to have been exorcised from her brain skating across her vision—another long hall, a terrifying red and yellow light, white clouds of cottony smoke. And she heard the crackling, the snapping of flames.

There was something else, something she wasn't certain she really heard. A humming. She concentrated, gripping the wall tighter and listened intently. Yes, there it was, a hum. Jeb, she remembered, often hummed at the mirror.

And then she smelled burning.

Before she lost her nerve, she threw herself away from the wall and turned the corner. There, in the distance, was a flame, a small bright lick of fire. Dancing, dancing. She was mesmerized by the skinny spurt of fire. In her mind's eye the tiny flame wooshed and flared, rose up, shrouded her vision until there was nothing but fire and the wall of heat pounding back at her. In the inferno she saw Tracy's brown curls turn orange and the daisies on Kathy's ruffled nightgown go black into ash.

Tiny hands were striking matches, one after the other, feeding fire into more fire until the flames towered, enveloping those other walls, the curtains charred and shriveling.

No! He couldn't have done it, never would have done it, wasn't such a baby even at four that he didn't know of the danger. And yet even as she was denying it, screaming, howling in pain and terror and rage—great bellows of sound beating down on the flames—she knew. She rushed down the hall, as if she were about to leave the ground and fly, as if she believed she could go back in time and put that other fire out by stopping this little, insignificant blaze.

"Maggie! Maggie! For Christ's sake, stop it!"

Hands were gripping her shoulders, fingers were burying themselves in her flesh. But out of her mouth the unending scream kept curling like the tail of a huge snake. Then her head snapped back with a crack, and she looked up at David, his hand upraised to slap her again. On her bottom lip she tasted the salty tang of blood.

They were standing before the mirror. She could see all three of them—David holding on to her, holding her up now, and Jeb there at their feet, curling into a small, tight ball, his face yellow and red in the glittering light of the small, dancing flame in the ashtray piled high with smoldering books of matches.

She stared at David, his hair mussed, his eyes still gritty with sleep, and then down at Jeb. "Why are you doing this? Why?"

But Jeb didn't answer her. He hovered over his pyre, the flickers diminishing until almost at once they were gone. Just a slight wisp of smoke remained, and then that too faded. He wouldn't look at her, just stared straight ahead into the mirror, where that other little boy stared back.

"He was playing with matches, David," Maggie said, surprised that her voice was so steady. The scream was gone. It had rattled the windows and seeped under the eaves and escaped in the cracks beneath the doors out into the night.

"That's no reason to yell like a crazy—" He stopped and she could feel his anger in the clasp of his hands. Slowly he relaxed and let her go. "What are you doing, Jeb?" He bent and pulled the boy into his arms.

"Playing, Daddy," came the muffled reply as Jeb curled against his father's shoulder.

"Don't you know you shouldn't play with matches?" he asked, lifting Jeb with him as he stood up. The slim arms gripped him about the neck, and Jeb's legs circled his waist.

He turned his head and stared at his mother, one eye blinking. "I'm sorry," he said.

"I know you're sorry, tiger," David said, carrying Jeb down the hall and up the stairs, "but children don't play with fire. It's dangerous. You can hurt yourself. You must never, never do that again. Promise me."

Maggie listened as their voices drifted away from her. She stood without moving, the smoldering ashtray at her feet, the memory of the little boy not below her but in the glass. She was certain in that moment just before she had taken flight down the hall, just before she had that terrible realization that this had all happened before with much, much worse consequences, with terrible consequences, one night high above Central Park—a realization she was already trying to bury deep within the slit of her mind— that Jebbie, the Jebbie she saw in the mirror, had been smiling.

It was chilly in the hallway even with her robe over the thin nightgown and she shivered. She turned and went back toward the kitchen where the light was on and Sarah was standing by the sink. Her long gray hair was tied back by a pink ribbon, and her face was shiny with cream, giving her the look of an aging child.

"Are you all right?" she asked Maggie, and for the first time Maggie thought—hoped—she saw a quiver of kindness in the remote eyes.

"Yes . . . I'm fine. Just—" she searched for a word and knew, not for the first time, that language was inadequate. She shuddered and sank down on a chair by the table and lowered her head to her arms. She was drained, sucked dry as though leeches had siphoned out her energy, her very blood.

"Would you like a cup of tea?" Sarah asked.

"Yes, please," she said. Anything, anything at all was all right now. She just wanted to sleep.

The kettle whistled, and then Maggie heard the clatter of cup against saucer, and in a moment she felt the warm breath of steam against her forehead. She straightened up, and Sarah was standing near enough to touch her, looking down, an unlit cigarette jutting from the corner of her mouth. She should have been menacing, but intuitively Maggie felt that things were beginning to shift between them, that—possibly—Sarah was no longer someone to fear. But perhaps it was only pity. I don't have to be afraid of someone who's sorry for me, Maggie thought.

"Go up to bed Sarah," David said from the doorway. "I'll take care of things."

Sarah left without saying anything more, but as she passed her hand just gently brushed Maggie's shoulder, leaving a lingering trace of warmth.

David came around the table and sat down. Maggie sipped at the hot tea. Her two hands cradling the cup were shaking so that the liquid seeped over the edge and splashed the tablecloth in big, dark stains.

"Well," David said.

"Well what?" She didn't look up.

"That was some scene, Maggie. Don't you think you overdid it just a little?"

She put the cup down and looked at him for the first time. "He was playing with matches in the middle of the night, David. If I didn't wake up, he could have set the house on fire." There, there, I said that fine, just fine, without a quiver in my voice, just the way a normal person would, she thought.

"But he didn't, and he wouldn't have." She knew that David was forcing himself to be calm. "He was wrong, and I told him that. What I'm more worried about," he said, reaching across the table and capturing her hand, "is that you went out of control."

"You slapped me." She yanked her hand back and rubbed her cheek, as if to remind them both, as though she could still feel the stinging blow. He might just this moment have stretched out and slapped her again.

"I had to. You were screaming like a banshee. There was no other way to bring you around," he said. "I know that fire scares you but—"

"What do you know?" She was up and off the chair, released. The chair fell back with a clatter. "You weren't there. It isn't your fault—"

"Maggie, Maggie." He went after her and pinned her arms to her sides with his own arms. She was crushed against him, rigid as a graveyard angel. "It's over. You can't bring the girls back." For a moment she thought he was crying, but when she broke away she saw his eyes were dry. There were no tears on his face. And she remembered that he hadn't cried at all, that he had yelled and carried on, slammed doors and been tight with rage, so that the veins in his temple swelled and his face was dark as death itself. But he hadn't cried. She had almost drowned in tears, and David hadn't shed one. If she held anything against him, it was that.

"Come to bed, Maggie, it's almost dawn."

She shivered, and David pulled her closer. She thought of telling him what she feared, but then knew she never could. Some things were not possible; and telling David that she now believed it was Jeb who had started the fire that killed his sisters was one of those things.

She had neither energy nor anger left and let him lead her away, his arm across her shoulders like a vise. Just before they climbed the stairs she looked back and saw the ashtray and the mirror and the corner of the ashtray in the mirror. And as they went up she remembered—but was she remembering or imagining?—Jeb's smile, sly and evasive, but most of all triumphant.

David walked her back into their bedroom and began untying the belt of her robe. Maggie didn't move as he slid his hands up to her breasts, and she realized that he was going to end the night by making love to her.

6

Klein came out to Four Oaks. He came a week after Maggie had been unnaturally frightened by the fat man, a week after Maggie had insisted she saw Jeb outside the study window, and David had maintained, no proved, the boy had been asleep in his bed; a week after she had gone hysterical over a wisp of flame. Klein came for two reasons: because David had come to see him unannounced at Greenwood, peaked with worry, his usually clear brown eyes cloudy with fear, and because Maggie had only reluctantly told him about any of those events. He was surprised by the first reason, but rather pleased. He was still firm in his belief that David not only had to help but had to change for Maggie to be truly well again. The second reason, however, worried him. He didn't like Maggie's reluctance, it weighed against her cure. She should trust him implicitly by now, be not at all inclined to secrets—or certainly not from him—and have less cause to fall victim to her own irrational fears.

"I know that Jeb wasn't outside the house, as well as I do know he started that small fire in the ashtray," David had said, settled deep in the armchair at the other side of Klein's desk—the patient's chair, though David didn't know that—"because I found him fast asleep in bed."

"Maybe Maggie saw someone else." It was just after nine and Klein had been summoned from a staff meeting when David had appeared at the sanatarium reception desk, insisting on seeing him.

"Who else could it have possibly been?"

"A neighbor, or what about the housekeeper?" Klein asked.

David smiled slightly. "There are no neighbors nearby. And Sarah? No way. She's too big to ever be mistaken, even in the dark, for a small boy. Besides, she came into the study from the kitchen a second, not more, after Maggie began to scream."

"I can understand her fear of fire, God knows, of Jeb's playing with fire, but why the other?" Klein asked himself more than David, settling back into his chair, his annoyance gone at having his morning disrupted. "Why say she saw him when she couldn't have seen him?" He patted his pockets looking for his pipe and realized that he had left it upstairs in the staff room. "Would you have a cigarette by any chance?" he asked. David retrieved a crumpled pack of Marlboros from his shirt pocket and tossed it across the desk to Klein.

"Why would she get so upset about a fat man? Why anything." He slumped further in his chair. Klein had to strain to hear him say, "She's worse not better."

"I told you she'd take patience and time."

"You told me a lot of crap!" David shouted. He couldn't sit still any longer and jumped up. Klein had never seen him so nervous, so worried. For the first time he wondered if he had been wrong about Maggie, if perhaps she wasn't securely fastened to sanity but was still drifting. Could she have fooled him so badly, been so duplicitous? No, he admonished himself, no, for to think so cut him on his one vanity, his certainty of his professional expertise.

Klein watched David pace back and forth, marking off the worn maroon carpeting in even steps, and said, "We're not talking about a disease that can be eliminated with a dose of antibiotics. Mental illness is a state of being from which a patient must be weaned."

"Well she's not. She's still got the tit in her mouth. And she's holding on with both hands," David said savagely.

"Do you want to recommit her? Is that what you're here for?"

"No, no, no," David said, shaking his head. "I love Maggie. Don't you understand that? I don't want her in the looney bin. I want her home with me and Jeb being a normal person." Even as he said the words, David wondered, oh God, is that true? Do I really mean it? The internal conflict brought pain to his eyes.

Klein was amazed. He would have bet a thousand dollars that nothing could make David Brace unravel. But something had, and it scared Klein. It was every psychiatrist's nightmare that was glaring at him out of David's eyes: that the insane would be clever enough to fool the expert and a lunatic let loose to do harm—if to no one else, then to himself.

Klein stubbed out his cigarette and automatically took another. Normally he didn't have two cigarettes a week. "Let's give Maggie the benefit of a doubt—"

David interrupted. "What did she tell you about Jeb playing with matches?"

For a second Klein hesitated. "You know I can't tell you what Maggie said to me during a session. Patient-doctor privilege. Why don't you tell me what happened, and I can compare your version with Maggie's."

David was about to balk. His face suffused with anger, but then he left out a long breath and said, "All right."

When he finished, Klein said, "More or less your stories coincide. Though Maggie seems to have some"—he searched for a word—"impressions of that mirror that you don't."

"The mirror?" David asked, surprised. "What mirror?"

"The mirror in front of which Jeb set the fire. The

mirror it seemed he talks to for hours, the mirror with the little boy in it."

"The mirror with the little boy in it?" David asked, as though Klein had lost *his* mind. "I mean, he plays in front of the mirror with his friend, as he calls his reflection, but . . ."

"A normal phase of childhood development, as I explained to Maggie. Perhaps a phase Jeb should have grown out of by now, but given the loss of his sisters and the fact that he seldom plays with other children, nothing to worry about."

"What did she say about the mirror?"

"It's not what she says, it's that she keeps bringing it up, making it more important than it is." Klein paused. "I want to hear more from Maggie on this, go into these events in more depth. See where these fears are coming from, besides the obvious. Let's hear her interpretations."

"I just told you what she'll tell you, what she thinks, and it's all nonsense."

But Klein held firm. "We'll see. We'll see."

Maggie of course, said nothing further, nothing more than she had, which was the bare minimum. Klein sat through the two sessions of the week waiting for Maggie to talk about the fat man, about her thinking she saw Jeb that night on the lawn, about the matches, but the closest she came was the mirror. How Jeb spent too much time with the mirror. How the mirror in the hall was like another person. That she was thinking of taking it down, but then she'd told Jeb, he threw an almighty temper tantrum that left her shaking, so she promised she wouldn't if he went outside more and if he'd play with real-life flesh-and-blood children. He agreed reluctantly, and most days he sailed around the property, wobbily riding his two wheeler or flying his Chinese kite if the wind was right.

Nothing, nothing at all about the events that had unnerved David so badly that he had come to Klein for help.

Which was why Klein was sitting in a canvas chair on the side lawn of Four Oaks, drinking lemonade and nibbling on a tuna sandwich. Maggie, at the other side of the small folding table, was smiling. She took Klein's excuse of being in Brighton to visit an aged aunt (he did indeed have an aunt, but she was neither aged nor did she live in Brighton) and was pleased, yet not pleased, to see him. Here in the folding canvas chair where she often sprawled to read or possibly catch a glimpse of Jeb as he skipped from side to side of the property, Klein played guest. Yet, she told herself warily, he's not a real visitor, he's a watcher.

"Where is the famed Jeb Brace?" Klein asked, smiling. His voice sounded false reminding her of the "ho, ho," of a department store Santa. And besides, she thought meanly, he looks ridiculous in a suit and dress shirt and tie, out in the sun when the temperature is near ninety. She wiped a trickle of sweat off her upper lip and smiled and glared and poured Klein another glass of lemonade all at the same time. He is not supposed to be here, her inner voice said. She wanted everything in its place, and Klein's place was Greenwood. It diminished him to sit on her side lawn in a director's chair, made him seem less important, more human.

Maggie shrugged. "Around."

"I'd like to meet him."

"I know you would. And I'd like you to." She paused, and they stared at one another. Here at Four Oaks, exposed on the lawn to the elements, they were—or Maggie thought they were—more equal. Klein was less imposing without his desk, his nurses fluttering right and left like harem dancers. He seemed, from this new perspective, less trustworthy, as if his conversation was without meaning. He *can't* be ordinary, Maggie thought. Because if she couldn't believe in Klein, then whom?

Klein twisted about in his chair, his eyes clicking with interest. "It's always revealing to see a patient in his or her own environment," he said. "No matter how well you see a place or a person in your mind's eye, reality is always different."

"I suppose so," Maggie answered flatly, refusing to be drawn. At times Klein could gnaw at her like a toothache.

"Is that Jeb?" Klein half rose from the chair. Angled toward the house, he had been the first to see the boy as he came around the front and stood motionless. The light was directly overhead, the sun noon high and unblemished by clouds, yet a shadow raced outward from the small figure, a long, thin puddle that oozed across the lawn almost to their feet.

"Jebbie," Maggie said, a thrill of terror caught midway in her throat, "come meet Dr. Klein."

The boy didn't move. Klein, standing now, started forward, reached the dark splotch on the lawn, hesitated, looked once at Maggie, and then moved to the side, calling with a voice so stagey that it rendered Klein a total stranger; "Hello, Jeb, I've heard so much about you." He thrust out both his hands toward the boy who drew back and then, just seconds before Klein was upon him, bolted and ran around the porch. There was the shuffling of the lattice being bent forward, then the slap of the wood and the rose vines against the side of the house as the lattice snapped back. Jeb was under the porch.

They were all marionettes with their strings being tightened, Maggie thought. She said, "I'll get him out." But she wasn't sure she could do it even as she went around to the front of the house, Klein trailing behind her, watching, always watching. She bent down and peered through the lattice, just vaguely making out Jeb way in the back.

"Jebbie," she said, "come here. I want you to speak

with Dr. Klein." There was no answer from the darkness, no reverberating response. "Jebbie," she tried again, "please come out."

"No," he finally said, so emphatically she was startled.

"Jebbie!" She could feel Klein in the distance pressing at her, and she gripped the lattice. "Jebbie, get out here at once!"

Still he didn't move forward. As far as she could see, he didn't even twitch. But she thought she heard a growl, like an angry animal would make. The very idea was so ridiculous she dismissed it at once. Yet that fueled her embarrassment even more, made her cheeks go red, so that she turned farther away from Klein, even though he couldn't see her face all that well, and she cried out in a momentary rage, "Jebbie, if you don't come this very instant, I am going to spank you!"

There was a rustling, the clunk of stone against glass, and a blur of movement as he disappeared altogether from her sight.

A hand came down on her shoulder and she reared up. *See?* she seemed to say to Klein, their eyes meeting, *I'm not making it up.*

"I never thought you were, Maggie," Klein said.

"Never thought I was what?" She hadn't realized that she'd spoken aloud.

They moved away from the house, and the slight breeze stirred the soft dress Maggie was wearing, the skirt drifting back and forth against her legs. The sun was behind, haloing her head, but her face was shadowed, and lines surged alongside her nose, dragooning her mouth, so that she looked older, haggard.

She tried to explain to Klein that Jeb was just shy, particularly around strangers, but neither believed that, or not quite. Klein in response merely patted her bare arm, the skin warm from the sun, but the physical contact wasn't reassuring.

After Maggie watched Klein's Mustang disappear down the narrow road, stirring up tides of dust that hung for a moment in the still air, then floated, settling, she went and again knelt at the far side of the porch and peered through the triangles in the lattice, but Jeb hadn't returned. As far back as she could see there was only a colorless haze. She sighed, feeling trapped by Klein's curious inspection, by her own child who inexplicably ran like quicksilver between her fingers each time she reached for him, and by a husband who was slipping farther and farther away than the farthest star in the galaxy. It was all supposed to be perfect. She had promised herself when she was in Greenwood that when she came home everything would be unblemished, that nothing would be mottled with despair, not ever again. David would be perfect, and she and David—though she knew that *she* was light years away from perfection, but that wouldn't matter to *them*—and Jeb, her angel child, her only child. She wouldn't think that he might have started the fire. She wouldn't allow that possibility to trail through her mind. And as day after day slipped by, the idea seemed more and more ludicrous. I was simply upset, she had tried telling herself, by his playing with matches.

Most times, her son was so heart-stoppingly wonderful she thought she'd die from the sheer joy of him. Yesterday, for example, they had blown up a whole bag of balloons and one by one released them up into the sky, running and dancing across the lawn with the very pleasure of the soaring blobs of color, and then rolling on the lawn, as if they had to anchor themselves to the earth or fly away too.

Yes, perfect, like the time before the fire, only the memories of those years were vague, as though they had lodged in someone's else's brain and could only be retrieved with surgery.

Upstairs she stripped off her dress and ran a shower, letting the cool water slide over her until she was chilled.

In her bedroom she pulled aside the curtains and threw up the shades. Even here, high up at the front of the house, the trees blocked the sun. Someday, if she had the choice—if David ever trusted her again to make choices—she'd move them all out of Four Oaks to somewhere sunny in a sea of light.

Opening the closet door, she reached between the row of blouses for her jeans hanging on a hook in the back and heard a rustling. Her hand outstretched, she looked down, suddenly afraid. There was something in the closet. Something alive. It moved again, furtively, and brushed against her legs. A scream gurgled just behind her lips as she frantically pulled at the cord dangling from the fixture in the ceiling. Light flooded the closet.

"Jeb?"

He was sitting on the floor cross-legged, his blond hair falling over his forehead. He stared up at her, his face as white as ivory except for the eyes. His eyes were dark, darker than they should have been, and they seemed not to see her. He might have been sleeping.

"What are you doing here?"

Then she noticed the scissors. How had she not seen the scissors that gleamed in the light? He was holding them pointed upward in his left hand, and in his right was a swatch of red material.

She caught her breath as the blades snapped shut with a loud click. A sleeve of the blouse slithered to his lap, joining the other sleeve like a banner across his thigh.

"You're cutting up my clothes!" she cried, more with surprise than anger.

The dresses had been slit from hem to waist, evenly,

almost surgically. Random sleeves of other shirts littered
the floor like streamers. Her slacks had been dissected
below the knees. It seemed that he had worked methodically from the back to the front of the closet, not sparing a
garment. She touched a powder blue ruffled sundress still
hanging by the straps, and it slid dismembered to the
floor.

"Why? Why did you do this?" She was screaming at
him, but he didn't answer. His bloodless lips didn't move.
She went to grab him just as he raised the scissors, the
blades spread. One sharp point pierced the palm of her
hand going in to the bone. The blood spurted in a thin
arc, flying and curling like a thread across his blond hair.

For a moment Maggie couldn't concentrate. The whole
scene had a gray, grainy feel to it like out of sync film.
Even the blood pouring down her arm seemed gray. Then
she focused on the bubbles pulsing out of the hole in her
hand and cried and pushed herself backwards, out of the
closet. She tripped and fell hard, striking her hip against
the side of a chair as she slid in a heap to the floor.

As though a spring had been uncoiled inside him, Jeb,
launched himself past his mother, who tried to grab one
wiggling leg. "Stop! Jebbie, come back!"

She rolled over, put her hand down, winced and left a
bloody print on the carpet. But he was gone, only the
scissors were left, just by the door. She could hear his
footsteps clattering on the steps, hear him running. In the
distance the screen door slammed.

Scrambling up, she tore open the dresser drawer, throwing out clothes until she found a pair of shorts. Quickly she
put them on. Grabbing a shirt of David's that he'd left
across the back of the chair, she ran, splattering blood.

In the kitchen she shoved her hand under cold water,
trying to staunch the bleeding. Sarah was nowhere in

sight. Thank God, Maggie thought. Who knew what she'd think?

And what do I think?

My fault . . . my fault. They'll say I was to blame again.

The wound was throbbing. It was a deep though narrow cut, looking worse than it was, but it pained like fire. Maggie felt giddy with the burning, and her eyes filled with tears. She picked up a dish towel from the counter and pressed it down on the cut. Sweat popped out along her hairline as she gulped for air, tried to force air into her heaving lungs.

Please don't let me faint, she thought as the window ledge with its parade of potted begonias shifted in and out of focus. Outside, the day, the green lawn, the yellow light lay flat as a painting on a museum wall. The time unfurled itself once more and Maggie could breathe.

She wrapped her hand in a clean towel and ran out the back door. She raced around the house and looked through the lattice but it was too murky to see more than the dim outlines of Jeb's neatly folded blanket and insect jars. He wasn't there.

He could be anywhere, Maggie thought, anywhere a six-year-old's imagination could take him, up the chimney or down the rabbit's hole or as far away as her bedroom closet. For a moment she wondered if it wasn't beyond her, the finding of him and the unraveling of the labyrinth of his child's scenario—the why and the because of what he'd done. She should tell Sarah and ask the older woman for help; and she certainly should call David and tell him what had happened, but knew she wouldn't. She had to do some things on her own. Besides, she was afraid, not of Jeb, nor even David, but of her own inadequacy.

She circled the house again, but he was nowhere that she could see, which meant that he had either entered the woods or gone down the dirt road to the highway. He was such a little boy that he could curl into the smallest place, and she could go right on by him without even noticing. Even now, he could be watching her.

At the edge of the lawn Maggie stood, shifting uncertainly, shaking. There wasn't a sound, just an eerie stillness, as though all life had been sucked out of the world and she was staring at reflections.

Where? Here or back?

She decided at last on the woods, feeling instinctively that he'd opt for darkness, somewhere out of the glaring light, away from the sun.

Plunging into the woods she found the path that led through the brush to the stream. The undergrowth was thick, and she felt plucked at by unseen hands as she pushed her way through. Overhead the branches bent and met, stretching a canopy that shouldered out the sun. Only here and there did the light interstice, speckling the path with baubles of color.

Almost at once she could hear the rushing of the water. It sang through the silence as she hurried toward it and broke into the clearing on the near side of the stream.

"Jeb! Jeb!" she called, going up the bank. She followed the curve of the water, passed the wide part they called the pool with the large flat rock like an immense table top ten feet out. Then she pivoted and looked back the way she'd come, listening, trying to hear with her body, with her arms and legs, with the back of her neck, as if her flesh could tell her where to find him.

There was nowhere, nowhere she could see or hear or feel.

There was too much, too many trees and bushes, and undergrowth too wild with tendrils and branches and needles, too seething with unseen life. He could have been swallowed up, interred in the lush foliage. She tried to remember how big the woods were, where they began and ended. In her mind's eye she tried to cast a map, to soar weightless over the trees so that she could discern the boundaries. But it was hopeless. He could play hide and seek here with her for hours, for days if he wanted to. She would never find him in these thickets if he didn't want to be found. And why would he after what he'd done?

Suddenly she felt so tired, so drained. She must have lost more blood than she thought she had. Besides, she wasn't accustomed to this kind of physical effort. These last months she had so retreated into herself that even her muscles had gone slack. Whatever energy she'd had was, by necessity, utilized to scale the slick walls of sanity.

Continuing upstream, she realized for the first time that she was barefoot. The river bank was soft, mucky, and the mud oozed between her toes. Then she saw that her feet were scratched from brambles, streaked with slime and red lines like protuberant veins.

Thirty yards further on, a large boulder jutted out from the embankment. She kept on until she reached it, gratefully sitting down and dangling her aching feet and legs in the water. It was icy. The shock was stunning but after a few moments, the cold water felt good, diminishing the pain which seemed to drain out of her with the swirling currents.

There was a narrow gap in the branches above and a splinter of light shifted down and flickered across the water. She unwrapped the towel from her hand and saw that the scallops of flesh had puckered. The angry cut was closing. She thrust the hand into the stream and watched the tiny minnows, no bigger than an inch and almost transparent, frantically dart by her in their terrified passage.

Bending forward eased the tension in her neck. Maggie thought she could stay there all day listening to the rushing of the water, feeling it slide over her like cool silk.

If you sit still and never move again you won't find him,

a voice in her head whispered, *and then you'll never know.*

She lurched, scambling up the rock, and then ran along the bank, the urgency pulling at her again with uneasy hands. What had she been doing just dawdling there, she cursed at herself. David wouldn't have done that . . . but then she knew with blinding certainty that Jebbie would never, ever cut up the clothes in David's closet, as if he were cutting the very skin off the bones.

The farther she went, the narrower the stream became until she reached a clutch of boulders and an oblong-shaped pool where, she remembered her father had told her, the stream originated from an underground spring, jetting forth with a spasmodic pumping. The water swirled and bubbled angrily as it thrust its way to the surface. She could feel the energy of the water, the unseen power within the ground as though an uneasy dragon rumbled beneath her feet.

What we lock in, must sooner or later come bursting out, she realized, and she circled the rocks, pushing her way through a copse of birch trees whose skinny trunks made her think of undernourished children.

The land was more solid now, less spongy. The visibility was better here, the bushes lower as she moved away from the stream. The trees became fewer, spaced further and further apart until she broke free and stumbled out onto a narrow dirt road. The sudden light was painful against her eyes, and for an instant the earth tilted, then lazily settled back.

At the other side of the road was a border of blueberry bushes, the fruit just starting to purple, beyond that a rolling field pocked with jagged rocks, debris from the long ago glacier. In the distance was a weathered barn, that seemed to be sliding sunward.

God takes care of idiots and little children, her father

used to say. Well, that's us, she thought, one idiot and one lost little child, and she wanted to cry as she scuffed up the dust with her toes. She wanted to throw herself on the ground and howl and flail her arms and legs and have her father come rescue her, or Klein—yes, Klein would do since her father had been dead too many years.

But no one was going to rescue her, not her father, not Klein, and certainly not David. So she scrambled down the other side of the road and then up through the blueberry bushes, which plucked with their scratchy fingers at her arms and shirt.

She'd go look in the barn because it was there, as good as any place to look. She knew she'd have to look until she found Jeb, if she had to search through daylight and darkness and then daylight again. There was no room for another defeat in her life, no corner where she could secret away one more failure, one more lost child.

No beast will eat you up, Jebbie.

She bit down on her lip, and her eyes once more filled with tears. She imagined yet again that she heard the girls tinny voices, their cries exploding with an impact like breaking glass.

I will find him. I will. . . .

Promises, promises, Maggie, her inner voice accused, beating against Tracy's cries, Kathy's screams. A whole chorus was carrying on an unholy howling in her head.

Crazyyyyyyyy. . . .

No!

She ran across the field tufted with spindly grass and weeds. Her feet, cut and bruised, stung from the lacerations. The wound in her palm began throbbing again. Blood once more saturated the already sodden towel. She ripped it off and let the blood flow more freely. Maybe all the blood would gush out of her, leaving her dessicated, a zombie, a living dead woman.

"Where is he?" she cried, knowing that when she found him she'd stop hurting, that then the bleeding would not only stop but the blood would be drawn back into her, and her wounds would close.

She tried to slow her thudding heart. Lost child . . . lost child . . . lost child. . . .

She tried to think of what Klein would say, how he'd tell her to proceed. He, Klein, more and more was the only one who understood (even if he didn't understand about Jeb, but then she didn't either). The one who was on her side.

Stop thinking my side, his side, their side. . . .

The barn loomed up on her unexpectedly, as though she hadn't been running toward it all this time, as if it had just appeared, conjured up in her imagination out there in the field. Out of breath, she swayed, hunched over, then finally straightened and looked about. There was no one, certainly not one small little boy, one wild-eyed little boy. But he hadn't been wild-eyed at all. On the contrary, he had seemed remarkably possessed as he scissored her clothes like paper dolls and then calmly, collectedly stabbed her. It occurred to her for the first time that if her hand hadn't been extended, the blade would have kept going, right into her midsection.

A pain sliced through her, just at the waist, doubling her over. Her toes dug into the stubbled grass. Stop thinking what might have been, what *is*, is bad enough, she told herself. Slowly she straightened up. She went around the barn until she found the doors, one of which was off its hinges and propped open.

Part of the roof had given way and a good-sized section of the opposite wall was knocked through, as though a gigantic fist had splintered it apart. Old bundles of hay were tuffed about in the corners.

Something darted from the darkness, black and swift, and disappeared under the remnants of a plow, rusted like a weathered piece of old sculpture left too long in the rain. Maggie flinched and scurried backwards into the sunlight until she could feel the warmth on her head.

If Jeb was hiding in the barn, he wasn't immediately visible. She forced herself back in and paced the length of the barn, shuffling at the dirt on the old floorboards in what remained of the stalls.

It smelled in the barn, a rotting dank odor. And out of the sun it was cold, with a chill that made Maggie shiver.

"Jeb? Jeb, are you in here?"

Of course he's not, and if he were, he wouldn't answer. She stared up, and overhead a curtain of cobwebs swayed in the slight breeze that drifted in from nowhere. "Ssss. . . ." It was so slight a noise that at first she wasn't certain she heard it. Then again: "Sssss. . . ." The hair on the back of her neck quivered. She held her breath.

It was whispering, so airy and light as to be almost undetectable. She heard it again, a flutey, sibilant whispering, coming from the loft above.

"Jeb?" She scrambled up the shaky ladder, ignoring the creaking of the rungs beneath her bare feet. Went up hand over hand, forgetting the pain in her palm, the wound opening yet a third time, dragging at the splinters in the wood.

A whisper: "Don't move or she'll hear you!"

"It *is* you, Jeb. And I can hear you. Who are you with?" Up, up until her head reached the top and she could see across the clear sweep of floor.

Here the hay was cleaner, new, not mottled with dank, wet spots. Light beams danced through the open loft doors and settled like an aureola on Jeb's golden hair. He was buried almost up to his neck in the straw and looked more like a broken doll plunked down by a child, than like a living child himself.

Whatever she thought she'd feel when she found him—relief, anger at what he'd done or worse, pain—was outweighed by a sheer joy that engulfed her. Oh God, she thought, thank you for giving him back to me, as if God himself had actually taken him away.

"Jebbie," she said, crawling off the ladder and onto the loft floor.

"Mommy!" he burst out of the straw and scrambled toward her, flinging himself so fiercely into her arms that they rolled in the straw, the dust.

"Oh, Jebbie, are you all right?" Enough time later to ask him why. He nodded and burrowed into her neck. The sweet, milky child smell of him, overpowering the dead smells of the rotting barn, invaded her. The puffs of his rapid breathing stirred her hair, and she knew his face was slick with tears.

"Who were you talking to, Jeb?"

He stiffened and held on to her so tightly that it hurt. Against her shoulder she could feel his thudding heart like a trapped bird.

"Who, Jebbie? I heard you whispering to someone." She pulled him loose with an effort and held him off, at arm's length. He shook his head swiftly back and forth and in one sweep, his eyes wide open and staring, he saw the blood on her, down her arms and patterned on the front of David's shirt like obscene trackings.

He wailed, "I didn't do it. Didn't."

"What, the whispering?"

"No!"

"The clothes," she stammered slightly, "in my closet? My hand?"

They stared at one another, as though from a great distance. She could almost feel him receding from her, swirling away, even though his arms were trapped by her hands.

"Didn't!" he cried.

"I don't understand, Jebbie," she said softly, brushing the hair off his face, and, leaving thin red streaks on his forehead. "I was there. I saw you. You stuck the scissors into my hand. You and nobody else, Jeb."

The tears gushed from his luminous eyes, sliding along his downy cheeks. "Not me, Mommy, not *me!*" Jebbie howled, as though he were being split in half.

7

There was a jagged pain in her palm, worse than the wound itself, a pulsing, throbbing ache that traveled insidiously up her arm. A young doctor, not much older than Maggie herself, had stitched up the gash, cheerfully accepting her story—told at David's insistence—of a kitchen accident. He whistled as he sewed, and though his hair was rumpled and much too long and there was a grass stain across the front of his gauzy Indian shirt, he was competent. When he finished he left a pursed red line, crisscrossed by almost invisible black trackings. It will hurt after the Novocain wears off, he told her as he handed over a fistful of codeine samples, cautioning her with a laugh not to become a druggie. Maggie longed for Dr. Meredith, who had treated her in this same office when she had been a child and had given her lollipops and pats on the head. Maggie hadn't wanted "hip," she had wanted coddling—but she couldn't dare tell David that— and now, even though the wound oozed pus and surely was infected, she hated to go back.

David had awakened and found her sitting up in bed, cradling the arm in much the same way she sheltered Jeb. The early morning light was ash against the drawn shades, and though he tried to be solicitous, he was distant. He seemed still asleep, still dreaming, and didn't like acknowledging the dark hollows and yellow stains of pain beneath her eyes.

It's all right to hurt, she told herself, yet she felt as though she was somehow at fault. But her hand was on fire, and even her forearm was hot to the touch. Little by little her body was being consumed.

David had wanted to take her himself, to stay home from the office and drive her into Brighton, but she couldn't have that. It was worse with David, because he didn't believe her, didn't believe that Jeb had actually stabbed her—not with Jebbie's litany, over and over: I didn't, I didn't. Wouldn't believe it had been Jeb, even with the evidence of severed sleeves and pants legs.

"I'll go with Sarah," she finally agreed, knowing she couldn't drive herself.

Which was what she was doing now, the sun hot and heavy already, and David long gone to the city. Sarah, her bulk squeezed behind the wheel even with the seat pushed back, had been noncommittal about this change in her routine, yet she had put on what Maggie supposed was one of her better outfits—a bright orange polyester pants suit that made her look like a huge carrot.

Jeb was in the back seat, turning the pages of a comic book, and Maggie rolled down the window, even though the air conditioning was on, and let the breeze blow across her feverish face.

Sarah, taking her eyes off the road for a moment, glanced surreptitiously at Maggie who leaned against the door, her lashes fluttering, her mouth agape. Sick she is, Sarah thought, burning up, and quickly gave her attention back to the road as she felt the front tire clip the gravel. For the first time since she had come to work for the Braces, Sarah felt responsible. The cooking, the cleaning, even the tending to Jeb were just parts of a job; she never had to think about them. But this variation from the everyday—for Sarah didn't drive that often, though she hadn't said so to Maggie—tapped into a vein of feeling

Sarah had long repressed. Maggie needed her, was relying on her for something, and so was he, she thought, quickly checking on Jeb in the rearview mirror.

He sat in the center of the back seat, his legs folded under him, a picture book on his lap. His face was shadowed but his blond hair, almost white, seemed to shine. To Sarah it was radiant, as though floodlit.

His fingers flicking the pages. Rapidly. She could tell he wasn't reading, just looking at the pictures.

Never. That baby couldn't do what she said he did.

A large brown rabbit darted to the side of the road and then hopped away as Sarah passed him. She shuddered, thinking she wouldn't have the stomach to roll over an animal, not even in self-defense, and that if some living thing ran in front of the car she'd probably swerve, and they'd end up in a ditch. You're too softhearted, Sarah, she admonished herself. Never used to be this way, and stiffened her shoulders against Maggie, against the Braces in general.

No, that little boy was innocent; for there were some things Sarah knew for sure, and children being innocent was one of them, which meant Maggie had made it up. And if Maggie had done such a terrible thing to her own child, her own *living* child, she was crazy. And while Sarah had already decided that Maggie had to be crazy because of the fire, because of the asylum, she really didn't like to think so. She couldn't be certain with crazy, because that was what crazy meant—uncertainty.

If Sarah hadn't needed two hands on the wheel, she would have crossed herself. If God was paying attention, that was all to the good, but maybe it wouldn't hurt to stop in at St. Agnes' before she drove them all back to Four Oaks. While not a steady churchgoer, Sarah was an undeviating believer. Yes, maybe she would stop by St. Agnes', and if Father Fallon was hearing confessions, that would be all right too, though Lord knows, she wondered, what it is that's weighing on my mind. I'm not crazy; I didn't do anything wrong. Just then she looked up again, as the road curled past a derelict farmhouse on the curve before the last stretch into Brighton, and saw Jeb gazing back at her in the mirror. His eyes were black holes, staring, staring, filling up the mirror, growing larger in the moment she was snared by them. She was a fish, being pulled up out of the water.

"Sarah!" Maggie screamed and with her good left hand yanked at the wheel of the Dodge just as the car bounced on the strip of dirt before the house, and then angled back. Automatically, Sarah's foot hit the brake, and the car shuddered to a stop in a diagonal across the road.

"For God's sake, what are you doing?"

Quickly, Sarah straightened the car so that it was once again fully in the right lane and headed toward Brighton. Yes, there was the curve, and they slid around it perfectly, like an eel in a barrel.

"I don't know what happened," she lied, and reaching over switched off the air conditioning. A deathly chill was starting up her legs and into her stomach. "Just daydreaming, I guess." She tightened her hands on the wheel, her knuckles white from the strain.

"We almost hit that old house!" Jeb said, his voice shaky with excitement.

"Nonsense!" Sarah flinched, hunkering over the steering wheel, away from the boy. He was leaning over the front seat, peering up into her face. "Get in back, you, before we really do have an accident." She shifted to the left, as far away from him as possible, and thought, forced herself to think, there's nothing wrong with him, nor me neither. It's *her* putting ideas into all our heads because she's crazy.

"Enough, Jebbie, sit down and be quiet," Maggie said,

but her voice was dreamy. She didn't have the strength to
scold him. She had taken two codeine tablets before they
left Four Oaks, and she was languid, shifting, like a sack of
feathers. The throbbing in her hand was far away, the hand
not hers, detached.

Brighton surged up on them, and they circled the
square to the municipal parking lot. Off in the distance,
spiked three blocks away was the steeple of St. Agnes' and
Sarah was reassured. She hustled them out of the Dodge,
forced herself to give Jeb a hurried but sturdy hug, the
weight of him pressing on her orange thighs, and was
relieved to find him flesh and bones, smelling of small boy.

Silly old woman, she said to herself, though she had
never considered herself old before and certainly not silly.
She took Maggie authoritatively by the arm, and with her
free hand grasped Jeb's shoulder, steering them all toward
the cedar-shingled building on Dumont Street that housed
the doctor's office.

They went down the far side of the square where
towering elms shaded the grass so that it was still green
and not blanched yellow by the sun. It had been a raging,
unremitting summer so far, the days seldom broken by
rain. The farmers were complaining about drought. Here
in Brighton and in the other small towns up through New
England there was a ban on watering lawns or shrubs or
flower gardens.

The grass was parched where the sun beat down upon
it, and the whole town was beginning to look frayed about
the edges. Not that the three of them noticed. Jeb's
attention was centered on a golden retriever that raced
back and forth across the square. Maggie moved, one foot
ahead of the other, in a bubble, cocooned by the codeine
and the pain. And Sarah, who came from the part of
White Plains that was a sprawl of gas stations and auto
repair shops, fast food outlets aproned by parking lots,

discount stores and blinking neon signs, didn't care that Brighton was dusty and desperate for rain.

"A good shot of penicillin is what you need. Fix you up nicely," she said as they went up the three steps to the screen door and into the waiting room. Maggie almost asked, is there a bad shot? She giggled, and Sarah's forehead creased like a washing board. "I don't see anything funny about penicillin," she said.

"No, no Sarah, I didn't mean it," Maggie said, hearing herself giggling again.

Around them, on chairs backed against the walls, people waited. The room was full. There were bandages, casts, canes, crutches, and several patients without any discernable signs of illness, which made them, Maggie thought, the most seriously sick of all.

"Yes?" The nurse was rigidly starched in the stuffy room, stationed behind a desk just to the side of the door to the doctor's private office. "Do you have an appointment?"

Maggie explained the accident, the stitching up, the pain now, and the possible infection.

The nurse sighed with annoyance, as if she blamed Maggie for not healing properly. "Well, I suppose I'll have to fit you in somewhere, Mrs. Brace, but you'll have to wait. Sit down." She pointed with a red-tipped nail to a chair by the window, and Maggie, as obediently as a schoolgirl, sat. Sarah towered above her, and Jeb balanced against her knees.

"Why don't you go do some shopping, Sarah," Maggie said.

"And the boy?"

"Could you take him with you? It will be boring for him here. I guess you could come back in an hour." She glanced questioningly at the nurse who shrugged and returned to her paperwork. "Try in an hour."

Sarah didn't want to take Jeb. She intended to go over

to St. Agnes' and say her rosary, even if she had left it in
her top dresser drawer under the new nylon nightgown
her niece from Des Moines had sent her last Christmas,
but she'd say it anyway, or at least several Hail Marys and
Our Fathers, and confess to Father Fallon if he was around
and willing to listen. She wanted to be alone in the
coolness of the old church, even if she wasn't spooked
anymore by the child. Gazing up at her, now, he was no
different from any other six-year-old—though maybe
handsomer—no matter that she remembered, hadn't really forgot, the time he spent under the front porch killing
bugs and frogs and God knows what else. He looked, in
fact, like a normal child, which as far as Sarah was
concerned was what he was. The only thing wrong was all
that tension—the mother's and the father's dragging at
them like a fast-running tide. It would be a miracle if she,
Sarah, wasn't a bit unsettled now and then. As Mr. Brace
said when he hired her: It wouldn't be easy.

Feeling seaworthy again, Sarah nodded her head, drew
herself up, and pushed Jeb ahead of her out of the office.

Maggie waited, her head lowered, her chin almost
touching her chest. Furtively the other patients watched
her, for even with the calligraphy of pain sketched on her
face, she was a flamboyant creature who had settled in
their midst, there in the slightly drab office with chairs
twenty years out of date, rugs balding and unraveling on
the edges, walls in need of a seasonal paint job under their
Utrillo reproductions. They expected her to take flight
momentarily. Even the nurse, scrutinizing her out of
narrowed eyes, found Maggie suspect.

The nurse knew all about that one, of course. Doctor
hadn't accepted Maggie's story, not for a moment, no
matter what he said or led Maggie and David to believe.
He recognized a good old-fashioned stab wound when he

saw one, for he had done his residency in a battered, run-down hospital not far from the South Bronx.

A suicide attempt, the nurse had suggested, but the doctor had rejected that one immediately. Nope, he had said, you can't kill yourself by sticking a potato peeler halfway through your palm. When you want to do the big one, it's the wrists or the throat, and you use a razor or a well-sharpened kitchen knife. He was warming to the subject when the nurse—a no-nonsense woman—asked, then what? But the doctor didn't have an answer, though he was certainly intrigued. The puzzle of it pleased him, as did Maggie herself.

A "townie" who had grown up in a pre-Revolutionary saltbox on Delaney Street on the other side of Elm, Jamie Evers remembered Maggie. He'd see her on summer afternoons, the light dripping like runny ice cream, shopping with her mother—a tall, imposing, steely-looking woman—or riding in her father's Lincoln, high up, her arm crooked in the open window. She always seemed to be smiling or laughing, impossibly pretty, more like a storybook character than a real-life child. Then she'd disappear, just as the leaves began to color, and magically return the following summer, a little taller, a little lankier, fuller breasted and more narrow in the hips, until the year he was sixteen, when he thought he at least had the courage to ask her out, which meant the movies in the stripped-down Ford he'd just learned to drive. So he watched for her, cruising Main Street, circling the square, spending hours when he wasn't bagging groceries at the Finest Food Market or swimming off the public beach at Lake Winoche or playing baseball on the scruffy diamond behind Central High, waiting for one glimpse of the Lincoln. But she never came back until pale, blood leaking through the towel wrapped about her hand, her hair just a shade darker than the fire engine red he remembered, she surfaced in his office, an Ondine rising out of the swirling waters of the past.

He still thought her pretty and arousing—though he hadn't known way back then that it was arousal he felt—but she had grown somewhat soft for his taste. He now liked his women harder, closer to the bone, still he was struck by a quick ripple of excitement when the nurse said she was waiting.

"Doctor—" Maggie realized with horror that she had forgotten his name. She stood just inside the examining room with its steely glittering surfaces and cold, hard look. "Doctor—" She stumbled, wondering, how do I say to him I've forgotten who you are except that you aren't Dr. Meredith, and you should be older, and comforting, and like someone I can trust. She meant like Klein, she understood. Klein fit her preconceived image, which was one reason she clung to him so.

"Call me, Jamie," he said, "all my patients do." She's skittish, he thought, and recognized that particular nervousness which he had come across so often. He had enough sensitivity to be saddened by a patient's fear, and sometimes he responded with a kindness that was natural to him as a person, but more often than not he grew angry, as if he were to blame for the disease, for the pain, which is what he felt now, that knotting inside that made him want to lash out. Maggie looked so weak, so wispy, like a wounded bird dragging a broken wing along the ground, that he broke out in goose bumps. God damn her, he thought, and grinned boyishly, crossing the room and taking her chin between his thumb and forefinger, forcing her head up. "Hey, com'on, lady," he cajoled, "you're a grown-up, not a little girl who's about to be yelled at by teacher."

Maggie flinched. She didn't like him teasing her. He firmly grasped her arm and led her to the examining table, helping her up. He wasn't a tall man, and as she sat between the stirrups on the high leather-covered table, they were almost eye level. They stared at one another for a moment, then another.

Christ, she really has turned into a beauty, he thought with the same detachment he would have given to a prize orchid.

He frightened her, for no reason she could put her finger on, except the way he looked at her, almost microscopically. "I think it's infected," she said, holding up her hand.

"Infected?"

"Yes. It hurts." Tears flooded her vision as she allowed herself to feel how much her hand did ache, even now above the narcotic. "And it's oozing pus. Look." She pushed her hand closer to his chest, but he kept staring at her face. His own face was a screen across which flickered an emotion that Maggie would have recognized as desire if she weren't so frightened and didn't hurt so acutely.

Looking down at last, he took up her bandaged hand. "Okay, let's see what's what." He cut the tape and gauze lengthwise, splitting open the bandage, carefully peeling it back like a delicate second skin and lifting up the pad that covered the wound itself. Pus had leaked through, leaving a wide moon of yellow against the white. His fine stitches were buried in a puffy mass of swollen flesh. The cut was an angry red, inflamed, rivered in pus that stank of rancid fish.

Jamie hissed between clenched teeth. "I don't like this mother *at all*," he said.

"I didn't do anything to it! I never touched it!" she cried as he tentatively prodded the inflammation.

"I never said you did. These things happen. Nothing's certain in medicine you know." He glanced up at her, but she wouldn't meet his eyes. She was mesmerized by her

wound, thinking it's as if there's something awful inside
trying to get out ...

*Stop! That's the kind of thing Klein wouldn't like, a
crazy thought.*

"The pus will have to be drained, and I think I'm going
to cut away those small stitches at the end. Then a shot
and you'll be just fine. Don't worry." He was trying to
keep his distance, but her vulnerability mitigated against
him. He wanted to comfort her, but he wanted to make
love with her too. He hardened standing so near her,
holding the damaged hand, and running over in his mind
the steps of the procedure he was about to perform.

"Okay, let's get this over with. I don't have all day to
spend over a little kitchen accident," he said, suddenly as
angry with her as he was with himself.

His moods changed so swiftly, he confused her. He was
a prism being revolved sharply in the light. First kindness
and concern, then a biting animosity.

"Have you taken any pain-killers?" he asked.

"Two, right before we left the house."

"What time?"

"I don't remember," she answered as he broke open a
syringe and quickly filled it with Novocain.

"Well, this probably won't hurt as much as last time
then," he said and quickly shot the needle into the base of
her hand. She winced and tried to jerk away from him,
but he just pushed forward.

He yanked out the needle and held onto her until from
the wrist down her hand was a piece of dead meat, then
calmly, methodically, he went about draining the poison
out of her. She watched from a distance as the yellow
faded and the wound grew white and pink and finally
spurted pure red blood. He didn't speak to her until after
he had rebandaged and taped her hand again.

"Now," he said, "I'm going to give you a shot of antibiot-

ics, and you're done. Oh yeah, you better take son
erythromycin every four hours for the next few days. I'l
give you a prescription for that. Now, let's roll up your
sleeve a little bit higher."

Maggie pushed up the white T-shirt to her shoulder.
Jamie filled a second syringe and circled her upper arm
with his hand, stiffening the muscle beneath a thin splattering
of freckles. He had a reputation, unusual for a doctor, of
giving a good shot, but he jabbed Maggie clumsily and she
cried out.

"Sorry," he said, the syringe quivering slightly as he
caught the scent of lilacs.

He moved away and tossed the empty syringe into the
garbage pail beside the small table on which sat a nest of
supplies. He kept his back to her, counting to ten, then
counting to ten a second time. She was coming at him in
waves, a sirocca, blowing memories in gusts that shifted
through the impersonal room. He thought, she is something left undone, time shuttered to a stop. Then all the
switches were flipped on fast speed, so that she was the
woman, the teenager, the child, and he was lost in an
endless Brighton winter, the snow piling up to the school-
room window as he wondered where she had gone and
why.

He knew in one of those flashes of insight that if he
turned back, everything would change, nothing would be
as it had been just a moment before, and as sure as the
sun set in the west and rose in the east, he was going to be
sorry. Worst of all, he didn't know what it truly was about
her—a combination of her beauty and that almost shameful air of helplessness, or maybe that elusive quality of
being there but being somewhere else at the same time.
Or maybe it just was the past and the memory of driving
up and down the Brighton streets that long-ago summer,
possessed by such longing that his mouth was always dry,

his heart lurching more than the old Ford every time he thought he caught sight of her in the distance.

"Am I finished now?" she asked, her voice barely above a whisper. A wave of nausea swept over her, and in an instant the room was launched upward, out into space, a whirlpool of metal tables, stools, bottles, streamers of gauze. Around and around. "I—" But the words went flying off too.

He turned just as she started to slip off the table, her bad hand thrust out, her hair sweeping sideways, and he jumped, grabbing her before she went.

And then it was too late, all his sane rationalizations evaporating under the heat of Maggie in his arms. He cradled her for only a moment before he let her go, setting her straight up, barely holding her arm. Sixteen again, not thirty-five, and finally he had touched her. Like any other patient she was flesh and bone.

Her eyelids fluttered, and she put the back of her hand to her forehead. In anyone else the gesture would have seemed theatrical, but she made it her own. He smiled thinking he was on the deck of the *Titanic* going down. Stiff upper lip, he said to himself, and listen to the music.

"Okay now?" he asked, and watched her eyes.

"I'm sorry. Just for a minute I thought I was blacking out."

"You were. It's nothing. Many people react that way to pain, to trauma. The mind just draws a curtain closed," he said, hearing himself babble.

"Can I go now?" she asked.

"Sure, if you're steady enough." He didn't want her to leave but had no idea how to keep her. Take out her appendix, vaccinate her, what? he thought wildly. And he said, "But why don't you sit for a while. Just until you're not woozy." Woozy, Jesus, he thought, I sound like someone's maiden aunt. "Com'on into my private office, and we'll have a Tab. I've got a mini refrigerator in there, good for keeping soda or ham sandwiches, which I also happen to have if you're hungry." He was helping her off the table, not waiting for a reply. Holding her good hand, he led her through the connecting doors into his office. He sat her in the chair beside the desk and dumped himself down on the old swivel, which creaked and protested like a wheezy asthmatic when he spun it around. Immediately, he jumped up again. "The Tab," he said, going to a small cube that looked like a vault in the middle of the opposite wall, bookcases built around it. "Maybe there's a ginger ale. Would you rather have that?"

"No, a Tab would be fine," she said. The office hadn't changed at all from when Dr. Meredith had sat in that same chair, which always tilted back so far she'd hold her breath, waiting for him to catapult to the floor. It wasn't at all like the examining room, which was new, shiny, all expensive, impersonal equipment. "It's like a time warp," she said, smiling tentatively. "I mean, I can hear Dr. Meredith saying, 'Now Maggie, you just be a good girl and listen to me.'"

Jamie laughed, sitting down and handing her a paper cup into which he'd poured the soda. "And then," he picked up, "he'd lean over and pat your knee."

She jerked away from him, his hand a flame on her skin beneath the skirt. She felt herself blushing and averted her eyes. "How do you know?" she asked.

"Same way you did. I was one of Old Doc's children. Grew up here in Brighton. You don't remember me," he said, rushing on, "but I remember you. Margaret Matherson, Maggie for short. You spent summers out at that big Victorian ark off Ice House Road. Four Oaks it was called."

"That's where we are now," she said, and then apologized. "I feel terrible that I don't remember you."

"No reason to, we never met. I just used to see you in

town and out at the lake. Last summer I saw you, you had a pink bathing suit. I'll never forget it because I'd always heard that redheads never wore pink, and there you were like some damn exotic flower. I was one of your better basic pimply-faced teenage sex maniacs with my tongue hanging out. No reason to have separated me out from the rest of the bunch of bananas that thought you were sexy city. God," he laughed, "listen to me, rambling on like an idiot. The good detached scientific image shot to hell."

"I'd better go," she said, half rising from the chair.

He bent forward hastily and stopped her. "No, don't go yet. I spent most of my adolescence getting up the nerve to ask you for a date, and then, poof you were gone, vanished without a trace, and I went for years wondering if I would see you again. No big thing, you understand, but every once in a while I'd think, what did happen to Margaret Matherson, Maggie for short. I heard you say that once to Silly Putty. Remember Silly Putty, the fat fire plug in O'Reilly's luncheonette, the one who dyed her hair so much her scalp had turned orange? She had asked you what your name was—oh, I guess we must have been twelve, thirteen that summer—and you answered. 'Margaret Matherson, Maggie for short,' like it was all one word strung together."

Maggie laughed. "You called her Silly Putty?"

"Yep, because of all those chins wiggling around." He swung the chair in a circle as a child would. "You never knew that?"

"No, but we were summer visitors. Summer visitors are special, my mother used to say."

"No time for townies."

"No time for townies," she echoed the old prejudice, "silly as it was. But things were different then." She glanced down shyly and said, "I'm sorry we never met."

"No more than I am." And then he asked without thinking, "How did you hurt your hand?"

The air went suddenly cold. He could feel the sweat dry up in the small of his back. All the lights went out in Maggie's face. Steel gates clanged shut. Warning bells tolled, beware. Oh shit, he thought, you really blew it this time.

"Peeling a carrot," she said.

He knew she was lying, even if the drop in temperature hadn't already told him. When he sewed her up, both she and the hotshot lawyer husband had said, peeling a potato. There were two kinds of accident victims, Jamie had found, those who recalled in instant replay every single detail right down to the last hair, and those who forgot it all. No middle ground sprinkled with some of this, a little of that.

"I really do have to go," she said in her best formal voice, puttering around herself as women did, swinging the leather shoulder bag up onto her shoulder, tugging at the waist band of the green skirt as she rose. Then she held our her good hand. "Thank you . . . Jamie."

He took hold, pulling her toward him, sliding his hand all the way up her arm to the elbow, until they were so close he could taste the small puffs of breath that came between her lips and smelled of oranges. The honey pot, he thought, not thinking, and brushed her mouth with his, feeling the softness, the trembling, moth's wings fluting the air. And then she was in his arms, his heart resounding like a cannon going off in his chest. Doctor dead of terminal teenage hot pants, he saw the mock headline, and said, "Margaret Matherson, Maggie for short, I don't do this lightly."

Jesus hung from his cross, chipped and faded, his big right toe flaked off to the bare plaster. His wounds looked older than time itself as Sarah, on her knees in the first pew just before the altar, prayed upward. Her lips moved with the wordless litany as Jeb just beside her concentrated on her pink cheeks and the flap of skin beneath her chin. It was difficult, in the dim church to pay attention with the weight of his intensity so near at hand.

"You go out and sit out on the steps and wait for me, lovey," she sighed.

"Why?" he asked, digging his fists between his knees.

"Because a person likes to pray in private," she said.

"Why do you want to pray?" He shuffled his feet against the railing, quickly moving away from her as she reached over to swat at his legs.

"Because I got things to say to our Lord," she snapped.

"What *is* praying?" he persisted.

"You know what praying is," she answered.

"Don't," he said.

He had that stony, peculiar look that sometimes glazed his face, a look that troubled Sarah, though she didn't know precisely why. "You say prayers before you go to sleep at night," she said, watching him. He turned away. "Jeb?" She put her hand on his arm, but he pulled out of reach. "Well, if that's how you're going to be, young man, just take yourself out to the steps and sit until I'm finished. Get now."

He moved along the pew, holding himself stiffly, his back to her. She waited until he pushed open the big oak door, straining against it, before she returned to Jesus, but the words were lost, as if the little boy had taken them outside with him. She couldn't arrange coherently what she wanted to say and slipped into a Hail Mary, but even that didn't calm her enough to unscramble her confused feelings.

Finally, she sat back and, clasping her big, white vinyl pocketbook in her lap, looked around the church. It was empty and chilly even on such a hot day, with a dampness that was bone deep. She hadn't been here for at least three Sundays, and then the church was as full as it ever got—fuller in the summer, with eight or nine rows of parishioners. The old building hadn't seemed during Sunday mass as abandoned and unused as it did now, nor had she noticed how run-down it had become, the white walls dirty halfway up, the runners in the aisles down to the threads, the railings worn to the yellow bone.

She heard a clatter from the vestry, then the snapping of steps and the swish of a cassock. She hadn't really expected Father Fallon to be hearing confessions in the middle of the week, late on a summer afternoon when the church was empty and the chances of anyone wandering in were minimal. Priests were no different from doctors, they liked you to make appointments, but when she looked at the confessional, the bulb glowed red, and she shuffled off to the booth feeling older and needier than she had in a long time.

"Father, forgive me for I have sinned," she singsonged to the invisible presence. Inside the confessional it was stiffling, unlike the cool, damp church, and she was claustrophobic in the gloom. The silence was deadly, as though there was no one living on the other side of the wire.

Quickly, she ran through a list of venial sins, searched in the swirls of memory for some transgression of substance. She wanted not forgiveness but assuagement of the uneasiness that tugged at her.

"I don't know how to explain this, Father," she began, "not being a person of words, but—" Just then the quiet was split by creaking, a fingernail-scratching-glass sound that sent the hairs on the back of her neck up and stopped the breath in her lungs. It was as if someone were shifting the stone door in the cemetery vault behind the church.

The hinges shrieked in pain from centuries of disuse. A dank odor of decay, of rot assailed her. Her heart fluttered wildly in her chest.

"Fa-ther!"

She thrust aside the curtain and stumbled out. The light at the top of the confessional booth sputtered red to gray and then went out. With no thought of the sacrilege, she thrust aside the curtain shrouding the priest's side of the enclosure. It was empty.

Sarah pivoted slowly, the menace of the whole vast interior space at her back. The front door was gaping open. Sunlight cut through in a narrowing shaft that dappled the last pew. And in the distance she could see Jeb sitting on the steps, slightly turned, just a little boy, his leg tucked under him, watching and waiting.

8

The old steamer trunk was cracked and scarred, the lining in thin shreds that were easy to peel back with his fingernails. And it smelled from moth balls, though he didn't know what the smell was, just that it made him think of being sick, of being tucked in bed as cozy as he was now on his folded up blankets and the second pillow from his bed. Lying in the closed trunk, the lid down, his nails scratching away at the sides, he saw in the darkness red striations. Whether he opened or closed his eyelids it didn't matter. The blackness was deeper than it was at night when he woke up because then there was always the tiny light plugged into a socket, the light in the shape of a smiling moon with eyes and a mouth and even two little dots for a nose. But there was no light now, just the red streaks and the darkness, the darkness that always scared him so much. And, cushioned as he was, there was no sound either.

Jeb knew about being dead and about being buried under ground, but he didn't understand how you got out when you were tired of lying there doing nothing. How did you move all that dirt? Wouldn't you have to wait until someone came and dug you up? And what if they forgot, if they got playing too hard or into their Mommy or Daddy business and then supper time came, and if they were having a fight or mad at one another and didn't notice you weren't there and went off to bed after television, how

would you get out then? Would you have to stay there all
through the night, though he supposed it didn't matter
about it being night since it was dark in the grave all the
time anyway. Just like it was in the steamer trunk in the
attic, with the lid slammed down and no light and no
noise.

He didn't really like being dead in the trunk, playing
corpse, and he wasn't sure why he was doing it. He
wanted to be away from the darkness and out on the lawn
in the sun, turning 'round and 'round, his arms outstretched
to the ends of the world, his feet barely skimming the
blades of grass, and Mommy in her folding chair that
always left marks on the backs of her bare legs when she
stood up—but just for a little while—Mommy smiling so
her teeth showed and her tongue made a little pink spot in
her mouth. Yes, Mommy smiling like that made him feel
as good as the sun shining on his head, made him feel
good most of the time anyway. No, he didn't like the
cemetery game much, really not at all when he thought
about it. It scared him, like the dark scared him. He
pushed at the lid with his fingertips and was relieved to
feel it give just a bit, which meant it wasn't locked shut.
But he was cheating, and he refolded his hands on his
chest and tried not to wiggle his bare toes, which just
reached the end of the trunk. He wished he knew what
time it was. Though he couldn't quite tell time well
enough yet to get it perfectly accurate, he knew enough to
know when fifteen minutes had passed, and when that
happened another fifteen, and then twice again, which
would make it a whole hour. He had to play cemetery for
one hour, and then he could push the lid back and go
down from the attic—quietly so no one would know where
he'd been—and talk to himself, to the other, in the mirror
for a while and then, at last, go outside and fly across the
grass.

He thought being a dead person would be simple; he'd just tuck in and go to sleep until he woke up, and then the hour would be over. It wasn't supposed to be hard, and he thought it couldn't be so bad because Sarah said that Kathy and Tracy were happy being dead with God. But that confused him because he didn't see how God could be down in the ground with his sisters, and if He was in one box with Tracy how could He be in the other coffin with Kathy. But then Sarah said that God was in a lot of places at the same time, and Jeb knew how that was possible, but then she went on to confuse him further by saying that only Kathy and Tracy's bodies were in the ground, their souls were in Heaven, and that he didn't understand at all. Not that it bothered him. Jeb realized that there were certain things he did know—even things that grown-ups didn't, and that he musn't ever tell them because they'd be awfully mad at him if they knew. Then, there were other things that were secrets and that he'd learn when he became one of them. Only he wasn't sure he really did want to be like them because, after all, they weren't to be trusted. They lost you if you weren't careful or lost themselves and went away somewhere, like that place Mommy went to, and you never knew if they'd return or not.

He shivered in the closed trunk and felt light-headed from the lack of air. Losing things scared him because he was always losing things himself, putting things in places where they disappeared to turn up miraculously in other places that he didn't remember at all. Sometimes he even lost himself, and that frightened him most, and he couldn't tell anybody because they wouldn't understand. He *didn't* really understand it. One minute he was there, and then he was somewhere else, and the hours in between had evaporated, and one of *them* said he had done a bad thing, a thing Jeb knew he'd never do and which he couldn't remember. Like Mommy's saying he cut up her clothes when he didn't. But they were always right. He could still hear Tracy telling him importantly that what made grown-ups grown-ups was that they were always right and what made children children was that they didn't know anything and therefore were always wrong. So he supposed he did do all those bad things Mommy said he did, even if he couldn't remember. But if that was true, then why didn't the other grown-ups believe her, like Daddy. He, Jeb, got so confused. He didn't like being confused. It was an inside-of-his-head way of losing things.

Was the hour up yet?

He wanted to turn over on his stomach, which was the way he usually slept, with the pillow clasped tightly in his arms, but he couldn't manage in the trunk. It was too narrow, and each time he tried to shift, he bumped his head.

Was it an hour?

Time on the clock was one thing, but inside the trunk time was as meaningless as light and sound; it was a factor he *knew* but had lost touch with since it didn't have two hands and a way of creeping along. He wouldn't be surprised if he discovered that it had stopped entirely and instead of being eleven in the morning it was still ten. Or, conversely, it might be tomorrow or yesterday, or even next week. He could remember the past, the past that is that wasn't shrouded in mist, like having breakfast with Mommy. But was that this morning? It could have been yesterday. He'd have to discuss that some more with himself to get it for certain—if the hour ever ended that was, and didn't creep along forever and ever.

Maybe he could fall asleep. Not that he liked to sleep either. He had bad dreams when he slept, dreams that he never could detail the next day; dreams that left him sweaty and with his pajamas twisted every which way, and sometimes he even screamed out loud, and either Mommy or Daddy came in the dark and curled him up until he could fall back to sleep again. If he fell asleep in the coffin and had a bad dream, who'd ever find him?

I got to be brave, he almost said aloud, like scraping his knee on the rocks in the driveway when he fell from his bike and not crying. But then he could think about the hurt and know what it was he had to be brave about, while here he didn't have one thing to concentrate on. It was all nothing and all everything, and before he could stop them, the tears began to trickle, squeezed out from under his sealed eyelids, and they dribbled down his cheeks to the curve of his chin, and if he stuck his tongue out, he'd be able to lick them. But he didn't, he just let them slither along and run down his neck until there were so many of them his whole face was wet. But he kept quiet. He didn't make a sound, not even a whisper. Jeb in his trunk was as quiet as a mouse waiting until time could scoop away all the dirt from the top of the coffin lid.

"I was sure it was you, Maggie," Lee was saying, leaning forward and tapping Maggie insistently on the knee. Maggie, her face in triangular shadows under a large straw hat, imperceptibly inched away from her, and stared across the lawn thinking of Jamie Evers, or how he had touched her. Her cheeks flamed and she bit at her bottom lip. She wanted Lee to go and leave her alone before she pecked out Maggie's secret, not because Maggie would tell her, but because she stank from it. It rose out of her armpits and from the bend of her knees.

"It wasn't me," she said. "I was in town, at the doctor's office, but he didn't walk me out to the car and hold me up. Why," she laughed, "would he have to hold me up? It's my hand that's injured," she said, raising up the bandaged hand as if Lee was mad for doubting her, "not my leg."

Lee sat back in her chair and lifted the glass of iced coffee that Sarah had given her to her mouth and thought: She's lying. You can tell she's lying. Why? She was so angry with Maggie she didn't want to shake her, she wanted to split her head with an ax, sever her skull, murder her right there on the side lawn in the somnolent afternoon. She could almost see her slumping forward, see her head cleaved in two and the blood spurting in a geyser all over the magnificent hair and down that porcelain, doll face. Lee wanted Maggie dead with a passion that possessed her, forced her heart to stammer out of control and made her breath come in short painful gasps. It wasn't enough for Maggie to be crazy. Crazy only meant being locked up again, and David wouldn't leave a crazy woman.

"I hope you'll stay for lunch, Lee," Maggie was saying, making an effort, "and meet my friend Janet. I did tell you she was coming up for the day with her daughter, Melissa, didn't I?"

"Yes, you did."

"Oh. Well, anyway, Melissa and Jeb were in nursery school together. I don't know if he remembers her because they haven't seen one another for"—she faltered—"well, for a long time. I think he needs to be out playing with children his own age. I asked David about the other children he went to school with last year, but, oh you know David. He didn't even know any of their names. He couldn't remember!" Sweat dappled Maggie's neck, and she spoke too quickly, rattling the ice cubes in her glass. "Where is he anyway? He should take a bath and get dressed before they come. I want him to look nice," she said, swinging back toward Lee and staring at her defiantly, as if Maggie had demeaned the child somehow.

Lee didn't like children, certainly not small children, not even ones who looked as though they had been painted by Renoir. But this child had been thrust upon

her, and she was smart enough to realize that she had at
least to manufacture a concern for David's sake. David,
she knew was worried about Jeb, not because he could
single out anything to worry about, but because Maggie
was. What, Lee surmised, he was really saying was: I'm
worried about Maggie because she's overreacting about
Jeb. She thinks there's something wrong with him because
there is something out of kilter with her.

"Oh, he's probably playing somewhere, Maggie. You're
too overprotective."

"Well, I think it's time he got ready." Maggie jumped
up, trying to get away from Lee and thinking: What if she
tells David she saw me with Jamie. What will Jamie say if
David asks him? Jamie had begged her to see him again.
Saying all sorts of silly things, none of which she believed,
of course. He reminded her of those college boys she had
gone out with at Smith, the ones who would huddle
against her in dark cars and beg, using their pretended
passion as bait. But Jamie . . . Jamie had the intensity that
David had had when they first met and married and
couldn't quench all their lust in lovemaking.

Maggie started across the lawn, her white skirt swinging
along her slim legs, clinging for a moment to the back of
her thighs and molding her buttocks. "Sarah!" she called
as she went around the back to the kitchen door. "Sarah,
where's Jeb?"

Sarah came to the screen and cracked it slightly. A wave
of heat billowed out of the kitchen. "Isn't he with you?"

"No. I haven't seen him for hours."

"Well, he's gotta be around somewhere. I'll look up in
his room, and you go look under the porch." The screen
snapped. Maggie was left staring at the thin configuration
of wires and then turned and went along the side of the
house, drifting by Lee who was absorbed in her own
thoughts.

But he wasn't in his secret place that smelled mildewy when Maggie bent to peer between the latticework. And he wasn't in his room, nor before the mirror, and he wasn't in the study, slowly turning the pages of the large encyclopedia volumes. Sarah came out onto the porch and called: "Can't find him, Mrs. Brace. When did you see him last?"

Lee left her lawn chair and joined Maggie, her hands thrust into her back jean pockets. Maggie said to her, her voice rising just slightly, so that Sarah reached down from the steps above and grasped her shoulder, "He's lost somewhere."

"There's no place to be lost to, so you stop getting agitated. You know how he is. Sometimes he just wanders off."

Maggie almost said, I don't know how he is at all. I don't even know how *I* am.

"Now he's got to be in the house someplace, since you would've seen him if he took to the woods," Sarah said.

"Oh, for Christ's sake, don't get in such a flap. He's here somewhere," Lee said. Sarah and Maggie looked at her without speaking. She shifted uncomfortably. "I mean, where else would he be? He's just a little boy, you know."

Sarah sniffed. "We know." And then to Maggie, "Don't you fret, we'll find him." She grasped the handle of the screen. "He just likes them quiet places, like closets" —she caught her breath then rushed on—"Mrs. Brace, you search downstairs and in the basement. I'll do the second floor. You," she gestured at Lee, "can do the attic."

The two women compliantly followed her inside the house, Maggie slinging her hat on the kitchen table in passing, and at the foot of the stairs they went their separate ways. In moments there was the sound of doors opening and closing, of voices calling, "Jeb. Jebbie, where are you?"

Maggie went down the long hall and peered into the

dining room. There was no small boy there. She came out into the hall and stopped before the mirror, captured there and saw herself, the bandage like a mummy wrap at the end of her arm. That hand was damaged, and it was Jeb who had done it, though nobody believed her, not David certainly, even after she had shown him her amputated clothes, had flung the dismembered dresses and pants and blouses across the bedroom rug crying, "See, this proves I'm not lying to you."

The woman so intently scrutinizing her didn't move. She might have been a stranger inadvertently conjured up and caught unaware. Could she speak to her and have her speak back, as Jeb did in the fantasy game he played with his reflection? Could you ask her if she, the mirror image, believed as David did that Maggie had cut up her own clothes and jammed a scissors into the palm of her own hand? And if she did manage to find the words, what would she hear?

There were vines and round globes of golden fruit in the mirror's frame and at the top, an undulating snake, his jaws wide, a slender tongue tipped out. Even under the gold paint his one, dark, beady eye was lethal. The snake circled the mirror in a malevolent curl, the edge of his tail just curving down to caress the top of a cherub's head. It was all an incongruous combination of images, as if the carver hadn't been able to make up his mind for good or evil. Or perhaps he was saying they are the same thing; they sentinel the world, because at the bottom of the mirror was a carved monstrous creature, not terribly big, who didn't in fact, stretch the length of the glass, but on whose back the whole creation rested. He had sharp pointed ears, and a wide, smiling grin that exposed honed fangs. He was a monster who existed in no mythology Maggie had ever read, an imaginary being so foul in appearance that Maggie could almost smell the fetid breath emanating from his gaping mouth. Why had she ever thought she liked this mirror, wanted it so much that she had moved it from place to place with her? She hated it now and drew back her arm in a snarl of anger, ready to thrust her damaged hand right through the glass. But the woman at the other side stopped her. The eyes locked with hers, the hair almost standing in straight lines out from the beautifully shaped skull. And slowly, the force of something beyond her, the force both outside and in, pulling, dragged her arm downward, and her arm descended half against her will yet with a sense of relief, as if she had stood at a precipice and gazed down and there was nothing there but an aching, impenetrable void. She knew now what the vast black hole in her own head was, where all was sucked in and destroyed, every neutron and proton eaten into ashes.

There were more places to look on the second floor, under beds and in closets, and behind doors. Lots of places a little boy might get lost in, which is why Sarah had taken the second floor for herself. She didn't trust the other two. Maggie would drift off, not out of unconcern but simply because she couldn't concentrate. Sarah sometimes thought that on top of everything else, something had been done to Maggie's head in that place, something with machines. As for the other one, well, she wanted to spit and cross her heart. She didn't like Lee McCann, not only because the woman was trying to break up Mr. and Mrs. Brace's marriage, and Mrs. Brace didn't know a thing about it, even thinking that Lee was her good friend, but because Sarah sensed that under all those smiles and gifts she brought out she was trying to do Maggie in. Which, Sarah had reluctantly to admit is what any woman evil enough to have set her sights on her married man would try. But still, she didn't like her. She was all front and no

underpinings, and not much of a front either. Oh, she was
smart enough, being a big business woman and reading all
them books, but she couldn't hold a candle to the Missus,
and Mr. Brace must be crazy himself if he didn't see it.
But Sarah wasn't going to tell. She had learned long ago to
keep her mouth shut.

Lee thought it was all nonsense and would have said so,
but Sarah's direct and unremitting gaze, something steely
in the faded gray eyes, had stopped her. Still, she thought
they were all making too much of this. Most kids did
wander off and then eventually wandered back. That was
what kids did. There was nothing to go off the wall about.

The attic was divided into two levels. There was a half
floor with a bedroom and bath that was Sarah's and then
up a short flight to the attic proper, with the exposed
beams and dormer windows and the accumulated junk of,
it seemed, half a millennium. There was a dressmaker's
dummy commanding one end, surveying her domain, her
stuffing curling out of her like leaky intestines, and next to
her, a husband through time, a curvy hat rack with a dusty
derby perched on top, its arms dangling scarves, canes,
even an old rubber boot. Boxes were everywhere, and
crates, and old bicycles, and a cradle, a highchair, a
playpen—all the paraphenalia of babyhood—as well as
neatly tied bundles of magazines and quavering stacks of
books.

The books attracted Lee's attention. She went through a
stack, thickly coated with dust. *The Hardy Boys*, *Nancy
Drew*, the *Bobsey Twins*. There was also a red-leather
bound set of Dickens, minus only *Oliver Twist* as well as
she could tell. That might be worth something. She'd tell
David. And a box with an odd assortment. Haggard's *She*,
an early edition of *Felix Kroll*, a volume of Tennyson, and
Sons and Lovers. Yes, she'd have to come back and do

some poking around. It was in such a place that you could discover a little gem, something that might bring a few dollars at auction. Lee couldn't see any reason why David wouldn't let her take it all away and keep what was valuable.

She was so immersed in her digging that at first she didn't hear rustling, like paper being crumbled. She was hunkered down on her haunches, her strong, tennis-firm legs barely feeling the strain, but when she straightened up, there it was. It had less the feel of menace than something ordinary, perhaps the scurrying of mice, pattering away in the old stacks of papers. But there was a rhythm to it, a sliding pace that didn't come from the haphazard scrambling of a mouse.

Something was in the attic with her, a presence. She peered through the curtains of gloom, the light a dusty, antique-white splattering the unwashed windows, sucking the color from the room, even from the floors and the walls where old landscapes hung swaying like dead men on their nails. Lee slowly turned, her arms extended for balance, feeling the air. Dust clung in lacy patterns from the beams. And still that noise, less a noise than a whisper.

At first she was curious, but then with that incessant sound, at once human and beyond one's comprehension of human, she grew afraid. A scream burgeoned in her throat. She wanted to run but couldn't move, and wouldn't, furthermore, let herself run away. Nothing, she told herself with bravado, nothing in God's green world will make me run.

Slowly, she put one foot in front of the other, leaving fresh tracks in the dust on the floor, and then, gaining courage, moved faster and faster, pushing aside racks and boxes, making such noise herself the rustling should have been drowned. Instead, it rose, fluty and in pace, to her own rhythm.

She was breathing heavily when she got to the trunk and slowed. It was an ordinary steamer trunk, years out of date, battered from voyages that no one would take anymore. There were stickers defiantly plastered on its sides, a whole history of Europe and back. Lee paused, her hands on her hips, and brought her fluttering heart under control, angry with herself for having been scared. It was just mice after all, mice who had gnawed their way into an old trunk, though she couldn't see where. They were probably having their damn babies in there, a real little city of mice. Christ, she thought, Maggie's making me nutty too. She turned to go, leaving the mice to their own maneuverings, but something tugged at her, as if she couldn't really be certain until she lifted the lid. Her faced creased with disgust. If she did that, they'd jump out all over her, and though she wasn't squeamish, the idea of the small animals running up and over the edge and across her feet made her slightly sick. But she couldn't go. She was held fast to the spot until she bent forward and slowly, carefully, lifted the lid up, letting the darkness swirl out around her.

And there, glaring up, his eyes wide, the pupils the size of BBs, in a white face of the long dead, was Jeb. His hands were primly folded over his chest, his legs straight as pipe cleaners; and there was a dark stain at the crotch of his khaki shorts.

A scream started in Lee's stomach. She felt it rising out of control like an exploding steam pocket. There was no way to stop that scream. It echoed out, bounced from wall to wall, reverberated, toppling boxes, splintering the spines of old books, divorcing the dummy and the hat rack as the scarves and canes all scattered.

There was a dead Jeb in the trunk, with a trickle of blood spiraling from the corner of his mouth, and he was clambering straight up, his hands stretched out before him.

9

It wasn't a telling thing. It was a secret.
I didn't tell.
They know. They have the right side out.
Oh no. I promise. Never.
Don't tell. Your ears will fall off.
I won't. I promise.
Remember.

Lee took a Valium to calm down, and then a slug of
bourbon, then stuck her head under the cold water tap
and came up looking like a wet otter. She was so enraged
she could barely speak, mad at herself, at Jeb, at Maggie,
and even at Sarah, though God knows why. What she was
truly angry about was her own terror, a terror that still
hunkered in the bones. Jeb had been a dead person, as
dead as she'd ever seen anybody.

Her shouts had brought Sarah and Maggie running. By
that time Jeb was out of the trunk, his face crumpled as a
wrinkled piece of silk and crying in torrents. The blood
was wiped away by Sarah, and the tiny cut in his bottom
lip healed almost immediately.

"I was just playing dead," he said when they forced him
to explain what he had been doing in the trunk. He really
hadn't wanted to say anything. He hid himself in Maggie's
skirt, leaving a line of pink blood mixed with tears and

spittle. He held onto her leg with a death grip and had to be forcibly pried away by Sarah.

Lee wanted to smack him. "He scared the shit out of me!" she screamed, and almost added, he's crazy just like you, Maggie, but even in her rage she managed to choke that back. Finally, she just left them and stomped down the stairs.

"I don't know what's happening in your house, David," she said later, just after seven, when he stopped by on his way home from the city, "but whatever it is, it's sick. And the cause is your wife. She's driving everyone around the bend, including your son. Now, what are you going to do about it?" she asked. Her voice was shrill, accusatory, and she stood in the middle of the high-ceilinged living room in a fighter's stance, feet apart, arms rigid as rods, challenging him.

David's head hurt. Lines of exhaustion like hatchet marks rimmed his eyes. Wherever he turned there were problems, not the kind of problems he was accustomed to dealing with every day, but situations that shifted like sand under his feet and which he couldn't get a good enough grip on to analyze, never mind solve. He had blundered into the middle of someone else's life over the last year, and he couldn't find the door to get out and return to where he belonged.

"It was just a game of Jeb's, Lee, I'm sure. Nothing but a game, and he frightened you coming on him like that." He had yet to hear what Maggie would say or Jeb himself, but already he understood that there was only one position he could take because nothing else made sense.

"You're damn right he scared me. You should have seen him. He would have scared you too. He looked like a corpse—"

"Stop it!" he yelled at her. "You're imagining things."

"Imagination has never been my strong suit, David." She sat down on a couch with a thud. If she didn't control herself, she'd hit him because she ached badly to hit somebody. "If you don't know by now that Maggie is mad as a loon and is making everyone else in your house— particularly Jeb—crazy too, well, don't blame anyone but yourself for what might happen."

"What do you mean?"

"You know what I mean. You've alluded to it often enough. The famous fire. Nobody, including the fire department ever found a reason for that fire."

"Hey, wait just a minute. Are you saying Maggie started that fire?"

Lee lit a cigarette, puffing smoke out at him in spidery columns. Unable to keep still, she stood up again and went toward him. "I'm not saying anything, but life at Four Oaks was smooth as glass until Maggie came home. And now it's the weekly edition of *Horror Comics*. What do you need, a blueprint?"

Somebody was going to get hit. This whole long day, Lee just knew it, that the anger had to explode in a palpable form. It could only be held down so long, but she had assumed she'd be the one who'd last, not the one who'd be thrown across the room as effortlessly as a down pillow. But David just swung. His arm came out with the same unthinking precision of a wind-up toy, right from the side, and his open palm went flat against her cheek. The speed and strength of the blow sent her sprawling backwards onto the couch. For half a minute she and David stared at one another in shock.

"Lee, Lee, oh God, I'm sorry! I didn't mean it!" He lurched forward, awkward, stumbling, and fell beside her, enfolding her in his arms, scrambling for her. He pulled her against his chest.

She had dropped the cigarette when he smacked her, and over the curve of David's shoulder she saw it burn a black hole in her Navaho rug, before it sputtered and went out. And she didn't care.

How could Maggie tell Klein everything? But not to tell him everything meant telling him nothing, leaving ellipses. So much had happened these last few days. With Jamie—and with Jeb. Oh, Jeb in that trunk, Jeb and how strange he'd become, and not one person believing her, or thinking at best that she'd made him crazy like she was, is—

Noooooo.

It was whistling in her head, and it came from down there, from that emptiness where she'd floated, unmindful, unknowing.

She sat obediently in Klein's office, waiting for him, not moving, a statue in her flowered dress, and counted her breaths.

My life is normal. I am normal. I have two arms, two legs. I see perfectly without glasses.

Klein had promised her that eventually she'd live happily ever after. He had said it would be difficult, that there were patterns to pick up where the stitches had been dropped, but that it would all be much as it had been before. *If* she could live with the acceptance of two dead daughters—whose ghosts would hover less and less but whose deaths would always loom like a mountain in the middle of her life.

Normal. She tasted the word. Yesterday was normal, wasn't it? she asked herself. Lee over to visit. A glass of iced coffee on the lawn. With Janet and Melissa due to arrive for lunch and the afternoon . . . before she had managed to stop them, putting them off until today.

It's all something I've gotten wrong, and I don't know why, Maggie thought. Through the open doorway she saw the butterfly people in their slow dance. She had been one of them not so long ago, one of the floaters who glided between sleep and awakening. You could always tell the ones who lived scenarios in their heads. They were the most languid, the ones with the softest, buttery faces. She tightened her muscles in case one of the nurses or doctors happened to look in.

She was still staring out the window when Klein entered the office and saw her sitting there, as if from a long way off, the light encasing her like a delicate and fragile piece of artwork. His stomach lurched. She was so still, so perfect, looking as she had in the early months when she'd sat in the recreation room against the window in deadly repose.

What if he'd been wrong after all? He banished the thought the very second he had it. He knew this woman as well as he'd ever known any patient. And he didn't make mistakes of such magnitude.

Klein crossed the threshold, hurrying now to get to her. Maggie rose half out of her chair, tentatively smiled, her lips arcing just slightly, then sank back and stared at him.

What, she wondered, should I tell him? What's safe?

Sarah didn't let Jeb out of her sight. She had him sitting at the kitchen table working play dough from flour and water and food coloring. She gave him the cookie cutters to form patterns and kept him in her peripheral vision as she sliced vegetables for stew.

Again she told herself, there's nothing wrong with him. She could understand, even if the rest of them couldn't, why he wanted to play dead in an old trunk in the attic. What did they expect? And *her* screaming like that! Well, that was more than enough to turn everyone into lunatics.

The phone rang on the kitchen wall, and she went to answer it, making sure that Jeb didn't escape behind her. "Hello," she said.

"Is Mrs. Brace there?"

"No, she's not. Who's this?"

There was a pause, then, "Dr. Evers. I—I just called to see how Mrs. Brace's hand is."

"Her hand? Okay I guess. She hasn't said."

"When will she be back?"

Sarah looked at the clock over the refrigerator. "In about an hour."

"Would you have her call me, please," he said and hung up. Sarah put down the phone and regarded it curiously, thinking, now what's that all about?

"Sarah."

"Yes, lovey, what is it?"

"The foot doesn't come out right. Can you fix it?"

Sarah leaned over the boy, centering the cutter so that the edge went down flat, hit the table through the dough, and pulled clear. She straightened up and felt the energy coming off the child. The air swarmed around him, and leaning back over him, she felt his head. He was hot to the touch.

"Do you feel okay, lovey?" she asked.

"Uh huh."

"Well, maybe you should lie down before your little friend comes. You want to be real perky while she's here."

"Do I have to go upstairs?"

"No, you can lie down on the parlor couch. Com'on now. But first wash all the goo off your hands." Jeb washed and dried his hands and followed Sarah into the darkened living room where she stretched him out on the couch and covered him with an afghan. That way, she thought, leaving him, I'll know just where he is.

When Sarah returned to the kitchen Jeb lay still. He didn't move a muscle and remembered the trunk. They were all mad at him for that, every one of them. He had done something wrong, but he wasn't sure what.

He was quiet for a bit, staring at the ceiling way, way overhead, then he tugged the afghan aside and swung his legs over the side of the sofa. He glided through the living room on tiptoes, his hands before him like a blind person's. From the hallway he could see Sarah at the other end, passing the kitchen doorway, going back and forth, and then the sink tap went on and off, and she didn't come back. He sighed with relief and sank down Indian fashion before the mirror. He pushed his face up against the glass, his cheek sideways, eyeball to eyeball with his reflection. His hands splayed out, grasping at the mirror, touching the cold himself, intent, and he let his breath fog the other Jeb and warm his skin.

The humming began. He liked the humming. It was a low keening that only he could hear, or so he thought. It was his private sound, and even when *they* were around he supposed that *they* didn't hear it.

It aroused him, the humming, like a faint tickle of electricity through his palms and the soles of his feet.

He couldn't remember when the humming had begun. He thought it was the night of the fire when he saw himself in the mirror in that other place. But he wasn't sure. There were too many blank places in his memory to be sure. Sometimes he thought he knew the humming in the inside of him and had always known it. And now he couldn't recall what it was like without it. The humming made him feel good, made his body vibrate slightly like a tuning fork.

So he pressed himself against the mirror, adhering to the glass like a piece of Scotch tape and let the humming flow through him and out as he slipped away.

The session with Klein hadn't been satisfactory at all, not on her part, nor she was certain, on his. She knew she had been elusive, slippery, and her dodging had alarmed him, yet how could she tell him she'd let another man kiss her and that she wanted to make love with a virtual stranger. And that the idea—just the idea—excited her as nothing had done for a very long time. And David? Of course I love David, she insisted to herself, and couldn't even remember what Jamie Evers looked like just then. But she could still feel the tug of his lips on hers, the quivering of his fingertips like tiny electrodes along her arms.

She had told Klein about Jeb in the trunk, and after she did, he visibly relaxed. "He's only acting out his fantasies about his sisters, Maggie," Klein said, feeling on firm ground now.

"He terrified Lee, and you don't know Lee, but she's not the kind of person who scares easily. And he did stick the scissors in my hand, Dr. Klein. He did. He did."

"Of course he did, Maggie," he soothed, his voice as sugary as cough syrup. Leaning forward, he rested his elbows on the desk. He had his "I don't believe it" look on his face, and she realized once again how useless it was to tell Klein something he didn't find palatable. Not that she liked the idea of what Jeb had done to her, but he had done it, and there was no way she was going to say differently. Her very sanity depended on believing her own perceptions, because if she let others define reality for her, she would slide like a snowdrift into fantasy.

Jeb had wanted, all of a sudden, to go to Greenwood with her. He had stamped his foot and scrunched up his face into a knot and held his breath until he turned red as a fire engine. But Maggie had said no. Even though she knew he was afraid she'd disappear into Greenwood and not return, she wouldn't have him sitting out in the anteroom alone. In that, she agreed with David. Jeb wasn't to be tainted. But she had promised him she'd drive back and pick him up, and they'd go to the farmers' market together before Janet and Melissa came.

It was a quiet Jeb she coaxed out of his secret place, a sullen child with a smear of dirt across his nose, and with flat, unyielding eyes. He lifted his left hand and ran a finger under his nose.

"Well, I thought you wanted to go. If you don't, okay," she said, ruffling his hair. He shrugged her hand away.

"Want to," he said, his voice as flat as his eyes.

She gave him a nudge toward the car, and even his back under her hand was cold and unyielding. He frightened her when he was like this, as though he had retreated to a secret place inside himself, the inner corollary to the hiding spot under the porch.

They drove in silence to the market just outside the village limits, stalls set back on a wide scruffy lawn, all stacked high with fruits and vegetables. Maggie pulled into the lot on the left flank, parked, and got out of the Dodge, slamming the door. Jeb came out the other side and trailed behind her, but when she reached back to take his hand his fingers were icy and slipped out of her grasp.

"Are you okay, honey?" she asked, but he skittered away and disappeared in the maze of stalls. Maggie shrugged and went ahead, her high heels crunching on the gravel as she circled the stands, filling her arms with fruit and vegetables. An apple rolled out from under her elbow. As she stooped to retrieve it, someone said, "Here, let me get that for you."

He was down in a crouch as she turned, his face so close to hers she could smell the aftershave lotion he used, different from David's, more astringent. She found herself thinking hysterically, he even smells like a doctor.

He was holding out the apple as a bride. As she reached for it, the cucumbers and lettuce rolled to the ground.

"You need help," he said.

*   *   *

At the other end of the aisle, just at the edge of a mountain of watermelons, Jeb stood watching. All the color had seeped from his face, and his hands clenched to fists in the pockets of his denim shorts. He focused on the man, and a siren shrilled "dangerous" in his head.

"I don't need anything, Jamie," Maggie said with more force than she believed she was capable of.

"You're the most beautiful woman I've ever seen, Maggie," he said, as if she hadn't spoken at all. "Do you know that? No," he went on, not giving her a chance to reply, "I doubt that you do. You don't have that arrogance or sense of the dramatic other beautiful women have." He had gathered up the vegetables and fruit and stood, pulling her up with him. "I never thought I cared much either way, for beauty, you know. But you're like that one work of art in a museum that you'd steal if you had the chance. The one you want to take to the bank and lock in a safety deposit box so nobody else in the world can have it but you." He guided her over to the cashier and waited while she paid for the produce, looking as if he belonged with her and she with him.

Jeb came sliding along, scenting the air, hiding behind shopping bags and large women. He was tensed, his hackles raised, his lips drawn back from his teeth, snarling. No one glanced down at the small boy, coiled like an attack dog, ready to strike, not even Maggie, who couldn't speak. She was a puppet in a dumb show. Whatever words came out of her mouth wouldn't be her own.

"There'll be another time, Maggie, and then a time after that. But you're going to have to come to me," Jamie said as he started to walk her toward the Dodge.

"Jebbie!" she cried, pulling loose from Jamie.

He was holding a tomato and as she ran toward him, he squeezed the vegetable between his hands, the goo and the liquid and seeds running over his shirt and down to splash on the ground.

"What are you doing?"

"You were going without me," he said baldly.

"Don't be silly. I was not. I was just going to put the packages in the car." But it wasn't true. She had forgotten, and she turned on Jamie sharply. "How could you do this to me?"

She grabbed Jeb by the arm, not even reacting as he wiped his slimy palms down the side of her dress, and yanked him to the car. "Com'on." She pushed him inside the front seat, the packages between them, and scrambled after him.

Jamie gripped the edge of the rolled-down window and leaned in. "Leave me alone," she said, turning the key in the ignition.

"You don't mean that," he said.

"Jamie, please."

Jeb curled into a ball in the angle of the door, all his edges flattened, and Maggie thought he had heard every word, that he knew everything. The set of his face, as wooden as a carving told her that. Would he tell David? What could he say? What could she say to him? Don't tell?

There was a terrible blackness emanating from him, right across her lap and through the window at Jamie, who saw nothing but Maggie, curve of her cheek, that straight slope to her nose, and the beautiful edge of her lower lip. He was oblivious to the child and to the laser of anger directed along the front seat of the car.

"Let go, Jamie," Maggie said. She shifted into reverse, pulled away, and circled back, leaving the lot. As she did, she saw him framed in the rearview mirror, in that cowboy slouch of his, a slight breeze just stirring the unruly brown hair, his too wide sensuous mouth smiling. And she knew he was right when he called after her, "I'll be seeing you, Maggie."

Melissa was just Jeb's size, a scrawny thing with a lean, bony face, and two dark pigtails that hung halfway down her back. Janet was bubbly and warm, yet Maggie recognized all the signs that read, let's be careful around the lunatic. She tried to relax, smiling, tossing her head, asking about friends they both once shared as they ate lunch on the front porch.

The children eyed one another suspiciously. If they remembered their days in nursery school, they gave no sign of it, but Maggie was relieved to see that the dark cloud had lifted from Jebbie. All the way home he had been silent, his face pressed against the window, staring out, but now he bounced around on his chair and chattered like a magpie, telling Melissa about his bike, his kite, about the dog he was after his father to buy him. He had come back to himself, and Maggie was so relieved she didn't wonder why or how.

"Do you think you'll stay up here or come back to the city?" Janet asked when they'd finished and were having coffee. The children had gone off to play Frisbee.

"Leave Four Oaks?" Maggie was surprised. She hadn't thought of moving. Each day was such a stone to be pushed uphill, and she was so frightened, that tomorrow didn't exist. "I don't know " she said. "Stay here, I guess. For a while anyway."

"But what about the schools?" Janet asked.

Schools, Maggie remembered, were the chief topic of conversation for mothers in the city. She had spent hours and hours in the Central Park playground discussing the pros and cons of one over the other, of structured schools versus progressive schools. With a shock she realized that she knew nothing now of Jeb's school, had never met his teacher, didn't even know where the school was. Somewhere in Brighton, she supposed.

"There's an excellent school here," she answered firmly, raising her eyebrows. "How is Melissa doing in Ethical?" She asked, and launched Janet off on her own tangent as she watched the children in their dizzy spinning, the orange Frisbee slicing through the still air like a knife.

Jebbie's a normal child. I am a normal mother. There is no Jamie. There wasn't a fire—But she balked at that; her mind shuttered down, and she closed her eyes, for a second hearing what a normal mother really sounded like, talking about ordinary things. In the moment her eyes were closed, the children had disappeared. She heard the kitchen door slam, the murmur of Sarah's voice, and then the patter of small feet coming down the hall. She expected to see a child burst out on the porch, but the footsteps had stopped midway. Maggie counted to ten but then, whichever child it was ran up the stairs. Almost immediately the door slammed again. Again, Sarah's voice called, and then Maggie heard the other pair of feet and Melissa's voice calling, "Hey, where are you?"

"Com'on up," Jeb yelled from a distance, and Melissa slowly climbed.

"Where are you?" She peeked around the corner of the stairs on the second floor but couldn't see him. The house smelled funny, old and dusty, but it wasn't dusty. She ran her finger along the bannister as she had seen her mother do after the cleaning lady left. It came away clean enough to stick into her mouth and lick.

"I'm in here."

"Where's here?" she asked, cautiously moving off down the hall, following the sound of the small voice.

"Here."

"Oh," she said, standing in the doorway and peering curiously around, "is this your room?"

"Uh huh."

"Is it your room all by yourself, or do you have to share like I do with Dolly, but she's in camp now. I'll go to camp when I'm eight."

"It's just mine," Jeb said. He was under the window so that the sun dripped across him, and splashed to a puddle on the toes of his sneakers.

"Don't you have brothers or sisters?" Melissa asked, inching further into the room. There was a model airplane on the dresser that David had put together for Jeb. Melissa picked it up and turned it upside down, suspiciously inspecting the underbelly while she talked to Jeb at her back.

"I had sisters," he said, "but they got ate up by a fire."

"You mean they're dead?" He had her interested now. She put the airplane back on the dresser and stared at him with awe. He might as well have said he was a Martian. But Jeb wouldn't discuss it further. He was rigid, clutching his elbows and glaring up at her, as if he had never seen her before. "Are they really dead, like grandparents?" Melissa persisted.

"You're a girl person," he said at last.

"What do you mean?"

"I never saw a girl person."

"You mean like with no clothes on," she said, coming over and sitting across from him, leaning back against the bed. Their sneakers kissed and they regarded one another warily. "Didn't you ever see your sisters? I mean before they were dead." Jeb didn't answer. "Why's your face look so dark."

"I want to see what a girl person looks like."

She sniffed. "My Mommy says it's a bad thing to take off

your clothes except when you're supposed to, like taking a bath."

"I don't care. I want to."

Melissa squirmed uncomfortably. She was a proper, unimaginative child who always did what she was told and never gave anyone any trouble. She thought Jeb was strange, and she wasn't sure she liked him. She didn't even remember him much from nursery school. At lunch he was okay, and then when they were playing Frisbee that was fun, but now he was being scary, and she wanted to go back downstairs to her mother.

Jeb's hand snaked out and grabbed her bare knee. Melissa was surprised and pushed at him, but he wouldn't take his hand away. "You don't have a thing between your legs like I do," he said.

"I know that. I'm a girl. Didn't your Mommy ever tell you anything?" She probed at his hand, but he held her fast, the fingers burrowing like little maggots into the soft, fleshy thigh. "I don't like that. Take your hand away," she said with as much dignity as a six-year-old could muster. "I'll tell your mother."

"I want to see a girl person," he said over again, as though he hadn't heard her.

"No!" she screamed and jumped away, shoving back as far as she could get in the confined space.

Jeb's face contorted, lines springing from corners of his eyes. A pulse as huge as a fist throbbed in his temple. He became an old man, wizened as a rotting apple, as the little girl watched him, her mouth opened in a silent scream, and then, exerting a tremendous effort, his lips pulled hard against his teeth, the cordons in his neck bulging, his face shifted, relaxed, worked like clay by an invisible hand. A little boy's face resurfaced from the deep. Only the voice had a mechanical whine to it. "I want to see a girl person."

Melissa jumped up, crying, tears running down her face, covering her cheeks. In a moment Jeb was up and after her. As he passed the dresser mirror he caught a startled reflection, the mouth wide, the eyeballs burnt out, the hair flying.

The little girl was just inches from his fingers.

On the porch Maggie and Janet heard Melissa screaming. Janet knocked over her coffee cup as she pushed back the chair, coffee cascading down her white pants. But in a second Maggie was through the door and at the bottom of the steps. There on the landing was Melissa with Jeb just two steps behind her. The stairs rose and Melissa came flying, soaring outward, her arms wings, and Jeb's two hands were palms up as they left the girl's back when he pushed her down the steps.

She tumbled and turned, rolling the length of the steps. Even with Melissa's screaming and her own cries, Maggie could hear bones snap. The child's face was the color of putty, and when Maggie grabbed her on the third riser, her eyeballs rolled back like marbles in her head.

"What happened? Oh my God, Melissa!" Janet, thrusting Maggie aside, cradled her daughter. "Melissa!"

"Sarah, call the doctor," Maggie cried, forgetting all at once who the doctor was. That was something she wasn't going to think of, not now.

Jeb stood silently at the top of the stairs peering down at the scene below him. He was limp as a shadow, his head lowered, and he didn't move, except for the fingers of his left hand which played over the buttons of his shirt, then reached up to tug at his ear.

Janet was hysterical, screaming, "Melissa, Melissa, say something. Baby, please say something!" But it was minutes before the girl's eyes focused and the color began to seep back in a pallid tinge to her cheeks.

"I hurt, Mommy. I hurt," she whimpered.

"Baby, what happened?" And to Maggie, "My God, where's the doctor?"

"He's on his way," Sarah said, wiping Melissa's face with a damp cloth.

Maggie couldn't take her eyes off Melissa's face. What would she say? What did she want her to say? Above her she could sense Jeb, a looming presence, and she remembered the fat man. Maggie shuddered, her skin crawling, and shrank back from Jeb, from the loathsome sight of those childish hands with the pudgy, dirt-stained fingers and of that curious dead look on his face. He might have been walking in his sleep.

"Melissa, honey, the doctor's coming. Tell Mommy now, what happened?"

She burrowed her face into Janet's breasts and said, "We were playing and I got scared for you and I ran away. And then I fell."

You didn't fall, Maggie wanted to yell at her. *Jebbie pushed you. I saw him. You must have felt his hands on your back*. But how could she say that? How could she accuse her own child of such a terrible thing? They'd think she was crazy. . . .

Oh, please Lord, what did I see?

10

Throughout the long afternoon and early evening of Melissa's accident, Maggie was stretched taut as a rubber band ready to snap. Jamie had come on the run and ordered Melissa to the hospital. From X-rays he found she had a fractured tibia and a mild concussion. Maggie sat in the hospital with Janet while she keened and cried until Barry, Janet's husband arrived, his suit crumpled, his tie yanked down at half mast, and a look of panic on his face.

"I didn't go under sixty all the way," he stammered. "I must've done it in forty-five minutes." They were huddled in the visitors' lounge with its Van Gogh reproductions on the wall, an ineffectual attempt at cheerfulness. It was there that Jamie found them, Janet wrapped in Barry's arms, while Maggie stared at their macabre reflection, like a two-headed person, in the darkening window.

"She's going to be okay," Jamie said from the doorway, professional now though he wore jeans and a striped boatman's T-shirt. "But she'll have to stay in the hospital at least overnight."

"I still don't understand how it could've happened," Barry said, bewildered, putting Janet aside and struggling up.

Jamie shrugged. "As far as I can tell, she just slipped on the steps and fell."

Janet shrieked, "She doesn't listen! I told her not to

148

run. I tell her all the time." Mascara ran down her face in bird tracks. Maggie reached over to take her hand, but she pulled away. "She's not used to stairs. There aren't any stairs in our apartment."

"Okay, honey, okay," Barry said, patting her head as if she were a stray dog that one had to be wary with. "You the doctor?" he asked Jamie.

Jamie nodded. "Dr. Evers."

"I'm Melissa's father. When can we take her home?"

"Like I said, she should stay here for the night for observation. So tomorrow maybe. Let's play it by ear. The latest, the day after. When we do release her, I'll see that you have all the records so you can take her to your own doctor."

"You'll stay with us," Maggie insisted.

"No, that's okay, Maggie," Barry said, lifting Janet to her feet and looping his arms around her. "We'll get a motel."

"No, Barry, please," Maggie said.

Janet was frozen. "I'd rather stay in a motel if anyone's asking me."

"Janet—"

The other woman turned on her. "It's because of you, you know. You're bad luck, Maggie."

Maggie began to shake. "Janet, I'm sorry. I never meant for Melissa to get hurt. I didn't do anything."

Janet came at her, like an ice floe of anger. Maggie's legs hit the back of her chair as Janet bent forward, her eyes wild, spittle flying in a curtain from her mouth and across Maggie's cheeks as she screamed in a terrible low voice, "You never mean anything. Nothing's your fault. And yet children get hurt around you. Children die! If we hadn't come up here, Melissa would be all right. Did you want her to die like your girls!"

"Hey, babe, com'on," Barry pleaded, grabbing at her

arm, "that's banana talk. You told me that Maggie was with you when Lissa fell. That's what you said on the phone. You told me that, babe. Maggie's not to blame. It was an accident."

"An accident!" she spat, turning on her perspiring husband now. "Everything's always an accident! And she is always so sorry!"

Jamie stepped in. He thought Maggie was going to crumble, and he parted her from the couple, leading her to the other side of the room.

"There's no percentage everybody carrying on like this," he stated flatly. "You people want to go in and see your daughter now, fine. Down the hall, turn right and ask the nurse at the desk. I'll come in tomorrow, and if she can travel, I'll release her. If not, the day after. Go on." There was no mistaking the weight of authority in his voice. He didn't say another word until they rounded the corner, then he put his arms about Maggie. She was a ghost next to him. Even her bones seemed soft. "Okay, they're gone. You can relax."

"Why was she so mad at me?" Maggie whispered into his shirt.

"What?"

"I was sitting with her on the porch, Jamie, when we heard Melissa crying."

"Yeah, that's what you said. What you both said." He ran his hand down her back, fingering the vertebrae like keys on a horn. "But she's a nut. Besides, she's got to blame somebody. Can't really say, I was feeding my face, not paying much attention to my kid, and the kid took a nose dive down the stairs. People need to blame somebody else. It's human nature."

"Jebbie."

"What did you say?"

She broke away from him and leaned back. He had

old-fashioned eyes, the color of faded silk, pale blue and fringed with dark lashes. "Jeb did it," she said slowly, looking into his eyes. "Jeb pushed her down the stairs. I saw him."

The lips move, the lids blink, the arms go up and down, even the legs step out in a march, Jamie thought, remembering the mechanical woman he had seen in the carnival one summer when he was a kid back in the third grade. He had thought her wonderfully humanlike, not realizing then that she was just a complicated toy, not a person. That was Maggie. She speaks, she moves, she even wiggles her hips, but she's all wires and spark plugs.

"Let's get out of here," he said. "I'll come back later and do evening rounds."

"I don't want to go home."

"Yeah, okay. Nobody wants to go to your house. What about your husband?" He walked with her to the elevator, and they descended in silence to the main floor. "Your husband, Maggie," he prodded when they went out the front door.

"I don't know where he is. I called his office, but he was gone for the day. Meetings somewhere." She shrugged. "David's big on meetings and deals and mergers and trusts and conglomerates. He's the perfect corporate lawyer. You know they even did an article on him once in *Business Week*."

She was mad at David now. Where was he when she needed him? He was never there when the bad things happened. And afterwards he always blamed her—just as Janet did—and said Maggie lied. An iron band was squeezing her head. She stopped and put her hands to her temples. Her brain was going to burst. If she told David that Jeb pushed Melissa down the stairs, he'd say she was crazy. Even Melissa said she fell, and she must have felt that feather touch of fingers on her back.

"You need a drink. In you go and we'll be off to my favorite roadhouse." Jamie helped her into his TR, and she watched the half of him she could see circle the front of the car to the driver's side.

He put down the top before they drove off through Brighton, the small car zig-zagging in and out of traffic. A large rig came up on their flank before they went left for the turnpike, and Maggie looked up at the driver who seemed like God far above them, and she was small, insignificant, pinned under his gaze. She was the incredible shrinking woman, and she was going to disappear. Frantically, she turned as Jamie shifted into second and the TR leaped ahead, away from the semi. She clutched at his arm.

"Whoa, that's dangerous." She spun away from him. "No, no, come here. I only meant since I'm in lust with you." He tried to get her to smile, but she couldn't or wouldn't.

But the truth was he didn't feel any lust whatsoever for Maggie at the moment. Sure, he wanted to put his arms around her again and have her fold right into his insides like an attack of the flu, but he didn't want to fuck her. Not that she, even in her half-alive state, wasn't as seductive—if anything more so—but there was a gut-wrenching feeling like the grinding of unoiled gears in Jamie's midsection that had nothing to do with lust.

The dying sun slid from the sky as they came up on the turnpike, and they rode quietly in the gathering darkness, Maggie's hair floating around her from the wind, to the next exit, where Jamie took the TR down and off the ramp. They turned under a feathering of treetops, into another small town, out the other side and onto a two-lane blacktop.

"Tell me about Jeb, Maggie," he prompted as they pulled up beside a narrow building like an Indian long house with a Miller's neon in the front picture window. "He's your son, right? The kid in the car with you at the farmer's market?"

"Yes, that's Jeb."

"Cute. How old is he?"

"Jebbie's six now."

"And you say he pushed Melissa down the stairs." He tried to keep his voice neutral.

"Oh, what's the use. You won't believe me either. No one does. It's ironic, Jamie, but proving that I'm not imagining things, that my word has *value*, means proving that there is something wrong with my six-year-old son." She shifted sideways in the narrow little car, the faint yellow light washing over her. "Don't you think that's ironic?" He didn't say anything, and then she sighed, "What do you want from me?"

"Right now, nothing, except to buy you a drink. Let's go." He got out of the car and went around to get her, but she wouldn't let him help. The anger had brought her back to life, pushed all her buttons, and she stormed ahead of him into the bar. He got a glimpse just then of what she had been, or maybe what she still could become. The gears inside him ground again, screeching, and he hoped that whatever was happening to him wasn't irreversible.

She surprised him by saying that she wanted a beer. He would have thought of her as a Dacquiri or a Whiskey Sour woman, but she drank off the Bud at one swipe and asked for another.

"I don't believe you, you know," he said. They were in a booth at the back of the bar, the only customers except for two beefy rednecks, their faces upturned to the television overhead. The bartender kept the juke box on low drive, golden oldies Jamie thought of them, though they were only from the seventies... "Send in the Clowns." "Feelings." Carly Simon trying to break your heart like she kept telling you hers had been.

Maggie wasn't going to talk, so he said, "Okay, Jeb pushed that little girl down the steps. Right. How do you know?"

"I saw him."

He wasn't her Jebbie; her Jebbie wouldn't do that. Her Jebbie wouldn't do any of the things he had done. Yet he had done all of them, and she knew it, and she didn't know why.

"Then how come the kid's mother didn't see him?" Jamie asked sitting back, trying to keep his distance, being drawn and repelled, pulled and pushed, as though Maggie were a magnet being raised and lowered and he could not resist.

"Because I got there just at that second. Janet was behind me. She only saw Melissa at the bottom of the steps. I saw her at the top, and I saw Jeb's hands—" She stopped. "Why would he do it? He's never hurt any—"

"What?" 'Round and 'round the beer glass danced on the scarred plastic with its bald half moons.

"Nothing." Why should she tell him?

"How's your hand?" He took the injured hand off the table and held it lightly. "Still hurt?"

"No, its okay."

"Taking your medicine?"

"Damn it, stop treating me like a child, like that little girl you remember. That's what they all do. A child or a crazy person. Why didn't I die, why the girls and not me! Why!"

She was back before Greenwood, in those first awful days, the funeral with the coffins so small she made the undertaker open them up, but David wouldn't let her look in. And then Kathy and Tracy's friends coming to the house afterwards, in dresses and Mary Janes, in blazers and shirts and ties, all spick-and-span, as though for a party, all saying how sorry they were. She wished them dead, everyone of them or any of them as much as she wanted to die herself. At night she lay tortured, unable to sleep, tormenting herself with the thought of saving one of the girls, and which one would it be. Tracy with her solemn face framed by spikey dark bangs, Tracy her oldest whom she had held first, or Kathy, her middle baby, the one who was to be a boy and instead was a gurgling, sunny girl child who didn't know how not to be happy. Which one would it have been? Was it better that they both were dead so she hadn't had to choose?

Jamie had slid into her side of the booth and was holding her. She was crying into his shirt, the tears drenching his skin right through the jersey.

She hadn't let go like this since the early days, before she realized that the tears weren't enough, wouldn't bring them back, and if she didn't go into death after them, she did the next best thing and ran screaming into the void of her own head. Klein had told her that, had made her understand that her breakdown was an escape, a way of not facing the girls' dying as much as coming to terms with her own sense of guilt.

She had wept then until she had almost drowned, but now she just ran down, a needle gliding from fast to slow to stop until finally she sagged against him, exhausted.

She nodded, and he went up to the bar and got two more drinks and a handful of napkins. The sports commentator was recapping the day's baseball—the Mets were still determined to self-destruct while the Yankees were committing mass murder up and down the American League. Jamie stood watching for a moment, imagining sitting in the bleachers with Maggie, popping peanuts and drinking beer and feeling the sun, while he wondered if right now, this very moment, she'd be in the booth when he looked back. And did he really want her to be? She was out in orbit and dragging him with her by centrifugal force, and he tried to pinpoint the exact moment he lost control of himself and begun the headlong, daredevil, death-defying dive. It had started as memory and unrequited lust, and now that lust was doing a fast dance into love, and the very thought of its evolution left him with a sour taste in his mouth.

He handed her the beer and the napkins and waited while she wiped her eyes. "How'd you hurt your hand?" he asked again.

She turned the wadded napkin over and over into a small square and then a smaller one. "Why do you want to know? You won't believe me. David doesn't. Even Sarah thinks I made it up."

"Try me," he said, "you might get lucky. Besides, I know from the wound it wasn't a potato *or* a carrot peeler."

"Jebbie stabbed me with a scissors. He was hiding in my closet cutting all my clothes apart, and when I found him, he stabbed me." She was canny and careful, and she tried to gauge his reaction, but it was too dim in the bar to see him clearly. Slowly she went on, "David thinks I did it in my sleep."

"Why does your husband think you're lying?"

But he knew why David thought as he did. He remembered enough outraged faces of disbelief, even his own, from those residency days in the Bronx. The mother who'd been told over and over that burns on the baby's buttocks came from the cigarette her pimp boyfriend had punished him with. Or the young Hispanic girl who'd been shot by her sister in a fight over a dress and who had seen the gun, had seen her sister fire, had even felt the bullet like liquid fire in her guts, and said, no, it couldn't be. It was all a mistake, they had gotten it wrong. The worst is what you dream about in the dark and call it a nightmare, and Jamie had seen hundreds of people deny their own senses, their loved ones, the cops, the doctors, to hold on to a shred of belief. But David's credulity didn't matter a hoot, one way or the other. It was like scratching on glass—only the sound came back, the nails didn't leave marks. Either the kid had stabbed Maggie or not. And either he pushed the little girl Melissa or he didn't. What David believed, or what Jamie himself believed for that matter, wasn't relevant.

"There are other . . . I don't know . . . things," she said.

"Such as?" he patted his pockets for a cigarette and remembered that he had given up smoking over two years ago.

"Jamie, I, well, there's something wrong with me." She kept her head lowered. In the darkness, her hair was an ebony shade, and her white shirt showing up even whiter, seemed to glow. "I've been sick. And I had to be away for a while—"

It was too painful to listen to her stumble on, so he interrupted, saying, "Greenwood. I know. I asked around. What's the difference. The important thing is that you had a breakdown and now you're better. Whatever's going on now, Maggie, you're better." He sounded so sure of himself, with his air of authority, that for a moment Maggie almost believed him.

"You think the world's a well-ordered place, and then your children die. Children aren't supposed to die, Jamie," she said as if he had argued with her. "And then you go to Greenwood, and whatever's real out here is different there. It's another planet. Everything backwards or upside down." She shifted her glass from hand to hand. "Sometimes I thought I was standing on my head." She laughed sourly. "There was one woman who believed she was a fetus waiting to be born. All day, every day, she kept stopping the nurses and asking if it was time yet. You see, what she was afraid of was not being ready."

"That's over," he said.

"What if it isn't? What if I'm not ready?"

Jamie slipped back to the other side of the booth and finished his second vodka. He wasn't much of a drinker but thought he could get drunk right then, roaring drunk as he hadn't been since college, where he'd fall down and sleep it off in some strange place, then wake up with mold on his tongue, his teeth stuck to his lips, and a clapper banging away at the inside of his skull. He needed that kind of drunk. Any sane person, he said to himself, would run off and leave her, or call that hotshot husband to get his ass over here and take her home. But Jamie couldn't move. He was nailed to the booth. He could almost feel the blood pooling under his thighs.

"Jamie," she said imploringly, "please listen to me. I see things that I can't see, and what I say happens hasn't happened at all."

"Like your kid stabbing you."

"Yes. David said he didn't. Even Jebbie said he didn't. And my cut-up clothes convinced nobody of anything, not even my doctor."

"But it's your hand, and you were there, and you saw him. Right, Maggie?"

"Well, maybe I was wrong," she cried. "Maybe he wasn't in the closet, and maybe I am crazy and did it myself!"

"Yeah, and maybe I'm Richard Burton. Maggie," he reached over and took the glass away from her, grasping hold of her hand, "I believe you."

"Do you?" She raised one eyebrow, a trick he noticed she had, and she tried to smile. "Why? Why of everybody do you believe me? Because I was your teenage wet dream, and you want to go to bed with me?"

The vulgarity surprised him. He didn't know what to say because he did want to screw her every which way to Sunday and then some. If it was the best of all possible worlds, he'd have a week with her in a motel. But the sex was only part of it.

"Maybe I believe you because nobody else does," he said. "I don't exactly swing with the tide." Which, he thought, was putting it mildly. His entire life had been one of contradictions. He had gone into medicine because his father had wanted him to be a lawyer. He had done his residency in the South Bronx when he could have stayed at University Hospital, which was antiseptic, clean, and not knee-deep in derelicts and junkies. He'd had an offer to join a group practice on Park Avenue, but instead he decided to come home to a small town in Connecticut and take over from an aging general practitioner. Most of the time he wore jeans and Indian shirts or a sweat shirt, and he had only one tie, which he couldn't even find. Yes, he never did anything the way he was supposed to, and even behaved stupidly—except in medicine—more times than not. He had been engaged to a blond, blue-eyed honey of a woman who was independent and had a portfolio big enough to keep the two of them for a century or more, and at the last minute he had decided she didn't yank at his heart strings nearly enough. Well, if he wanted some woman to turn him into Jell-O, he had found her now. Maybe that's why he was going to believe every damn word she said. Given the kind of sleigh ride he'd been on all his life, he didn't see how he couldn't.

Later, driving back to Four Oaks, Jamie put the top of the TR up as a fine rain, soft as baby's breath and too delicate to burst the heat spell, pattered on the canvas. The wipers swished in sympathetic harmony to a medley of Beatle songs, and Maggie, for the first time since coming home from Greenwood, was at rest. She had told Jamie of Jeb, of his strange and bewildering behavior, and the telling was a catharsis. It flooded out, and she wasn't sure if she sounded crazy or not, if what she had said made coherent, logical sense or instead described the underbelly of derangement. It didn't matter, just the telling did, and the wonderfully empty, purged feeling she had. Not even Klein knew as much as Jamie did now, and David, in comparison, knew nothing.

There were no other cars on the turnpike. They were alone in the night, in the singing rain, the dull green of the TR's hood glazed bright in the wetness. Jamie had had one vodka too many, and his head ached way back behind his eyeballs. Maggie was slumped in the embrace of the passenger seat, sleeping. He had seen her visibly relax as she finished her story. She had almost nodded off in the bar. God knew what he'd do with her now, though there was no question what he wanted to do.

As if she could tell what he was thinking—and why not, he'd told her often enough in the short time they'd known one another, and his desire was palpable—she awoke saying, "I think you better take me home, Jamie. David must be there by now. It's late, isn't it?"

"Late enough. And, yeah, I guess Four Oaks it is."

The TR ate up another few miles, and as they spun down the exit ramp and hit the auxillary road going into Brighton, she whispered, "What am I going to do now?"

"Nothing, Maggie," he said without thinking, not that thinking about it could change anything since he had no answers for her. "Just take it day by day. It will all work out. You'll see."

And to himself—because he knew this was meaningless advice worth nothing—he said: you shit.

Four Oaks was lit up like Macy's at Christmas time, each window blazing with light, the doors wide open behind their screens, drawing in the night through the mesh while swarms of moths frantically struggled to get to the source.

"David's going to be mad at me," Maggie said, resigned. "I'm always wandering off and getting lost, and he's always waiting for me to come home. He doesn't like that much. In David's world wives, like children, should be decorative and silent and in their place."

"David doesn't seem to be your favorite person." Jamie pulled up behind the Mercedes, which was parked in the drive.

She looked at him in surprise. "I love David. He's my husband."

She was as matter-of-fact as a mugger, clinical and passionless, and it was only the monotone that kept him from feeling that she had shot him in the chest.

"This is getting to be a bad habit, Maggie." David had come to the door at the sound of the TR and stood, backlit, behind the screen, his face bisected by tiny lines that made him seem in the dimness, old and weary.

"It's my fault, Mr. Brace," Jamie said as they entered the front hall.

David wasn't sure for a moment just who he was. "Oh, Dr. Evers. I didn't know it was you."

"Yeah, it's me. You probably heard from your housekeeper about the accident. Well, after I took care of the little girl, I had to spend some time calming your wife down. She was—as anyone would be," he emphasized that, "—pretty upset. And the kid's mother didn't help much, acting nutty and slinging around accusations. So, I took Mrs. Brace out for a drink and drove her around until she felt better." He was putting on his good doctor act, trying to appear safe and professional, and for one of the few times in his life he wished he was of the suit and vest and tie school, with hair trimmed up over his ears.

David stared at him for one long, sizzling minute and then dismissed him. Jamie recognized the arrogance of a mover and shaker, for that was what David was. He had known enough of them at Cornell. If you weren't an integral piece of their life, the hell with you; your significance was little less than that of the milkman.

They stood awkwardly in the hallway, almost touching, until Maggie left them, hooking her pocketbook on the newel post of the stairs and going into the kitchen. Jeb, in his pajamas, was sitting cross-legged on the kitchen chair. A glass of milk stood half empty on the table. Maggie reached out for him without speaking, and his arms went up to her. She lifted him and he wrapped himself about her. He was washed and powdered, his hair still damp and smelling of baby shampoo. "My love boy," she whispered the old baby name to him, but he was solemn and hid his face at the side of her neck, the lashes tickling her skin.

"You left him alone at a traumatic time, Maggie," David said, "so don't be all loving and wonderful to him now."

"I didn't leave him alone. Sarah was here. And we couldn't very well take him with us to the hospital."

He wouldn't let go now that he had his teeth in it. "There was no reason you had to go with Janet. Your responsibility was here. With Jeb."

"I know what my responsibilities are, David. Please don't lecture me."

To Jamie they were characters in an off-Broadway play where meaning underlies each word spoken, meaning that will be unraveled if you manage to stay to the end. Right then he didn't want to wait it out, but he didn't want to leave Maggie either, not while her husband was determined to punish her.

"I think that Mrs. Brace handled the situation quite properly," Jamie said, somewhat pompously, as they both both turned to stare at him. He wanted to defuse the anger and resentment, and if he had anything to do with it, Maggie would take a hot shower and sleep for twelve hours and get up in the morning, not a whole new woman—Jesus, he didn't want a molecule of her to change even if she was crazy—but with a whole new world. Gunshot wounds and melanomas, hepatitis and lead poisoning notwithstanding, Jamie believed that you painted life the way you wanted to see it and then lived it that way. So what if you did it by numbers and weren't Rembrandt.

Maggie came toward them carrying the boy. His bottoms had slid down and the top had scrunched up and there in the middle, the twelfth dorsal Jamie thought automatically, was a vulnerable expanse of child flesh. Maggie's fingers crept around and touched the skin.

But David was not to be be moved. "Do you realize," he asked, "that once again I didn't know where you were?"

"I'm sorry. I should have called and let Sarah know. But I did try to find you, David, and as always you weren't to be found."

"What does that mean?"

He was on the boiling point, just ready to go over. The skin around his mouth puckered, the tendons in his neck stiffened.

"Where were you, David?" she shot back. Her spunk jolted Jamie. He hoped it was because of him that her fuse was lit, because she either had to fight and lash out, or he was afraid she was going to go under again. People who get angry and stand up for themselves seldom end up in the booby hatch, Jamie remembered. It's the passive ones who most often get eaten alive.

"I was working, as I am supposed to, while you were running around the countryside with this hippie doctor," he yelled.

All right folks, here we go. Jamie sighed with disgust,

and said, wishing all the time that he had left, "Let's not get rude or overimaginative, Mr. Brace."

It was all too much. David saw himself breaking away, saw himself spin off into anger, the white walls rising to engulf him. He seldom lost his temper because that relinquishing of control so badly frightened him. It was dangerous to give into rage—passion, love, greed, hatred, but never rage—because rage could sweep you right over the falls, strand you on foreign terrain with no face-saving way to return. But he was gone now. He could feel himself flying alone, the wind bruising his face, tearing at his clothes. For a moment he tried to grasp hold, thinking, they have all pushed me into this, Maggie, Lee, the gods that for some reason he didn't understand had decided to attack him.

It was useless; he was screaming. Sarah came to the upstairs hallway and peered over the bannister. Maggie was sculpted in stone. Jamie grabbed David's arm and said, "Stop it, you're acting nuts."

"What the fuck do you know?" He spun on Jamie, knocking him off balance. "And get the hell out of here anyway. All you were supposed to do was sew up her goddamn hand, not play shrink. She's got her own expensive shrink and thirteen months in the funny farm. She doesn't need you to moon over her and think, 'poor Maggie, so sad, so awful.'" His voice boomed until Jamie's ears hurt, but David was so close to the truth—just inches from it—that in just a few sentences he was going to stumble over it.

Maggie's mouth was opening and closing. Jamie could see the flash of her white teeth, the pink of her tongue. Insanely he thought, if I kiss her, she will shut up, because if she forced the words up and out of her larynx, then they were all going to be destroyed. For the first

time he was sorry about his feelings for Maggie, and what
he hoped her feelings might be coming to be for him.

"Hey, listen, Brace—"

David shoved at him. It was inevitable that they were
going to touch one another. The stench of desire, of
longing, was so strong in the hallway it was impossible that
David didn't get a whiff of it.

Maggie moved forward and backwards, unable to think,
as Jeb clutched her more tightly. The mirror was behind
them both, and from the curve of her shoulder and neck,
Jeb blinked rapidly at himself. He saw himself; he saw his
mother's back in white stripes; he saw the opposite wall
with its tiny pink flowers and green pointed leaves, and he
heard his father raging, cursing at his mother, at the
doctor. He didn't understand the words, but with every
breath he swallowed his father's anger like poison gas, and
he couldn't breathe. Smoke was pouring into his nostrils.
He heard them screaming and heard the whooshing, and
his heart was beating in rapid, machine gun beats. He
cried to his reflection, to that other little boy and that
other mother in that other place, where the gusts of white
smoke were ruffling the glass, climbing up insidiously, the
heat churning far off down the hall, coming toward them,
attempting to make its claim as it was doing on Tracy and
Kathy. . . .

"*Mommmeeee!*"

Just then Jamie struck out at David, hit him in the
mouth with a clenched fist, the blood spurting in all
directions as David went backwards and bounced up on
the wall, his hands rising in self-defense and rage to
grapple at Jamie who hit him again, this time in the
nose—

"*Mommmeeee!*"

And Maggie was screaming too, trying to pry Jeb off her

neck where he hung on her in that death grip until she smelled the acrid, terrible stench of burning—

Noooooo!

She flung him from her, right at David and Jamie, away from her body, from the mirror, where she thought for a thousandth of a second he was grinning and laughing and not screaming at all. And then she flung herself after him.

11

Lee's bedroom was surrounded by trees, branches splayed outside the windows and hovering over the skylight, a green web that always made David feel he was above ground, high up, and with a long way to fall. He lay naked on top of the down quilt and listened to the comforting sounds Lee made in the kitchen. In a few minutes she'd bring up a steaming pot of coffee and a plate of buttered toast.

He rolled over on his stomach and hugged a pillow beneath his head. He'd have to go back to Four Oaks. It was Saturday and he'd been here since Thursday night. He couldn't stay much longer. Maggie didn't know where he was. He rolled over again onto his back and stared up through the skylight at the blue sky and the narrow streaks of white clouds that trailed behind the trees like streamers from a gigantic kite.

The swelling in his face felt like it had gone down as he tentatively probed his nose and upper lip with his fingers. His cheeks were bristly, since he hadn't shaved in two days, and his skin itched. Shit, I must look like a bum, he thought, but didn't get up to glance in the mirror that hung over Lee's dresser at the other side of the room. Whatever he looked like, it would be ghoulish. It might be days yet before he'd be able to return to the office.

But he had to go home. He wasn't sure whether he wanted to or not. He'd come on impulse, not the moment

167

after Jamie had knocked him to the ground and all the screaming had begun, but later.

He jumped up and went to the small triangular window near the bed. Below, beneath all the foliage, he could just pick out a swatch of bright yellow, that flower, the name of which he constantly forgot, trimming the side of the house like a ribbon. He wasn't good at flowers, but he knew he liked this one because it was dignified. A dignified flower was a ridiculous idea, and he laughed aloud.

"Hello, you must be alive and well if you can laugh." Lee brought in a tray with the pot, cups, and the toast and put it on the small, low table beside the wicker lounge chair with its plump canvas cushion almost the exact shade as the flower.

"What's the name of that flower? You know, the one along the side of the house."

"Dahlia. Why?"

"Just curious."

She poured him a cup of coffee, and he stretched out on the lounge, naked as a jaybird, he thought, and sipped it. It was just right, not too strong, not too weak. Maggie couldn't make a good cup of coffee if the Gestapo threatened her. She had finally learned to cook, and not badly either, after almost poisoning him the first few years they were married. But, she never did learn about coffee.

"You look very somber for a naked man," Lee said, sitting down at the edge of the lounge. Her robe flared, and the whole bottom half of her body was bare.

"I thought I looked more like a patchwork quilt," he laughed sourly. He wanted to kill Jamie Evers. He hadn't been in a fight since he was seventeen and he was jumped behind the public high school as he was leaving a dance. The other boy had a pig sticker, but David hadn't known that right away, so he'd lashed out, and then felt the slash across his knuckles. Anyone else would have turned tail and run like a rabbit, but the rage had erupted out of him. . . .

He scuttled backwards from the memory of his rage, as he did from those last confused minutes.

Had he smelled smoke? No, of course not.

A kaleidoscope of images shifted through his mind, but he refused to look at any particular one except Jamie swinging. The rage was buried once again, but a stinging anger sang in his bones. He wanted, if not to kill Evers, at least to kick the shit out of him.

When he stopped thinking about Jamie there was Maggie. David couldn't put her aside. She was a burr in his mind.

And yet he'd had to leave Four Oaks that night. He didn't want to think that he ran away, but rather had gotten away. He had called Maggie Friday morning, then again at night. He'd have to phone soon, and say . . . what? In the other calls he hadn't explained his actions, and she hadn't asked. They just solemnly assured one another that they were fine, no problems, and Maggie would say that Jeb was fine too. He didn't, she added in the first phone call, remember much of all the confusion, or at least he said he didn't.

Neither Maggie nor David said anything about the smell of smoke, about fire.

They were both very polite. David took comfort in that. Still, he knew he'd been wrong, that he was the culprit this time. He'd lashed out at Jamie because the doctor was there, and David could hit him. Not that he had, which was another thing that made David mad. He'd wanted to hit Evers, and Jamie had hit him instead.

"I better get dressed," David said, though he didn't move.

"Any particular reason? You've been wandering around my house, in and out of bed, without any clothes for some time. I'm not unhappy about that, are you?"

She put down the coffee mug and lay next to him, untying the robe's belt so that turquoise velour parted and her pendulous breasts tumbled against him. He liked the feel of her breasts on him, the weight of them.

"I have to go back."

"To Four Oaks?" She wouldn't say to Maggie.

"Yes, where else?" He teased at her nipple with his thumb and watched it swell.

He hadn't told her why he'd come, nor what had happened, only that there had been a fight—which she could certainly see in his battered face—and that he needed a few hours rest. The few hours tumbled into a whole night and then the next day and another night. Lee hadn't asked any questions, just told her assistant in the store that she had a fever—which was true enough—and she'd be in when she felt better, and then kept herself and David in a perpetual state of heat. When they weren't making love they were sleeping, almost comatose with exhaustion. Lee knew this was some kind of purging for David, but of what or of whom—Maggie?—she didn't know. It was enough to love him and make love with him.

"Again?" She was whispering at his ear, nibbling the lobe, his hand trailing down her belly. She lifted one leg and raised herself toward him, and thought she really was a bitch in heat, pushing her swollen sex to her lover, never satisfied, never fulfilled until the fit had passed. Only this fit hadn't passed in almost a year.

Their bodies warmed, slicked with sweat, and they rubbed up and down, the velour robe tangled around them.

I'll go home to Maggie in a little while, David promised himself, plunging into Lee, into the warmth and comfort of her, her insides soft as velvet, but this is for me. I must have something for me.

*   *   *

Maggie wasn't worried about David, nor about David going off and leaving her, something he had never done before, and something which was antithetical to his personality. Nothing was as it once was, despite Klein's promises, so why shouldn't David be different, stepping out of character like an actor on stage who plays a dual role.

If anything, Maggie was pleased with David's vanishing act. It showed, for the first time in their marriage, that David wasn't as tough as the hundred-years oaks at the edge of the drive that neither lightning nor dynamite had been able to budge.

When Maggie thought about Thursday night one part of her was vaguely reassured. Jamie had stood up for her. Other men, including David of course, had insisted they cared, but none of them had ever fought to prove it. It stirred something primitive in her, and she was childishly pleased.

The rest of that night she, like David, had put in cold storage.

When, on Friday morning, she had rolled awake and found herself alone in bed, her unguarded thoughts stirred with drifts of smoke, and she shot straight up in a web of sheets and blankets, as if Jeb's arms were around her neck again. *There was no smoke and no fire.*

Oh yes there was, someone else's voice inside her head insisted.

She had jumped out of bed, took a cold shower, and didn't see the note propped up by a box of Chanel dusting powder until she was already dressed.

I went out for a while. I'll call you later.

Now it was Saturday and as she looked over at David's side of the bed, she saw his pillow was still smooth and unwrinkled. Again he hadn't slept at home, and for a moment she wondered where he was. But she didn't care. She didn't want to see him right then. Too much debris lay between them, cluttering their lives, refuge that had to be sluiced away if they were going to survive.

She startled herself with that last thought, and vigorously brushed her hair, her head thrown forward, the blood rushing to her brain, as if she could beat or drown the disloyalty out of her mind. There had never been any question but that she and David had to go on. How could they not? Why wouldn't they? Didn't they love one another— oh not in that wild, passion-filled way that Jamie came at her and she, God help her, she wanted to respond too— but with authenticity built on years and children and possessions and loss. They had tied one another down, and if now they were pecking at each other, wasn't that to be expected? They had lost two of their children and thirteen months of their marriage, and right now were at ground zero. But the very fact that David had exploded, had been stripped of his Mr. Perfect façade gave her hope for the first time. David having faults made her feel less inadequate, and she smiled.

The phone rang. As she came down the steps, Sarah was holding out the receiver from the wall phone in the kitchen so that when she walked through the doorway she felt as though a gun was pointing at her midsection. Maggie didn't have to ask who it was; Sarah's expression told her that. There was nothing Sarah had missed, and some things she might have seen that the others, too busy yelling and flailing about and being terrified, hadn't understood.

"Hello," she said, turning her back on Sarah, who furiously beat pancake batter until it was runny.

"It's me. Are you all right?"

Had they come that far that he could say, *It's me*, and she would know who it was?

"I'm okay."

"Heard from Mohammad Ali again?"

"He called a second time. Late. About ten or so." She could hear other voices, and background static, and sensed that he had his lips pressed right against the mouthpiece, kissing it as he spoke, kissing her. "How are you?"

"I want to see you. I can't go another day without seeing you."

The batter sizzled on the skillet; then Sarah slid the spatula under each perfectly rounded circle, not a frayed edge anywhere, and flipped, just a half inch, and caught it landing. Jeb was watching her juggling act with intense concentration. Maggie hadn't even noticed him sitting at the kitchen table drinking his orange juice through a crazy straw out of a Big Bird glass.

"Maggie, can I see you?"

"What? Oh yes, I guess so." Should she see him? She locked her gaze on Jeb, as if the very fact of his existence kept her grounded. Did she want to see Jamie?

Sarah served Jeb a neat stack of pancakes, patted a piece of butter on top and cascaded syrup over the pyramid. He dug into the pancakes, cutting and chewing, butter and syrup dripping down his chin. Sarah sat and watched him, wiping away at his face as if he were a much younger child.

"When? Where?"

"Today." She didn't want Sarah and Jeb to hear her. There was something shameful in making a date to commit adultery—because that's what she was doing whether or not she and Jamie actually made love, though she knew without a doubt that if they met again they would have to—right in front of your child and your housekeeper. Even if they seemed to be absorbed in one another and in the pancakes. Sarah had made another batch and sat eating next to Jeb.

"Where?" Jamie asked.

"I—"

"You can't talk?" he asked.

She blushed furiously, feeling cheap. "Yes, that's right."

"Listen, I'm at the hospital now, and I don't have afternoon hours until two. Can you meet me now if I cut it short here?"

"Okay."

"I have a cabin out at Lake Winoche, about fifteen miles from town. Nothing much, just a lean-to that keeps the mosquitoes off, but nobody's around for miles. Meet me in the parking lot behind the Shop-Rite, and I'll pick you up. By the back fence. I'll find you." Without waiting for an answer, Jamie hung up.

"There's fresh coffee," Sarah said as Maggie hooked the receiver.

She ran the water until it was freezing, then drank a full glass. "No thanks, I don't want any."

"It's another hot one today if you're going out," Sarah said, "a hundred again. At least that's what they're promising." She shook her head. "This is a bad summer. But you knew it had to happen sooner or later, all that fiddling they're doing up there," she pointed at the ceiling, "with space ships and such. I read in the newspaper there's a whole garbage dump going 'round and 'round the earth. It's a wonder that junk doesn't fall down and brain us."

"Where are you going, Mommy?" Jeb asked, though Maggie hadn't moved except to put the empty glass in the dishwasher.

Methodically, he cut a fresh stack of pancakes into quarters and skewered them, shoveling them into his mouth until his cheeks bulged. Yet he didn't look at her.

What had he heard? What could he have heard? She hadn't said anything. Jamie had done all the talking.

"I have some errands to do," Maggie said.

"If you get to the Shop-Rite, I've got a list," Sarah said.

A flutter of dread moved up Maggie's spine. "I'm not going near Shop-Rite."

"Then you'll have to go in tomorrow, or let me have the car." Sarah liked the idea now of driving the car. "We're out of detergent and low on coffee and grape jelly. He does like his grape jelly sandwiches, don't you, lovey?"

Jeb gazed at her solemnly and nodded his head. "I don't want any more," he said, pushing his plate away.

"All right then. I think you've done your duty. Go upstairs and wash your hands and face. And what about changing your shirt? You've got a trickle of syrup right there," she poked at his collar, "and we wouldn't want a bee to find you. Bees like sweet things just like little boys." Once again the balance between Sarah and Maggie had tilted. Jebbie seemed more the housekeeper's child than hers.

He slid off the chair and going over to Maggie asked, "Can I come with you, please?"

She shook her head, feeling guilty. "No, not this time. But later, honey, we'll do something special. I promise." She couldn't meet his eyes, and he went out of the kitchen shuffling his feet.

"He's a delicate child, moody," Sarah said, gathering up the plates, not looking at Maggie. "One minute this way, the next that. He takes careful handling."

"I think I'll have a cup of coffee after all," Maggie said, sensing a rebuke, though it had been given kindly. She poured the steaming coffee into one of Jeb's Snoopy mugs and sat at the clean end of the table. "Has he said anything about the other night?" she asked.

Sarah cleaned up, scraping the leftovers into the garbage disposal, rinsing off the plates before she stacked them in the dishwasher. "What could he say? Everybody screaming and yelling. He got upset and screamed and yelled too. It's a wonder I didn't howl like a banshee myself." There was no mistaking the disapproval in her voice.

Maggie's mother used to say that Maggie wasn't any good with the help, that she forgot that they received a salary every week for doing the work she, Maggie, didn't choose to do and could afford not to do. The fact of that salary automatically put a distance between Maggie and whatever woman it happened to be. They were decidedly not equals. Color and class had nothing to do with it, but money did. Once you paid someone, you were better than they were, and they had to listen to what you said. And, if they disagreed with you, well, that was too bad. They could always go elsewhere. But you never, under any circumstances, treated the hired help as anything but hired.

Only Maggie had never learned, and now she sat in the kitchen with Sarah and said, trying to smile, "Come sit down and have a cup of coffee with me."

Sarah glanced at her suspiciously and sniffed, "Well, I have the wash to do, but a few minutes more or less won't make no difference."

Jeb was uneasy. There was a current in Maggie's voice that he picked up, a current that troubled him and that he didn't understand. He went through the gray light, down the long hall, and paused at the bottom of the stairs looking up. He put one sneakered foot on the first step and started to raise the other when he turned abruptly and hurried to the mirror.

Small, sticky hands went up and grasped at the cool surface that warmed almost immediately. He fitted his body against himself and felt the humming prickling up his legs, heard the comforting sound inside his head, his lips moving, kissing the glassy surface, his breath misting his blurry, softening features.

He stared into darkness and whispered, "Himself."

Half a breath later he was flying up the steps, into the bathroom where he spilled water on his hands, splashed it across his face. He barely dried his skin and then was off again. He wanted to change his shirt but hadn't time. It took too much attention not to tangle his head and arms. But he knew he should have put a clean shirt on because he was supposed to do each thing they told him, the Mommy person, or the Daddy person, or that Sarah person too. He was supposed to listen and follow their orders. That was the way he learned. And he had to learn because he had to be ready, though when he tried to puzzle it out he wasn't sure what he had to be ready for.

He rushed down the steps on his tiptoes, avoiding the mirror in the hallway, averting his head so he couldn't see the other little boy, and raced out the front door and around the house to the garage. The small door at the side opened on squeaky hinges. He stopped, holding his breath, but nobody seemed to have heard, and he slipped inside, letting it close lightly behind him.

There was the Dodge. He went over and peered in. It was dark inside and empty, except for an old newspaper and the picnic basket and a blanket. He scrambled into the small space behind the front seat, curled into a ball, and pulled the blanket over him. He was a little boy, and he didn't make much of a lump under the blanket, and if he didn't sneeze, she'd never know he was there. He closed his eyes and tried not to sleep, waiting for her. He didn't like to sleep. It was a bad thing. It was dangerous too because he never knew where he went, and if he traveled someplace different and foreign he might not get back. And he had to get back. He wasn't sure how long he could be gone, but it was longer and longer these days, like a tunnel that stretched out into nowhere the more he walked into it. But he had to be careful not to get caught, to be able to reverse and return.

The garage door swooshed up, and from under the corner of his blanket he got a peal of daylight. The tap, tap of feet on the cement, then the driver's door opening. Boom, it slammed shut, and all of a sudden they were in motion, backwards and forwards. Bump, bump. Over the drive. Stop. And out onto the highway. He could feel the road close under him, banging on his bones. He clutched the blanket, brought his legs against his chest, and coiled tighter than a spring, every muscle stiff as a bent hairpin.

Click. Snap. There was music. The kind without words. He knew the Mommy person could do something in the front of the car to make music. He had heard it before. There was a caroom, caroom, and an icy sound that scratched the inside of his ears racing along. Caroom. Scratch. Jeb listened intently though he didn't know what it meant. But he didn't think *they* knew either because *they* always talked when the music was on, except if *they* were alone as she was now. Sometimes if there were words, they'd stop what they were saying, as if the words were a secret message, but then they never said anything about the words or the music. Why did they play it if they didn't listen? He decided that if he ever got the chance to do it himself, the music that is, he'd try to find out what it meant, even though he might have to play it backwards, put the end on first and reverse all the sounds so that the ups were downs and the clicking which was over his forehead became a clunking down in his belly.

Jeb was lulled along and despite his resolve found himself drifting, rocked in the car. And then they were stopping and starting again until at last the car stopped completely, and she shut off the motor, and he could no longer smell the stink of gas. For the longest time there was silence, the music off and no horns or the plunking of their tires along the road or the rumbling of trucks like big beasts. Then Jeb heard that man's voice.

"Sorry I'm late, but there was a cardiac alert just as I was leaving, and I was the closest doctor they could grab," Jamie said, opening the door and helping Maggie out. He had parked the TR next to the Dodge and left the engine running.

"That's all right. I've only been here a minute." They were painfully shy with one another, like teenagers. He took her elbow gingerly between two fingers, afraid to touch her, and walked her over to the TR. There was a flash of bare legs as she slid inside that made his stomach twitch. He thought it was a long time, if ever, that a woman had so excited him, kept him hungry and permanently erect. He ran around the car and scrambled in, eager as a boy on his first date, and floored the TR getting it out of the parking lot.

It was hot in the Dodge, stifling, the heat creeping up his nose with the floor fuzz. He was going to sneeze after all. He didn't like to sneeze because he thought his insides would fall out, but he couldn't stop himself and sneezed twice, puffing up the blanket. Tentatively, he poked the blanket aside and uncoiled, getting to his knees. Pins and needles stitched up and down his thighs and calves and along his arms. He blinked in the heavy sunlight, thick as butter, and peered over the front seat. There wasn't another person around. The Dodge was parked way back by a high fence rows away from the rest of the cars. Far off there was a line of buildings like those old blocks from the second shelf in his room, the ones you could line up tall or low, flat down or on edge.

Jeb tried to remember what this was, this place with the little ants scoodling back and forth in front of the blocks, and he ticked off his list of words and phrases, curling them like sucking candy on his tongue. There was a sign on the biggest of the buildings, but he didn't know what it said, all the letters going backwards. He concentrated harder until there was a pop in his head: shopping center. Yes, he was at the shopping center.

And the Mommy person was with that other person whom he should remember, only for a minute he couldn't. That part always scared him, that he knew something because he had *seen* it and it had *happened* to him, and not to the other; and then he got it misplaced like a forgotten sock somewhere in the back of his skull. He thought it would have been better if he could have reached right inside his brain and turned all the knobs and dials that he was positive had to be in there and bring up the picture like on the television set. He scrunched his eyes shut until he could lock the voice with the person. The doctor person. Yes, he remembered him now. He was a *bad* thing, not a *good* thing. Jeb felt smug with himself because he had been right. The Mommy person was doing something bad, something dangerous going off with him when the Daddy person wasn't around. He had gotten one thing as straight as a line, one given that must never be deviated from: The Mommy and the Daddy were a together thing, and the sky was going to fall right down and the earth buckle up and swallow them as it swallowed the sisters if the Mommy and Daddy ever came loose from one another now that the Mommy was back.

He didn't know where they had gone, nor, of course, when they'd be back, and he wondered if he should stay right there without moving. Except he couldn't breath.

There was no air in the car, and he knew if you didn't get air, bubbles rose up like soda in your brain and you exploded. He cracked the window and put his nose to the slit and sniffed in, but the air out there stank with heat and gas fumes.

He looked again at the big blocks with their backwards lettering and twitched. He could go down there and investigate in case *they* had gone into one of those places. Not that he thought they really had. He was smart enough to know if they were going to poke around the inside of one of the blocks, they didn't need that other car, the toy one, to do it. They could've walked, just like he could do, even if it was a long way. So they probably weren't up there, and if he went and poked around on his own, what if the Mommy person came back and drove off in the Dodge without him?

He pondered the problem awhile, turning it upside down and sideways, but the heat decided for him. It was too hot in the car. His shirt was stuck to his back and he was light-headed. And besides, he was curious. He was like a vacuum cleaner when it came to information. He sucked up everything that came his way and then attempted to make order out of it. To make order he first had to deal with chaos, little blobs of information that assaulted him like meteors.

He pulled up the button and opened the door. Even the pavement was hot, oozing sticky globules of tar that stuck to the bottoms of his sneakers as he piloted his way on a direct course through the parking lot. As he passed the shiny cars with the burning skins, the heat bubbled around him. The ants inflated, grew larger, metamorphized into people who loomed bigger than he was, a small boy in a green T-shirt, with a nibbling alligator to the left of the buttons, and khaki shorts and white socks rimmed in a wavery line of color, socks that had lost their elastic and sagged down on his Keds.

The most gigantic block was a supermarket with people sluggishly pushing carts back and forth, down long aisles towering to the ceiling with boxes and cans. Gusts of frigid air came off the refrigerator cases of meats and cheeses and yogurt and margarine.

The sweat evaporated, and he was clammy, wiping his hands on his shorts. He wandered into the produce section, and when the man-in-the-white-apron person had his back turned, Jeb ate a handful of grapes. No one paid him any attention, and he cruised, up one aisle and down the next, marveling at the pyramids of cereal boxes.

After a while, he got tired of the supermarket block and decided to see what the others were like. There were big windows top to bottom on all the stores, which made it easy to peer inside, his nose flattened at the glass, and he walked along, stopping, looking, until he came to a shop filled with toys and other children persons. This door he had to pull at, and it was heavy, which didn't seem fair, but inside it was just right, not too hot nor too cold.

He intently inspected each shelf, gazing curiously at the dolls, the games, the boxes with promises written along the sides. There were big wire baskets filled with curved sticks. He picked up one of the sticks and turned it over and over in his hands.

"That's a boomerang."

There was a little girl person just level with his eyes, like that other one who got hurt, only this one had curly hair the color of chocolate pudding and skin that was so brown it reminded him of the darkness in the back of the closet.

"You throw it, and it comes back to you," the little girl pointed out.

He contemplated the boomerang with wonder. "How? How does it come back to you if you throw it away?"

"It's a scientific principle," she said smugly.

"What's that?"

She put her hands on her hips and regarded him as though he was stupid. "It's something that's true, even if you don't like it or want it to be."

"Oh," he said, nodding his head, though her words buzzed at him in a kamakaze attack of confusion.

"Zia, what are you doing?"

And there was another chocolate person, but a lighter one, more like the color of syrup he poured on pancakes, and Jeb supposed she was a Mommy person too.

The little girl went away, and Jeb's attention returned to the boomerang. What had she said, that you couldn't throw it away because it always came back to you? He liked that idea. He liked that idea a lot. And he wanted to see how it worked. He looked around and was going to throw the boomerang but decided he'd only knock over all the toys, and then maybe they'd *all* come back to him, charge at him like an army. It would be better to do it on the lawn and see it whiz through the sky and clip the corner of a cloud and, when he put his hand up in the air, settle back down next to his palm.

Jeb took the boomerang and went right out of the toy store without anyone noticing him, even though he vaguely knew you were supposed to give something in a store before you took anything outside. But since he didn't have anything to give, it wasn't important.

Back on the sidewalk he thought about the Dodge and the TR, and he compressed his lips, narrowed his eyes, and thought again about that doctor person who was being bad, just like he had been bad at the fruit stand. He better get back to the car because even if the Mommy person didn't drive off without him, they might return and do something he should know about.

He wandered up to the Shop-Rite, drew an invisible line down the parking lot to the Dodge and stomped back over the steaming macadam. The car was still there, but the TR wasn't. Jeb climbed into the back seat, fitting the boomerang next to him, and carefully covered the both of them with the blanket. It was even hotter now, but he'd just have to wait. He was awfully good at waiting, he decided, as he stroked the boomerang, sliding his fingers up and down the bend until he heard the screech of another car, the murmur of voices in lapping waves, and then she was back. The windows were rolled down, and the heat lifted a bit. Jeb held his breath.

"I'm always saying I've got to see you again, Maggie." The doctor person was right over his head. "But I do."

"Not now, Jamie, I've got to think."

"Tomorrow. Any time. Anywhere. You name it."

"Tomorrow's Sunday. And David...oh God, I don't even know where he is. But he has to come home some time, doesn't he?"

"Not if you don't want him to."

"Let's not go into that. I love David. I told you that."

"Yeah," he said sarcastically, "and elephants have wings and fly. I'll call you tomorrow. And if a man answers, I'll hang up," he snapped, and then Jeb heard him drive off.

For a few minutes she sat quietly in the front seat while Jeb lay curled behind her. Finally, she started the car and they went bump, bump all the way home, but without music this time, just the sound of crying. And Jeb, cradling the boomerang, was glad she was crying, because he just knew she had been bad.

12

The heat wave had finally broken, and the rains came, just as immoderately. In twenty-four hours the temperature dropped fifteen degrees, and a high wind sweeping out of Canada blew across New England with gale force, bringing a deluge. It had been raining for the better part of two days, a cold, unremitting rain that sank into the marrow.

Four Oaks creaked and shook, rattling its window panes in a windy fury. The old boards groaned, as if the house were a raft on a stormy sea, rising and settling with the waves. The lights flickered, and in the cracks left by warping and age, the wind crept uninvited.

David had come home. He had returned almost a week before, as though nothing had happened, as though he had simply gone to the office in the morning and now it was time for dinner. Why he had come back, or even why he had left, Maggie didn't ask. And it didn't matter. She just wanted life to smooth itself out like a freshly ironed sheet. He had come home and walked with her through the woods, down to the stream, helping her cross over to the other side, and sat with her on the far bank and said he wanted to try, he wanted to work things out between them, that he thought they had to do it for Jeb if for no other reason. And that he loved her and worried about her and wanted her to be well, to be again the woman he married. He wasn't, he was honest, even sure why he wanted all of this, or if it was the right thing to want or right for them and Jeb, but they had descended into chaos all three, or at least the two of them, and if they were to save themselves, they had to get back to firm ground.

"That's an image I used with Klein, or he did with me, you know," she said.

"What is?"

"Firm ground. Klein said it was as if I had been walking along the edge of a cliff and had fallen off, and I had to climb back up the mountainside to firm ground."

David didn't say anything. He dug into the soft dirt warmed by the sun and trickled it over his fingers. The water was low. Gray rocks grew in the river bed.

He hadn't known he was going to say any of what he just had to Maggie until, leaving Lee's and trapped in the Saturday traffic jam, heat shimmering around him in a cloud, he forgot for just a second where he was going. Was he on his way to Lee's or back? Was he dreaming? He shook himself, sweat dripping down into his eyes, and tried to push it all away from him—Lee and Maggie and Jeb—and see the canvas unrolled on the windshield of the Mercedes. Where was he in all of it?

A car behind honked impatiently, and he realized that traffic had come unraveled, the cars ahead speeding off leaving him behind. He shifted gears, and in the click of that second made a decision, like flipping an interior coin, and it came up Maggie because it had to come up one way or the other; it couldn't stand on its edge without rolling away.

"At any rate, Maggie," he said finally, "let's try."

"Weren't we trying, David?"

He wouldn't answer that because it stirred his guilt with a heavy hand. He wasn't ready to give up Lee. Pushing the thought down, the thought which even on that hot afternoon gave him shivers, he said, "Let's try harder."

Maggie didn't know then what trying harder meant and couldn't ask without appearing perverse. Now, sitting on the living room floor with Jeb playing Chutes and Ladders, and David in the chair behind them reading *Time*, she decided that this was what harder meant. David home more often, hovering at their backs, reaching forward every now and then to caress her shoulder, to make an offhanded remark to Jeb. David playing normal father to her normal mother and Jeb the normal child. If it smacked of theater, she had no one but herself to blame, for how could she try harder to put together a family that had shattered into a thousand pieces while all the time she was making love with another man.

The rain crashed against the windows. The wind howled dementedly. The curtains quivered, pulled tight to lock the darkness outside where it teemed with demons. Then the lights went. They all sat waiting, but they didn't come on again.

"Christ," David said, "it's for good this time. The wires must be down."

"Daddy," Jeb said in a quaking voice, "what's wrong? Where did the lights go?"

"It's just the storm," David reassured him. "It will be okay in a little while."

Thunder rolled so close it seemed in the same room with them. In the crack between the drawn curtains lightning glowed, converting the night into a blue-white cariacature of day.

"Daddy!" Jeb screamed.

Maggie grabbed at him, knocking the board game aside, and took him in her arms.

"Hey, Tiger, it's okay," David said, his voice booming like a cannon in the darkness, "that's only thunder and lightning. Do you know what my daddy used to tell me thunder was?"

"No, what?" he asked, curious in spite of his fear.

David laughed, "God rolling bowling balls in the sky."

"Mommy," Jeb asked suspiciously, "is that true?"

Maggie laughed, "Would Daddy make that up?"

"I guess not," he agreed reluctantly, "but how does God get all those bowling balls up there? They're heavy."

They all laughed then, Maggie inching backwards until she rested against David's legs. They sat that way in the darkness, listening to the pounding storm, hesitant to move, to leave the small, magic circle they formed, all touching, locking out the night. Nothing could happen to them if they stayed together.

"Well, we can't sit here forever," David said at last. "And it must be past some people's bedtime."

"Not yet," Maggie said, scared to let go, to break the connections. The black house was an abyss waiting to claim them.

"Not yet, Daddy," Jeb echoed. He knew there were monsters waiting, with gaping mouths and sharp teeth and foul breaths, ready to eat them up. He could smell the monsters and snuggled closer to Maggie, the curve of her breast warming his cheek.

"Hellooooo."

The voice echoed, came at them out of the darkness, fell back on itself, hit the walls like a ricocheting tennis ball. The hair rose up on Maggie's arms. Jeb's fingers dug furrows into her flesh. Jeb knew it was a monster calling.

"Sarah," David said, "we forgot about Sarah."

"Is everyone all right?" the voice asked, coming closer, Sarah's voice now, not a monster's after all.

There was a little pinpoint of light, just a flicker, a firefly that wavered and danced, skipping closer until a dim, hazy Sarah appeared behind it. Sarah entered the living room carrying a candle, wearing her chenile robe, her feet in shower thongs, her hair rolled on thick pink sausages. In the candlelight the creases and lines of her face were thick, turbulent rivers, and her eyes were hooded like a snake's.

"I heard on the transistor that power lines are down all over this part of the state," she said. "Won't come back until the storm's over most likely."

"We better go to bed then. There's not much else we can do," David said, pushing Maggie aside as he left the chair.

Maggie loosened her grip on Jeb, and he spilled from her lap, rolling away into that part of the room where the thin sputtering candle couldn't reach. He was going to be lost, but Maggie stretched out her hands for him, scrambling across the floor on her knees, until she had the tail of his shirt between her fingers and pulled him back. Then, he was gone, out of her reach.

"Tiger," Jeb heard his father's voice far above him, at least up there with God and his bowling balls that were cascading through the alleys of heaven. "Let's go tuck you in."

But he was too frightened now, even with his mother's hand creeping up his arm, an alive thing that wasn't a hand of flesh and blood and bone, but a strange creature, a monster tentacle that was going to slide right up his nose and down and out his mouth and ears, filling him up with slime. He smelled the dead smell like the spot at the far end of the yard that oozed and seeped in a thin puddle on the grass, as though if he dug down, he'd uncover rotting bodies whose lifeless arms would reach up to grab him.

The light moved nearer and there was a tall, hulking monster right out of one of his comic books, a monster that walked on two feet and crushed you in its thick, beefy hands and ate you like a chicken, crunching your bones.

There were monsters all around in the terrifying darkness, monsters with wavy lines who changed shape and form the minute you recognized them. The house shook with them, and Jeb frantically pawed at the chair, crawling behind it, trying to get underneath and hug the floor, but the chair was too low to the ground, and he backed off to the wall, away from the light, the monsters. He wasn't thinking clearly, and he had to get to a safe place where the monsters couldn't find him. He had to reach the mirror.

"Jebbie, where are you?" Maggie called.

"Tiger, it's bedtime," David's voice was sharper now, coming at him like a knife.

Jeb knew it was his father as he knew that had been his mother's hand, but fear invaded him. Fear was marching in his head, thumping. In the darkness even Mommies and Daddies and Sarahs turned into monsters. In the dark everything was different. There were no safe people. Dark was a nightmare that he tried to fly away from in sleep.

"I better get more candles," Sarah said. "Here," she handed the one she was holding to David. "We have a box in the kitchen somewhere."

"You'll need this to see," David said, handing it back. "We'll be okay for a few minutes, won't we, Jeb?" He was jocular, hardy, a ha, ha, booming father.

Jeb knew that was a lying voice, that one that said it won't hurt before the stingy stuff went on a cut. Even if he weren't so scared that he was dizzy, he wouldn't have believed that voice. So he quietly, carefully inched along the wall, feeling the reverberations of the storm through his fingertips, behind the end table, which just whispered at his backside, until he hit the corner. The joining of the two walls was a resting point, and he stopped, catching his breath.

"Where the hell is he?" David asked, impatient now. "Jeb, stop hiding and come here."

"Jebbie, what's wrong?" Maggie called from a long way off. And then to David, "What's the matter with him?"

"Jesus, I don't know. Frightened of the storm and the darkness I guess. Jeb, hey, Tiger, com'on. Daddy will carry you upstairs and tell you a story."

Sarah had gone, taking the candle with her, the light dancing in front of her, leaving the darkness thick as mud. Jeb could feel it surging, buckling around him until he reached the couch. There were just a few inches between its bottom and the floor, but it was enough room for a small boy to slide underneath. Jeb crawled along, the voices muffled outside.

He was in a secret place, another secret place like the one under the porch where he often found ashes and dead frogs, their limbs severed. He knew the ashes had once been living things, and when he saw the remains of the bottles he'd have a mass funeral, tucking the ashes and the frogs into a hole further back beneath the house, patting the dirt and putting pebbles on top. He was never certain how the frogs got separated from their legs, or the bugs became ash, but he felt oddly responsible to dispose of the remains, as if their dying was all his fault.

He finally got to the far side of the couch, the doorway just ahead, and then the hall. If he got across the field studded with mines and booby traps, reached the hall and the reassuring surface of glass, he'd be safe. He could smell safety like a breath of fresh air. He had to get there, he had to get to the mirror or he'd be torn apart like the frog.

"Jeb!" his father called. Then, "God damn it!"

"What's wrong?"

"I just bumped into the coffee table."

"Sit still until Sarah comes back with more light, David."

"Jeb, I'm getting pretty angry."

The monster pretending to be his father was out of his cage, loose now, in the center of the room, but even if he jumped, he wouldn't be able to get this far in one swoop unless he was one of those flying monsters, the kind Jeb saw in the encyclopedia, with the enormous wings and the tiny, little heads and the teeth all sharp and pointy. That kind of monster could come right down from the ceiling and fold him into the scaly wings, the nails digging holes in his belly.

Jeb ran in a crouch, scuttling to the hallway until he bumped into the wall at the other side. The monsters didn't know he was there. He could still hear them talking and creeping around the living room after him.

Where had his Mommy and Daddy gone? Did the monsters have them?

He lay down on the carpet, its tufts scratchy on his face, and moved crabwise, crossed to the far wall, running his fingers along the baseboard, then traveling another few inches until he rose up and pressed himself full length against the mirror. He knew where he was now, though he couldn't see himself, himself as black as he was, blackness washing in and out of the mirror, but he held on, sagging onto the glass. And he began to hum. The humming was like bouncing lights inside his head, dispelling the darkness, chasing it away. He pushed at the cool, slick surface of the mirror, worked at it with the tips of his fingers, softening it like play dough left too long in the box.

The fear drained away, sluiced out of him, as the humming grew louder, louder than he had ever heard it before, so loud that it was deafening, obliterating the noise of the storm. And he felt himself begin to go slack, the weariness entering his limbs as heavy as sleep, just as comforting, and in a second, no more, he knew he was going to be safe.

The wind was gusting around the house. Rain pounded at the roof, the walls, trying to force its way inside. The lightning collided through the sky and split into the earth.

Sarah had never experienced a storm like this one. Nature was on a rampage, blasting away, and it gave her the willies. Just calm down, she told herself, but there were shadows everywhere and ordinary, familiar things like the refrigerator were suddenly menacing. She found the box of candles in the pantry and lit one, hot wax rolling down the sides, burning her fingers. She winced but determinedly went back toward the living room. Midway in the hall she saw Jeb before the mirror, the faint glow as she approached lighting up his image.

"There you are, you," she said, bearing down on him.

He saw her coming, the monster with fire burning in each hand. But monsters didn't scare him. *He* knew about monsters now.

She awkwardly shifted both candles to one hand and grabbed him. "Now I've got you. He's here," she called out to Maggie and David. "Let's just get upstairs to bed."

Her fingers tightened into his skin. He didn't like that. He didn't want her holding him; it made him feel trapped, cornered, with no way to get out.

"Let go," he ordered in a dead voice, struggling with her, the lights bobbing up and down, corks in the darkness. Hot wax dripped over and splattered on his face. He screamed and lashed out, kicking at her, smashing in a rage with a closed fist into her stomach. The blow startled her, and for such a small hand it hurt. Sarah released his arm and clutched her midsection, dropping one of the candles which sputtered on the hall carpet, burning a hole in it, before it flared and died.

And then the storm, which had all her nerves jangling, roared even louder, the voice of an angry god, and something in Sarah snapped, as if all the strangeness and shadows had risen up in one suffocating cloud of madness. Though one part of her mind said it was ridiculous to think of a small boy as being dangerous, she found herself striking out.

Her open palm landed on the side of Jeb's head, and he fell screeching to the floor, kicking his legs, flopping his arms.

Maggie and David crashed into one another coming out of the living room, and Maggie almost fell from the impact, but David saved her, and both of them went down on their knees beside Jeb who was tossing on the rug, his limbs spasming, like a fish out of water.

"Stop it!" they both ordered at once.

Maggie took his arms and David his legs, and they held him pinned to the rug until the fit passed and his sobbing snuffled into silence.

"I don't know what came over me, I truly don't!" Sarah was crying herself now. "I never hit a child in my life, as God is my witness. But he kicked me and then—"

"It's all right, Sarah," David said. "Just calm down. This storm has us all—" He almost said crazy, but even at the moment when he couldn't think clearly, he couldn't bring himself to say the word. It was the truth or so close as to be the same thing. "—Hysterical," he finished, but neither of the women was listening. Maggie was bent over Jeb, stroking his face, soothing him, all his nerve endings quivering beneath her fingers.

"You're going right to bed," David said, scooping him up, "and we'll have a talk about your behavior in the morning." Cradling the little boy that seemed in his arms to be no heavier than a crumpled tissue, he stared down into his son's glassy face, the eyes dark as the storm outside and no more revealing than the black pips on a teddy bear.

Jeb didn't say anything, stony as a catatonic. He let the Daddy person carry him upstairs and let the Mommy undress him and tuck him in. He refused to listen to her milky voice, or bend to her caresses, and went down on his bed, his head on the pillow, the sheet and thin blanket up under his chin, like a doll whose parts had to be arranged by hand.

They said they would leave the door open, and if he was scared in the night, he could call them and they'd come running, even her, that Sarah person who burned his cheek, who hit him. There was a fire burning in his belly about her, and it was crawling up and up, until he knew it would singe his brain. Then they were gone and he lay there. Enclosed in darkness, he waited.

Maggie and David were too tired even to speak. They merely said good-night to Sarah at the foot of the steps leading up to the third floor and assured her again that they understood why she'd hit Jebbie, that either of them would have done the same thing, and that they knew she cared about him. He was a special little boy, and nothing like what happened tonight would ever happen again.

They fumbled with their clothes in the faint light, then slipped naked into bed, Maggie sliding into David's arms. His body, so familiar, was different with the ghost of Jamie lying between them. He was bigger than Jamie, fuller in the chest, and hairier too, and she felt, as she drifted off to sleep, his one arm under her head, the other curled about her, that she was being unfaithful to Jamie.

David lay awake for a long time, not stirring, weighted down by Maggie. He couldn't sleep trying to understand why Jeb had run from them. What was it that had frightened him so? He worried the situation back and forth, but he didn't get anywhere. Finally, he let it drop, deciding that in the morning everything would be different, everything would be settled again.

Watching the darkness as though there was something to see, he listened, hearing the storm battering upon the walls, thumping on the roof, and his rage was as violent as the howling winds outside. Only he knew that the storm would end, storms always did, but the anger against that Sarah person wasn't going to go away. If he went to sleep it would still be in his chest in the morning when he woke up. Even if he went back *there*, he'd carry the rage with him.

She had hurt him, and he had to get her back.

He thought for awhile how to do it, counted the possibilities, and then he smiled. There was really only one way to get even.

He left his bed and raced down the steps, not bothering to keep quiet because *they* would never hear him with the noise of the storm, even if they were awake. As he reached the mirror, the humming, uncoiling, began, riding along with the lashing of the rain, the growling thunder. He threw up his hands and slapped the glass, hissing, as his breath misted the surface.

"Come out," he said. "There's something that has to be."

Sarah, like Maggie, went right to sleep, climbing down into oblivion, eager to relinquish consciousness. She slept tilted slightly upward, thrown back against the headboard, and awoke with a stiff neck, a pain in her shoulder that radiated down into her chest. Her mouth was dry, and she licked at her lips, her face a sagging balloon without her teeth.

She didn't think she'd been sleeping more than a few

minutes, except for the dream. She was running up and down stairs, being chased by a black dog who snapped at her heels. He was big, with fur that swept the floor, and his eyes glowed red as traffic lights. Even awake she smelled his old dog breath with its stench of death.

It was cold in the room, freezing, wintry even, and she tugged at the blanket, pulling it around her, but the cold seeped right through.

Her mind told her it was too cold. Even with the storm whose demented howling she could still hear, it was too cold. She was in a deep freeze, frost creeping up her varicosed legs, ice rivering in her veins.

Something was wrong, but she was afraid to open her eyes to see what it was. Or maybe her eyes were open already, and there was such blackness it blinded her. Cold sweat rolled in waves under her nightgown, along the soft fat of her rib cage and between her legs, drying immediately into sheets of ice. Yes, something was wrong, with the cold and her heart pounding almost to the point of explosion.

She was so scared she was stapled to the mattress. Maybe she was still asleep, still locked in that bad dream, hiding from the hound. But she knew she wasn't asleep, that she was as awake as she had ever been, her nerves screeching. It was cold in the room, cold to the point of death. And she wasn't alone.

She didn't hear anything, not a rustle beyond the beating of the rain and the surly whine of the wind that ripped along the roof, but she was certain she wasn't alone.

There was another person bearing down on her, coming nearer, and though she didn't want to open her eyes— Dear God, how she didn't want to open her eyes!—she had to. It was the only act of will left.

And so she did.

There was a double image, like a ghost on a television

screen. It wavered and flickered in the white flashes of
light that slapped the window, the thick curtains not thick
enough to keep it out, and the room lit up in the dead
glow. Then the image began to separate so that she
realized with horror that there wasn't one, hadn't been
one, but two, two standing one behind the other, just the
edges visible. And now they moved apart, and she saw
four small hands, four bare feet padding over the rag rugs
to her bed. Four dark eyes watched her remorselessly, and
two little mouths opened, and two little tongues like
snakes darted out.

The ice raced in a current through her veins into the
chambers of her heart, and a litany of Our Fathers began
automatically to whirl in her mind.

Her eyeballs bulged, ready to pop. A detonation went
off in her chest, circuits fusing. And suddenly, the paralyz-
ing cold gave way to a roar of heat within her, like a fire
burning, *burning*. . . .

At the last minute, digging in at consciousness with her
torn fingernails, she howled in her head, I don't want to
know this! God, God, she prayed, sweet Jesus, oh please
help me! The fingers, all twenty of them, wiggled at her
face, bore down, and just slightly dusted her skin.

She tried to scream, but the scream merely gurgled in
her throat, and though she begged God again, begged
Him a third time as the irrevocable darkness began its
final slide, it seemed that God wasn't listening.

13

The kitchen was empty. The back door was still firmly shut and locked. There was no coffee pot steaming away on the rear burner of the stove. Sarah must have overslept, Maggie thought, hitting the switch and seeing the lights come on.

She opened the door and looked out. The rain had stopped, at last, though the grass still sparkled with shiny rhinestones of water. Overhead the sky was as clear as a china plate, not a cloud smudging the blue. It was going to be a perfect summer day.

There was a slight, early morning chill to the air, and a deep silence that was deafening after the storm. Maggie rubbed her arms, thinking a cup of Sarah's coffee could warm her up. She was cold to the bone, worn out, but she couldn't—like Sarah and Jeb, a buried mound under blankets—sleep anymore.

David had already left for the office. He had kissed her awake, leaning over her as she opened her eyes, and she hadn't been able to fall back to sleep again, anxiety coiling in her stomach like a snake.

She measured carefully, tiny scoops of grains into the basket and filled the pot with freezing water from the tap. Then, glancing up, she saw him through the window above the sink. Jeb. He was out on the side lawn near the thick fringe of woods, a mite tiny enough to be obliterated by an upraised thumb. He was throwing something into

the air, something that rose and arched and circled grace-
fully back to him. It was a boomerang. He leaped and
caught it on the return then heaved it, left-handed, again.
There was a stumbling awkwardness to his motions, a
puppet's jerking.

She dropped the pot, and it clattered at the bottom of
the sink, spilling water and coffee grains. There, watching
him throw and catch, a silent movie framed by the bright
geraniums, she grew afraid. Dread swept over her in a
tide, awakening the snake that slithered, hissing, along
her insides.

Maggie was scared, frightened of her own son, of Jebbie,
far off, silently tossing the boomerang. Her Jebbie asleep
in his bed. Her Jebbie out on the lawn.

Thoughts spun like pinwheels in her mind. *He's not in
bed. All I saw were blankets. He went out the front door
without my hearing him.*

Tears gathered in the corners of her eyes, rippling her
vision, making the boy and the lawn and the trees and sky
blur in runny water colors.

The tears finally overwhelmed her. She put her wet,
cold hands to her eyes in fists, as a child would, and wept.
But even crying, great hulking sobs that bent her double
from the waist, contorted her like menstrual cramps, she
was afraid. The fear played on her spine like a xylophone.
She held onto the edge of the sink, then let go, groping
her way around the kitchen, spinning off across the tilting
linoleum to the table, where she collapsed in a chair,
putting her head down on her arms. She was faint from
the fear and the crying that tore through her, rushing
along her veins, another storm out of control.

It was as though everything had come together in the
one moment that stretched on and on without stopping,
all the pain and terror and anxiety for herself and Jeb and
all of them. She couldn't have stopped crying if her life

depended on it. Like a car with the brakes gone, she went careening along, banging her fists on the wooden table, beating at it, moaning, her head waving side to side.

She should have raised the dead with her keening, but no one came running. Finally, she ran down, her head slipping foward again to rest on her folded arms, and a curtain swept over her consciousness so that she might have passed out or just fallen asleep, worn raw with exhaustion.

Minutes went by, perhaps an hour, before she came to, surprisingly refreshed, as though after a long, untroubled rest. She felt as she had after Jamie drained the poison from her system, weak, and if not renewed, better. She wasn't going to die from this. She sat at the kitchen table, drifting, remembering, sifting through pictures of the past.

She was a child again in this very house, her mother making her breakfast on the housekeeper's day off. The clink of the spoon against the side of the glass as she stirred the thick, chocolate syrup through the white milk. The pop of the toast coming up in the old toaster, which if you didn't watch carefully would burn the bread. The smell of bacon as it sizzled in the frying pan.

At night, curling in her father's lap as they watched television, Lucy and Desi. Jackie Gleason. Ed Sullivan. She rode her father's stomach when he laughed, feeling the up and down of him.

The click, click of her mother's knitting needles.

There were always people coming and going in the summer, an endless string of guests, friends from the city, friends from far away who were passing through, people from Weston or Greenwich who'd had too much to drink at one of the lawn parties and had to sleep it off in a guest bedroom and who the next morning were sheepish—green around the gills her father would say, laughing.

Where were the gills? She had wondered as a child.

Parties, all those parties, with Chinese lanterns on the
grass and once a small band, only three elderly men in
shiny suits from Brighton actually, who seemed to Maggie
gazing down from her bedroom window better than the
whole symphony that her mother would take her to hear
in Carnegie Hall when there were children's concerts. The
dresses were brighter then, more feminine, the women
prettier, the men handsomer in their white summer jack-
ets that gleamed luminescent in the dark.

Then she was old enough to stay up for the parties.
There had been a white piqué dress the summer she was
twelve, with a frilled apron and little puffy pale blue
sleeves. She could almost feel the starched collar scratching
her neck. And her father had danced with her that night,
thrusting her out the length of his arms, twirling her
carefully around the lawn as the records played—there
hadn't been any band for that party—while everyone
watched and told her mother how pretty she was. What a
beauty she was going to grow up to be. Anything was
possible.

But then nothing had happened. All the promises seemed
to shrivel up, to blow away like last year's autumn leaves.

They left Four Oaks and went to the Cape, to Truro,
where from the top of the house the ocean was visible and
where everything had a salty smell, and sand crinkled
between the sheets at night. The Cape wasn't the same, as
if in looking for something, her parents had left whatever
was important and magical behind. Or maybe Maggie was
just growing up, and they guarded her more. It was the
sixties then, and life was suspect to her parents, the world
had become a treacherous place where, if they weren't
vigilant, their Maggie would be sucked away, metamorphized
into one of those grungy, long-haired types who never
wore shoes or brassieres if they were girls—and sometimes she'd hear her mother muttering, you can't tell the

difference. They closed their eyes to change, to the world outside, and put blinders on her. And because she was all they had and they all she had, and because she wanted nothing more than to be one of those ladies—just as her mother was—who floated light as a summer moth through the moonlight in arms as strong as those of her father, Maggie listened.

She had listened right through high school at Hewitt, and four years at Smith, and into marriage with David who was as tall as her father and just as broad. The Mathersons had approved, so had their friends. Maggie had not gone out with the tide as so many others did to an apartment of her own—five floors up with cockroaches and a super who wasn't reliable—or a boring and slightly demeaning secretary's job, or an ambiguous sexual arrangement, or worse, a protest movement or even a commune. Instead, Maggie was safely married in a ceremony brought off in Christ Church on a Saturday with a long, specially designed gown and bridesmaids and morning suits and orchid bouquets and baby's breath.

Maggie had survived. They had carried her through the shoals to David and the two grandchildren they had lived to see, and they were satisfied. They had done their duty—as Maggie would do hers and her children after her—and when they died later in a plane crash Maggie was certain, their consciences were clear.

What would they think of me now?

Disappointment. Disapproval. She could sense the shades of the long gone shaking their heads.

"Mommy?"

Aiiiiiii

She was off the chair, her heart racing, thrust against the refrigerator, her legs wobbly like overcooked spaghetti.

Jeb was standing in the door, wearing his pajamas, his

hair tousled from sleep, watching her curiously, "Mommy, I'm thirsty."

Maggie's head swiveled to the corner of the window she could see, but there was only sky and lawn. She propelled herself to the sink and looked out, searching for the boomerang as it flew toward her then away. But there was no boomerang cutting patterns in the air, no small boy.

"Mommy," he said, padding up next to her, reaching for her arm, "where's Sarah? I'm hungry. Can she make French toast?"

She pressed him to her, his head along her stomach, and wanted to pull him inside, back to the womb, to start all over again and be heavy with him.

She wanted to feel him under that heart already slowing to a normal beat. Her fear was removed, at a distance, carried off by the friendly specters who noiselessly moved about the house. Yet, still, she couldn't bring herself to ask, were you outside? Do you have a boomerang?

Her father often said, don't ruffle the water. What you don't know won't hurt you. And she listened to his presence, whispering, now, Maggie, pay attention.

It was ten by the kitchen clock on the wall over the refrigerator.

Maggie decided not to wake Sarah, thinking the older woman needed her sleep. So she made the French toast, with Jeb propped up at the table watching, and then they sat and ate it together. Maggie was being bright and cheerful, doing penance for her fear, for her silliness as she now saw it, as she would describe it to Klein. But for all her good intentions, she didn't know how to talk to her son and compromised by telling him a story, the three bears, which he dismissed when she finished as "for babies."

"Excuse me, big shot," she laughed, clearing the table.

"Can we go swimming today?" he asked.

"Sure. Here, put the milk in the fridge."

It made him feel like a big person to help out. He took the carton and positioned it just right in the center of the top shelf. "Sarah never lets me do anything. She says it's her job."

"Well, I guess it is, but Sarah's sleeping."

"Why's she sleeping?"

Ten fifteen.

"Because she's tired, that's why," Maggie explained, stacking the plates in the dishwasher.

But she should be up by now. Sarah never slept late. "Why don't you go and—" Something stopped Maggie, a thin remnant of dread. She shook herself, shrugged away all the fears crowding in. "I'll wake her up. You go get dressed."

They went up the stairs together, Jeb to his room and Maggie to the foot of the steps leading to the third floor, just where she and David had stood with Sarah the night before and reassured the housekeeper, calmed her down before sending her off to bed. Maggie wished David were here with her. On the landing above she could see the closed door. There were no sounds of drawers opening, of closet doors, of water running in the neat little bathroom. The morning droaned away in stillness as she poised, one foot on the first step, her hand gripping the railing.

There was something terrible waiting at the top of the steps. She could feel it in each jangled nerve ending.

You're being silly again.

There was something behind that door, beating its wings upon the wood.

Step by step Maggie pulled herself up, her heart racing again, her mouth dry and sour with fear.

This is nonsense. The woman is just sleeping.

But it wasn't sleep hovering in that room. Maggie knew it in every molecule, yet she still climbed. She couldn't go back down and call David and say, "Come home; Sarah's still in her room, and I'm afraid to go up there."

She reached the landing and put her unbandaged palm flat against the door, as if she could feel what was waiting for her on the other side.

I don't have to do this. Nothing is forcing me to do this, she thought. But something was.

She grasped the knob and turned. The door inched away from the jamb without a sound, and the stench hit her, the foul smell.

Sarah had soiled herself, and the stink of thin, watery excrement rose in a cloud. Maggie gagged, bile rising in her throat.

Something was in the room, death, and it lay in a sheen over the old woman with her sunken cheeks and white frozen skin the color of the sheets. It sat on her face with the bulging eyes like enormous marbles; aggies Maggie thought giddily, we used to call them aggies. And it rode her arms off which the fatty flesh was already dissolving, to the hands like claws that clutched the blanket as though she had tried to wrench it, death, away.

The mouth formed an almost circle. The mouth now, not Sarah's mouth. That wasn't Sarah on the bed, hard as alabaster and twice as cold, Maggie knew, to the touch. It was a foul, smelly thing that Maggie wanted to slam the door on and run from, an awful thing, not just a corpse, but an agonized vision of death.

From now on, Maggie had a terrible thought, when I have bad dreams that face will hover. And then she moved, backing out of the room to the landing where she gulped in deep breaths until her lungs hurt. She pulled the door behind her, hanging onto the knob to keep herself upright and to hold death away from her, from Jeb down below whom she could hear singing, "Row, row your boat."

Sarah has rowed away from us, she thought hysterically, rowed through the night, through the battering storm into tomorrow and all the tomorrows there will ever be. She was clenching her jaws so tightly her teeth ached.

She let go, and the door stayed shut as she backed away, went down the steps without turning around, afraid to see *it* coming after her. But Sarah had seen it as it rode out of the darkness toward her, and it was terrifying. It stopped her heart, slammed a fist into her chest with such power life left its moorings.

I don't want to know. I don't.

She turned around then and raced down the few remaining steps as though the icy chill was at her neck.

The funeral was in White Plains after a three-day-and-night wake at the undertaker's where Sarah lay painted and powdered in her best navy dress shirred white at the neck, in an open coffin banked by flowers—*in memory of*—a rosary twined in her dead hands. And that came after an autopsy and a rather heated argument between the coroner for the county and the Brighton police chief, who cursed the fact that Four Oaks was just one mile within his jurisdiction.

The cause of death was what they argued about. Fear doesn't kill anyone; the chief was firm about that. But the coroner said it did, since she was dead. She hadn't been damn *near* scared to death, she had *been* scared to death. Fear had stopped her heart. Then it was heart failure, the chief insisted because he didn't like complications, problems, unknowns. And if fear had killed Sarah, then it had to be fear of something. Which meant in his slow and tortuous thinking, a crime. But there was no crime. No breaking and entering. No assault. Not a mark on her, he said to the coroner. Just that gruesome look on her face with those eyeballs popping half out of their sockets. And the body all contorted, the top part going one way, the bottom the other, as if she were two different people. And the fists clenched so tightly they had to break the fingers to get the sheet free. Could have been the force of the coronary, heart going off so suddenly, so painfully, the chief insisted, I know enough to know that! Sure, the coroner agreed, smiling broadly. It could have *just* been a coronary, and it was, but it wasn't. It's *why* she had it that counts. And that's where the scared to death part comes in. And he laughed because he didn't like the chief one bit and was landing him with a real headache the way he, the coroner, saw it.

"You didn't hear anything at all, right?" the chief, a fat balding man of about fifty, prodded David and Maggie. He was sitting on the edge of her father's old chair in the study of Four Oaks, sweating profusely, and wiping away at his face with a not too clean handkerchief. "I mean, you didn't hear anyone walking around up there?" He bent even further forward until Maggie was certain that like Humpty-Dumpty he would lose his perch and topple over.

"We wouldn't have," David tried patiently to explain, as he had when the chief first asked them a week before, "because of the storm."

The chief nodded his head. "Right." He looked at Maggie out of eyes set far back behind creases of skin. "And nothing was taken, right?"

She thought if he said "right" one more time she'd snap. There was nothing right about what happened, and even this gross fat man who looked more like a child molester or a flasher than a cop, wasn't *right*. "No, nothing was taken. We told you that. We checked immediately."

"So check again," he barked. He didn't like pretty women, they made him tetchy. He liked women who reminded him of his wife, cushy and comfortable in house dresses and sensible shoes. Women you knew you'd find in the kitchen or pushing a vacuum cleaner. No women like Maggie.

"We did check again and again Chief Kessel. Nothing is missing," David said, hanging on to his temper with both hands. "And I don't see the point in asking us repeatedly. No matter how much you want this house to have been broken into, it wasn't. When I left for the city that morning the front door was locked, and I slammed it behind me which meant it was locked again. And," he said to the chief, as if he were the village idiot, "when my wife woke up the back door was bolted."

"What about the windows?"

"Chief Kessel, all the windows were closed and locked because of the storm. When we went to bed it was pouring outside. We never would have left a window open. Right?"

The sarcasm went by Kessel like a fast-floating cloud. He was thinking again. It was almost possible to see the brain cells bumping into one another.

"Okay," he said at last, dragging his bulk upward, the sagging stomach loose as gelatin slopping over his belt and holster, "okay, that's it," as if the Braces had defeated him. "Doc can say something scared her to death, but maybe it was something she dreamed about. You know, like a nightmare?"

It was a nightmare, Maggie thought as David saw the chief out the front door and watched while he drove off. But it was a nightmare that they not only slept with but woke up to. It was a nightmare that didn't splinter and dissipate at dawn. It wouldn't go away, just spread like cancer, eating up whatever healthy cells remained of their lives.

Maggie had called David, and he told her to call the police. Then, even knowing how angry David would be when he found out, she called Jamie. She didn't want to be in the house with *that*, wouldn't stay with Jeb inside with *that*. Childishly, she wanted someone right then.

It turned out that Kessel came first in a black car with a revolving light and the siren on full blast, scattering gravel as he and his deputy pulled up at the front steps where she waited with Jeb.

She wouldn't return to the house, and just stood there in the sunlight, shaking and saying, no, no. And then Jamie came. She didn't care what any of them thought, not even Jeb whose hand she had held onto from the moment she had hung up the phone and hurried them outside. She threw herself at Jamie, sagging like a rag doll.

It was Jamie finally who went up to Sarah's room with the two cops and declared her dead, as if there had been any doubt about it. "She died sometime during the night, rigor's just setting in," he told Maggie when he came out again, putting his arm around her. "Natural causes, as far as I can tell," he had added because even though he half suspected from the look of terror on Sarah's face what the coroner would later verify, he wasn't going to go near it with a barge pole.

"Sarah's dead," Maggie had said to Jeb right away, and said it baldly, without flinching. Not that she wouldn't have sugarcoated it, but she didn't know how. Sometimes, she added, though he hadn't asked, people just get old and die in their sleep. She was trying to be strong for him, as she hadn't been when his sisters died, but he wasn't shaken. He simply asked, "Can we still go swimming?"

"Where's Jeb?" David asked, returning to the study after Kessel had gone.

"Up in his room. Rebecca was reading him a story to keep him out of the way."

Rebecca was the new housekeeper whom David had

immediately hired from an agency in the city. She was the antithesis of Sarah, tall and lean, all angles, with a hawkish look to her. Though Rebecca was nearer to Maggie's age than Sarah had been, Maggie knew she'd never sit comfortably in the kitchen with this one drinking coffee. Rebecca didn't sit, at least not on the Braces' time. She moved incessantly, with short, geometrical motions, never at rest. She wasn't a woman Maggie would have hired, but as David had pointed out, she was available.

David went to the liquor cabinet under the bookcase and poured himself a tumbler of Dewar's, neat, and stood drinking.

"You never drink during the day," Maggie said, surprised.

"I never used to do a lot of things," he answered.

"Are you going to the office?"

He looked at his watch. It was twenty minutes to noon. He shrugged. "Yeah, I suppose so." Where else could he go? He couldn't stay here, the two of them sitting and staring at one another, strangers waiting for a train that had already been derailed.

"I have to get the bandage changed," she said, holding up her hand.

"Fine," he said.

Silence hung between them, a dead weight. Neither moved. The light trickled through the window.

He finished off the scotch and asked, "How is you hand? Does it still hurt?"

Maggie shifted on her chair, blurring as David watched her, swimming in and out of focus like some exquisite tropical fish in a murky tank. "It's okay now."

"Listen," he said, as though there were truly was a sheet of glass between them, "about Evers, I'm sorry. I mean about the fight. Stupid, like a kid. There was just so much pressure, I blew like a faulty gasket. Stupid," he said again, banging the empty glass down on the shelf.

"It doesn't matter," she said, then, "David—"

"Yes?"

"Nothing. No, everything. What I mean is," she took a deep breath, "I'm scared."

She wasn't supposed to be scared, but then Sarah wasn't either.

"Scared? Of what?"

"What did Sarah die of? What was so awful that her heart stopped just like that?"

"Ah, Christ, Maggie," he said, crossing the room and standing over her, absently running his fingers through her hair, "I don't know. Maybe that dumb bastard is right. She had a bad dream."

"Bad dreams don't kill people." She was emphatic, but couldn't have explained why, only that she knew it was life that killed people, not dreams, as terrifying as they might be.

"Well something did, and that's as good an explanation as anyone's had so far." Suddenly she laughed. "What's so funny?" he asked.

"You're the practical one, so hardheaded about things. No imagination, David Brace. And I'm wishy-washy, seeing bogeymen in every dark corner, thinking things happen which you and Klein tell me don't, and now—" She stopped and laughed again in little puffs. "You're saying it was a bad dream, and I'm saying, oh no. Don't you think that's funny, David?"

He wasn't smiling. "I don't think anything's funny these days."

She reached up and grabbed his hand. "What are we going to do?"

"Just what we've been doing. Go on. Life doesn't stop because one old woman dies."

Life doesn't stop because your children die, Maggie was thinking. You might die, but the world revolves on its axis; the seasons change; the sun shines; rains fall; there's snow and sleet and wind. The gravitational pull remains in force. Yes, life goes on as indifferently as it always had, though you might not. You might slide off into space.

"For the longest time I would wake up in the morning and not remember," she said. "There'd be that one moment just before I opened my eyes when everything was about the same. I thought of it as the safety zone." David knew she wasn't talking about Sarah's death but about their daughters. He gripped her shoulder and could feel her trembling, a seismic vibration below the skin. "I'm all right now, David. Don't worry about me." Again she had skittered off, and he realized that she was trying to tell him she wasn't crazy. "Klein taught me that I have to live without walls that I can touch, that I couldn't carry the safety zone around and live in it like a box."

"Don't, Maggie," he said, for the first time feeling sorry for her.

"Don't, Maggie," she mimicked him, pushing his hand away and jumping up. "You never want to talk about it, about anything. With you it's all in neutral. The girls won't go away, and neither will Sarah, poof, vaporized. They're going to haunt us forever."

"We have to go on," he said woodenly, an idiot repeating a line he'd learned by rote, yet wondering as he said it if that was totally true. Lee hung just in his peripheral vision, and he thought, I have options, I can change things. I don't have to live with ghosts. But almost immediately he pulled back, remembering his decision, the contract he had made with himself. "I've got to go," he said. "Don't wait dinner for me. I'll probably be late."

Maggie didn't answer him. She spun out of the study into the hall, shaking with anger, angrier than she had

been in a very long time, since before the fire and before
Greenwood. The light that danced in through the windows of the living room opposite flaked in dusty gold spots
across her vision, and she halted abruptly for a moment
and saw Jeb by the mirror, hugging the glass as though the
mirror were a person. And that made her more furious
yet.

She screamed, "I've had enough of that mirror! Get
away from it!" She ran down the hall and grabbed him by
the arm, dragging him forcibly behind her to the front
door.

"Stop it, Maggie!" David yelled, appearing in the archway, but she was already out on the porch, the screen
banging behind her and Jeb, and she refused to turn
around. "God damn it, come back here!"

She swept to the Dodge that was parked in front of the
garage and opening the passenger door, flung Jeb inside
and slammed the door after him.

There was a sharp pain between her breasts, and she
kept gulping for air, as if her lungs were working only
sluggishly. But she switched on the engine and stepped on
the gas. The car shot ahead. She sped down the drive
going far too fast—rocks churned up by the tires clunking
against the underbelly—and turned onto the road without
even checking for oncoming cars.

It was only as they were approaching the old farm house
that the tension in her neck and across her shoulders
began to ebb. And she thought, that wasn't me. I never
lose my temper. My God, what if David tells Klein! Klein
will think I've broken loose again, that I'm falling. I
shouldn't have done it, shouldn't have, she silently cried,
as if she had a choice. And Jeb . . . She glanced at him out
of the corner of her eye, feeling guilt slither around inside
her.

"Mommy's sorry, sweetness," she said humbly and reached

out with her bandaged hand to pat his knee. He jerked away from her and stared sullenly ahead. He had that flat, cardboard expression that made her wonder if he had any bulk to him, whether if she turned him around, he'd just be a paper doll, nothing more than a photograph. "I just lost my temper, Jebbie. Sometimes grown-ups do that. I didn't mean to hurt you. Forgive Mommy. Please!" But he still didn't reply, just pulled even further away from her.

Why, why, did I have to yell at him? He didn't do anything. Not this time.

In a brief flash she saw again the whoosh of flames, smelled smoke, heard the terrible crackling. And Kathy and Tracy screamed their eternal cries inside her skull.

No!

The car swerved to the right, rolled up and over the verge of grass, and Maggie flinched as a pickup truck came flying up behind her, whizzing by.

She drove back onto the road and listened to her hollow, false voice as, the rest of the way into Brighton, she tried to coax Jeb out of his sulk. But he had withdrawn from her as surely as though he had swept off into space. When, getting out of the car before Jamie's office, she tried to touch him with quivering hands, to rebutton his shirt that he had gotten wrong again, he fiercely moved out of her reach. But he did go with her right into the examining room, fast by her side. He sat in a chair clutching himself and watched while Jamie removed the dressing from Maggie's hand, inspected the wound, probed at it with his fingertips and pronounced it healed.

"It's fine, Maggie, and there will only be a thin, white scar," he said, taping a narrow Band-Aid to her palm. "All right, Champ," he said to Jeb when he finished, "wait in here for a few minutes. I want to talk to your Mom privately."

"No," Maggie said, but Jamie took Jeb firmly by the

shoulder and steered him into the private office and closed the door.

Jeb stood on the other side, leaning against the wood and listened, but he couldn't hear very well, the voices were muffled, the words indistinct. That Mommy person, he thought, cold with rage. She had yelled at him, pulled him by the arms, and all that gave him a flashing pain at the back of his head. But he knew instinctively there were worse things than what she had done. Her and the Daddy person fighting was worse. Yes, that was *bad*. That frightened him even more than her raised voice. And the Doctor person! An icy sweat broke out on his upper lip, and he strained to hear what they were saying in there. He had to know what they were saying, what they were doing.

Cautiously he clasped the knob, curled his fingers about it and slowly turned. There was a click, and he eased the door ajar just enough to see through the crack.

"I haven't seen you for a week, Maggie," the Doctor person was saying.

"There were things to do," she replied. "The wake, and then the funeral. And getting Sarah's things together for her brother."

Jeb's lips turned up and he ran his tongue over his teeth. He remembered that Sarah person all right. Listening, he thought he could hear the thunder once again, feel it as it ran along his bones, and he shivered, squirming with momentary pleasure.

"We had to get a new housekeeper, Jamie. And, well— oh, her name's Rebecca and Jeb seems to like her quite a lot. It has something to do with her reading him stories, I suppose, and telling him tales about her grandfather or father—I can't remember which—diving for sunken treasure off south Florida."

Jamie interrupted. "You're babbling, Maggie. What's the matter?"

"Nothing, nothing's the matter."

Jamie leaned forward and ran his hands lightly up and down Maggie's arms. He said, "I have to see you."

"You're seeing me."

"Don't be cute, Maggie."

He sounded mad to Jeb who, holding his breath, was so tense he thought he would shatter, break apart. He knew better than to storm into the room with all the shiny equipment and the big, black table upon which the Mommy person sat, her legs dangling off the floor. The Doctor person pressed in against her. And there was badness in the air. The room was alive with it, sizzling like static, and it flowed through the crack. Jeb tightened up his face.

"I can't see you, Jamie. My life's a mess and this . . . this makes it worse," she whispered.

"You can and you will." He wound a strand of her hair around his hand and gently pulled her toward him.

"Oh Jamie, don't," she moaned, but she lifted up her arms, winding them around his neck.

Then the Doctor person put his face on top of hers, his lips just where hers were. His hands were like little mice walking all up and down her. Jeb felt sick; his eyes smarted with tears of rage.

The sky is going to fall right down!

And under his feet he was certain he could feel the earth already starting to buckle.

14

Rebecca had turned out better than Maggie imagined, unbending slightly, loosening invisible corset stays, though Maggie had yet to see her really smile, except with Jeb. And then it wasn't much of a smile, just a minor upturning at the corners of her mouth. Her eyes never wavered, muddy brown eyes discreetly lowered behind the half glasses she often wore.

Maggie stood outside Jeb's room in the dusty shadows of early evening and listened to the steady, sensible drone of Rebecca's voice. She was reading him *Alice's Adventures in Wonderland.*

From the lawn she could hear the caterer setting up the buffet table, and from the kitchen the jumble of voices as the two cooks and their two helpers put the final elegant touches on the food. She tried to remember what menu she had chosen, but couldn't. Whatever it was, however, she knew it would be perfect. If she had any talent at all, it was an instinct for what was stylish, about food as well as clothes. In this way—and now looking back, in this way only—she had never disappointed David. Oh yes, she thought bitterly, I always was the quintessential *Better Homes and Gardens* wife. And it had all returned, that meaningless ability, those worthless skills, when David insisted they have a party.

A party wasn't possible, so much the wrong response to what had happened in their lives, to what was going on, that to David it made perfect sense in some convoluted way that Maggie didn't understand at all. He was going to set them all on an even keel, he said, stand them upright and march them into normalcy like a platoon of soldiers.

Standing now in the upstairs hall, Maggie thought, as she had done all the time she was preparing for it, that a party belonged to the world of that other Maggie, the one who had such fluidity of motion, such gliding power, that she had moved through life like a skater on smooth ice. That was a different Maggie, with her Chanel bought by the ounce, with her face creamed at Arden's, her hair styled at Kenneth's, and with the perfectly crafted shoes on slender heels like exclamation points that she always wore, never expecting to fall. That Maggie went to fashion shows and got her picture in the paper as one of the smartest of the smart young marrieds. That Maggie was now to this one—listening to the preparty sounds and attempting to move her inner self into alignment with her outer image—elusive. That one had never done anything important at all, had never held a real job, pursued a career, gone out into the world with her spine as straight as an ironing board. But then, that Maggie didn't see things which weren't real, like a little boy in one place when he so patently was somewhere else.

Already she was getting a headache, a tightness at the nape of her neck, that was creeping upward.

She knew she should move, set herself in motion like one of Jeb's mechanical toys, but didn't, couldn't. She stood clutching the railing and drifting with the voices that wafted upward, unfurling the past. She could almost hear her mother's tinkle of laughter and wouldn't have been surprised to lean out the window and see her father slowly fox-trotting across the lawn with a twelve-year-old Maggie.

She shut her eyes and tried to believe at least for one brief moment that change was in the wind, that all the windows had been thrown up, and all the doors left gaping wide, so that the accumulated sadness would be swept out into the gathering dusk on soft strains of music.

Jamie's face rose against her closed lids, and she felt her heart lurch behind her ribs. She hadn't had the courage to invite him and tried now to imagine him firmly planted on the lawn, drink in hand, wearing his one tie—probably with a gravy spot—being polite, making conversation. Jamie made people better, made the pain go away, made love with such intensity that afterwards his eyes were bloodshot, but he couldn't make small talk.

She wondered where he was now, and looking at the minuscule hands of the tank watch on her wrist, saw it was after office hours, after late rounds, after all the sick and injured, the maimed, dying, and diseased were put away for the night, barring accidents. Where would he be now? And what would he be doing? She didn't know where he lived or how, except for the lake shack with its single cot and army blankets, kerosene lamp and stack of paperbacks. The shack where she wanted to be with him this very moment rather than waiting to descend into swirls of conversation and laughter like a dead woman going down into the nether regions.

Jamie. He clung to her thoughts like a bat in a dark cave.

"You look like the old Maggie," David said, smiling, coming out of their room in an Armani suit the color of weak tea, the Larouche shirt unbuttoned at the neck.

"Thank you," she said, and Maggie, pretending to be that other, long ago Maggie, tried to smile back. She thought her face would crack like delicate glass and net of fine fissures would spread over her cheeks and forehead under the eyes.

"Ready?" he asked. "People should be arriving soon."

"I just want to say good-night to Jeb," she replied,

afraid to touch even the lapels of his jacket when he bent
to kiss her like a benediction.

Why doesn't he see he's kissing a dead woman?

"'. . . Thank you, its a very interesting dance to watch,'
said Alice. . . ."

"Jeb, it's time to tuck you in." She approached the bed,
cutting Rebecca off from view.

"Not yet. A little bit more, Mommy. Please." He squirmed
away from her.

"Nope, it's time, Turtle. Under the covers." She pulled
him down by the legs, laughing.

How could she still laugh, have parties, make up her
face in tones of burnt umber? Because Klein said she
could, must, had no choice if she was to outrun the
darkness snapping at her heels. Because David insisted.

She blew in Jeb's ear, making him giggle and bounce
with pleasure. "That tickles, Mommy," he cried gleefully.

Rebecca coughed discreetly behind her, and Maggie
spoke without turning around, her resentment taut in her
muscles because Rebecca was not Sarah, was alive while
Sarah was dead, and Sarah's death meant fear and the
howlings of demons. Sarah's death still hung in the room
over Maggie's head, though Rebecca now occupied that
space, slept in that bed, put her clothes with sachet in the
dresser drawers. Yet, like an invader who had seized
enemy territory, she still hadn't made it her own, and in
the crevices and corners it smelled like Sarah, that com-
mingling of scents of the living and the dead, talcum
powder dusting her skin, and excrement in riverlets leaking
down the sheets.

"Why don't you check on things in the kitchen, Rebecca,"
Maggie ordered, her voice her mother's voice.

"Certainly, Mrs. Brace. Good-night, Jeb." The old rocker creaked when it released her.

"Will you read me more tomorrow?" Jeb asked.

"Of course," she said flatly and left.

"Mommy, why can't I stay up for the party?" Jeb asked, walking his fingers up and down Maggie's arm.

"Because it's a grown-up party."

"I've never been to a grown-up party."

"That's because you're still a little boy."

"Will I be a grown-up one day?" he asked, looking up from his intense concentration on her fingers that reminded him of beetles, tiny insects that were protected from the world by their armor but not from the mysterious fires that burnt them to death, into ash, and eventually landed them—or what was left of them—into a hole in the ground. Just like Sarah. Before Maggie could reply, he said, "Doesn't the ground get crowded with dead people?"

He was always coming at her like this, obliquely, glancing off her blind side when she least expected it. She didn't understand him any more than she understood any of them, or herself if it came to that, and all of Klein's expensive treatment washing over her psyche in hope that something would stick, didn't change that.

"Jebbie," she said, whimpering, "Jebbie." She enfolded him in her arms, held onto him, for besides everything else he was, the future rested uneasily in the crook of his elbow, the curve of his brow, in the hollows under his eyes with the faint blue veins. He was the past, present, future rolled into one of those little puzzles with interlocking pieces. "Yes, you'll grow up, just like everybody does."

"Tracy and Kathy won't."

There was no end to the devastation he could bring down on her, even if unwittingly. He was six years old and knew almost as many dead people as living. "I can't talk now, sweetness," she said, kissing his hair. "I have to go down to Daddy and the guests."

"Are you sure I can't come to the party?" he asked again, but without much hope, already admitting defeat.

"Positive. Now go to sleep and have a funny dream about the White Rabbit."

He reluctantly let her move off to the center of the room, the doorway, and then down the hall and finally to the stairs where he heard her descending, escaping, out of reach. He closed his eyes and tried to evoke the White Rabbit, to pop it out of the hat of imagination, but the rabbit who came was as big as a house and twice as wide, flooding across the screen of his mind. And it was a black rabbit with yellow eyes and bone-white teeth sharper than the razor blades Daddy used to scrape the beard off his face. Jeb opened his eyes. He didn't like the rabbit as undefined as spilled ink. He dived under the covers and retrieved Scottie, his gnawed stuffed animal of indeterminate species and gender, and put it inside his pajama top where it lay reassuringly upon his heart.

The sound of the party rose and fell in little waves like bathtub water when he splashed with his feet, and he sought sleep in the drift, but it eluded him. He didn't like to be alone. If he had thought about it, he'd have realized that he liked to be alone less and less. The moonlight puddled on his floor, and he wished he had a dog, something alive and breathing, at the foot of his bed for company. But there was nothing but Scottie, and Scottie didn't speak, being nothing more than a lump of old cloth and pulled threads. So gradually Jeb got up, a little bit of him at a time. First, his two arms over the blanket, the blanket neatly folded aside in a triangle, then his legs bending up at the knees. Up into a sitting position. And finally feet on the floor. When he stood, Scottie rode down his chest and flopped on the carpet. Jeb nudged the

stuffed animal aside with his toes and crept stealthily to
the hall.

There was a mosaic of voices now, and little bits of
sound climbed the steps.

"—so glad to—"

"—it's been—"

"—isn't the country just—"

"—lovely—"

"—the hottest—"

"—summer—"

"—of them all—"

Step by step, not a board creaking beneath him, he
went down, into the watery voices like a swimmer into a
sea of sharks. The voices nipped around the house and
danced up and along the lawn. They bounced in the living
room, the study, and wove in and out of the music from
the stereo.

Down, down he went.

It wasn't fair. They had all their friends, lots of friends,
and he had only one. But that one was special, and Jeb
knew he had been lucky, so very lucky, to have found him,
even if the finding was the night of the fire when himself
was so scarey. He had frightened Jeb so that first time.
But that was before he had understood, before himself had
explained it. And Jeb knew too, that that night he'd been
bad, awfully bad, though he never thought about *it* anymore, not even when he made the little flames dance in a
dish or an ashtray, just the way himself liked to see them.

Another step and then another until he was in the
downstairs hall, floating closer to the warmth, listening to
the humming begin and grow louder. He just wished he
had his matches so that he could make them burst into fire
and watch himself smile as the tiny curlicues of smoke
would spiral higher and higher up the glass.

*   *   *

"Everything's falling apart," David was saying by the bar on the front porch as a young man in a dress shirt and black bow tie handed him a scotch on the rocks, "the whole of Central America."

"The domino theory again," a short man, square as an ice cube, said. They moved off the porch and onto the lawn, where David glanced about approvingly at the small tables covered by white linen, lily pads in a lake of candlelight.

"Bullshit, George," David said. "The domino theory cost fifty-seven thousand lives in Vietnam."

"And made us a ton of money, I hate to admit," the other man, George, said with feigned reluctance. "We had ball bearings coming out our assholes, and the more we made the more the government wanted. I've never had that kind of production level before or since."

"Was it worth it?" David couldn't get annoyed tonight as he would have been some other time with George, a Mayflower descendant, impeccably ancestored, schooled and mannered, whom he knew from Yale. Not even George, who was rabidly to the right and twice as ignorant, could make him flare up tonight. He searched for Maggie in the crowd, now thirty people or more, but he couldn't find her.

George answered primly, his mouth pursed, "I don't make policy."

"Is that like making book?" David said. Then, "Oh, hello, Matthew. When did you get here? Matthew Orenstein, George Whittier." The two men shook hands, warily sniffing each other's scent, George more dubious because he was genetically uncertain about Jews, even when some of them were friends of friends.

"Matthew's in the Manhattan D.A.'s office; George manufactures ball bearings, among other things," David explained. He saw Lee a long way off, all in black like a raven, flowing in darkness, her face a white flower above a caftan that blended in and out of the night. He willed her to look at him, and he felt a tingle of pleasure as she turned his way. Then he edged his shoulder to her like a knife blade and said, "Did you get a drink, Matthew?"

"Right here, thanks. Where's that gorgeous wife of yours? I haven't seen her yet, but I hear she's as radiant as the Hope Diamond. Maybe I can convince her to run off with me."

"There she is," David said, laughing. "Maggie, com'on over here; Matthew wants to elope with you."

"Matthew!" she cried with genuine pleasure, tears coming to her eyes. She loved the soft, squishy little man who seemed tossed together by an inept doll maker. What hair he had left dusted a baby-pink skull above a face in which the nose was a brush stroke off center and the eyes impossibly close together. His shirt had a button undone; his tie was twisted aft.

"Oh boy, oh boy," he yelped, hugging Maggie, "this is worth coming to the country for and risking mosquito bites or poison ivy, God forbid. How are you, chickadee?" he asked, his eyes narrowing with concern.

"You know, Matthew, it's day by day." She shrugged, not needing to pretend with him, for Matthew had handled the investigation of the fire and had seen her revolving faster, a dervish on high speed who had finally disappeared into inner space. "Why haven't we seen you?" she asked, plucking at his sleeve with nervous fingers. She remembered one time he'd come to Greenwood, and she hadn't been so far gone that she was unaware of his pity.

"Why haven't you asked? I'm available for Saturday nights and any summer weekends. Forget the winters. Snow in the city is bad enough; in the country, fegh," he spat the word, "it stirs some vestigal memory of the steppes."

David left them bantering, George watching with disapproval, thinking, David was sure, dark thoughts of miscegenation, worldwide conspiracies, Zionist plots. Lee saw him slip away and followed.

Fireflies danced on the rhododendron at the side of the house. At the bar David added more ice to his scotch. "Let's fuck," Lee said at his shoulder, her voice so soft he had to stoop to hear her. "It's been forever."

They were always after him, the women, wanting something. His mother in the nursing home: Come see me, come see me. His sister out in Colorado: Help his brother-in-law get a better partnership, get his nephew into a more prestigious law school, make her portfolio flush with higher yield tax free bonds. And Maggie worst of all because he wasn't certain what she did want from him.

"Don't start," he said through clenched teeth. "There are people around."

"Oh really? I thought they were robots," she snapped and wandered into the house, glancing back at him, huge eyes glistening with lust, as he followed her inside.

"I'm sorry, but you know how I feel about this, you and Maggie, you here."

"Good old, compartmentalized David," she swiped at him.

"Lee," he said patiently, "I've tried to explain. I'm uncomfortable with this friendship. Maybe that makes me a son of a bitch, but I can't help it. I won't leave Maggie; I don't want to. And I want to see you. I love you, but it makes things worse to have it all run together."

"Don't be mad at me," she said. She was so close to him that as she slid her hand all the way down the front of her caftan, she brushed his crotch.

He groaned. "For Christ's sake, Lee, somebody will see us."

"Then let's go where they won't." She smiled and

stepped away from him, the tiny diamonds in her ear lobes glittering with light, sending off sparks.

David wasn't sure, right at that moment, that he even liked her, but her lasciviousness meant danger, and it was only there, in that deep, bottomless pool where he could escape. Lee was his excuse, he suddenly comprehended, not for indecision, but for not thinking. She pushed away all the pain, remorse and anger over the girls, about Maggie, all the dangling participles in a life that was slowly, inexorably sinking.

As long as he clung to his lust like a man going down for the third time, he wouldn't drown.

"Go upstairs to the second guest room at the end of the hall. I'll be there in a minute," he said, pinching her arm through the sleeve, feeling childish and hungry, his heart pounding with excitement. How had he come to this? "Just make sure that nobody sees you."

But he didn't see her, he heard them through the half-opened doorway of the closet under the stairs where he was hiding behind the winter coats. Their talking together gave him a pain in the head, as though someone had put a clock inside his skull, and it was going tick, tick, the pendulum swinging side to side, cracking against bone.

All he could see in the darkness was his own anger, the color of blood. The party sounds came and went in undulating currents, agitating the coats on their hangers. He cracked the door still further and peered out. Women passed him, their dresses dancing. Men's legs scissored by. If anyone cared to look, they would have seen two eyes staring, luminous as moonlight.

Where was the Mommy person?

What was the Daddy person doing upstairs?

The smells were all tangled up together—perfumes,

flowers, food from the kitchen. He wanted to see more and silently inched forward in a pause when the hall was empty, clung to the steps, raced along the walls, and slid into the study. He was a small boy and nobody noticed him, or if they did, he wasn't worth much attention. In a blink he was gone, behind the leather couch.

He heard people come and go, the cushions whistling when they sat down restlessly or rose in almost the same movement. They spoke in whispers, words muffled by leather fuzzy as the carpet licking his toes.

". . . a tragedy . . ."

". . . you never know . . ."

". . . how terrible . . ."

". . . and crazy as a loon he said, but he's a fruitcake himself so who'd believe him if you know what I . . ."

What were all these big persons doing? What did their squooshy words mean? Where was the Daddy person? And her? That *her* person made him even angrier than when the lights went out.

All at once he was alone, hearing nothing but the whistling beneath the furniture. He slithered along the back and came upright at the edge of the couch with its rounded arms, a small animal scenting the wind. There was nobody in the room—just tables and chairs and the leather couch and the lamps dripping light. He picked up a glass with water in it and took a sip, his face squeezing tight. It had a bitter taste so it wasn't water. Water felt like cellophane gliding across his tongue.

He wanted to get outside, and the only way was through the window. He unlatched the screen and pushed at the mesh with the flat of his hand. There was grass below and soft dirt when he fell into it and lay on his back looking up.

The sky was a mess of stars, bright dots punctuating the blackness. The sound now, coming from the other side, trailed over him in ribbons. The earth pitched and surged beneath him, and he couldn't lie still. There was too much he had to know, to see and hear and smell and do. He got up, creeping around the house in a guerilla crouch, drawing nearer the party until, squatting by the rhodedendron, he rolled.

There were cars bumper to bumper all along the drive in front of the house and down the long dirt road, cars bunched together silently waiting. Jeb didn't know it, but almost all of them were expensive cars: Mercedes like the one David drove but shinier and black, Lincolns, Cadillacs, Mazdas, a Bentley, and three Jaguars with extras—tape decks, telephones, and in the one Rolls even a bar that stocked Couvoisier and Dom Perignon.

He scooted between a Jaguar and a Cadillac to the far side of the drive, away from the party, which popped in and out of view as he stalked from car to car. They were the wagons; he was the Indian—he had seen that once on television, the bullets flying, the arrows zinging through the air in flaming streaks that burst into fire when they hit the canvas coverings—and he could almost smell the smoke, feel the warmth that tingled up his legs and into the pit of his belly where the warmth sat as contented as a lazy cat.

In one of those incidents that became acts of fate, while he was thinking about all the wagons burning, listening to the war whoops—all of which he remembered himself, which made him feel especially good—he saw the matches. A book of matches dropped at the door of a bright blue Lincoln. The matches advertised a popular restaurant on West Fifty-Seventh Street, but he didn't know that because the letters didn't form into the two or three words he had learned to read.

He pressed the book between the palms of his hands, and all he could see was the fire starting, whooshing upward into sheets of flame that became bright walls of red and yellow, each agitating cone of fire eating its way into the black sky.

All at once he knew what he was going to do. He tucked the matches carefully away in a small pocket over his heart.

The gravel hurt his feet, and he hurried on tiptoes to where the drive went straight and the trees began, the underbrush sniping at his pajamas. It was a long circle around the perimeter of the lawn, the party ebbing then rising up again at his left.

Mosquitos buzz-bombed him, stinging his face and neck, burrowing as far down as the first button on his top, and he slapped at them, paddling his hands, pushing aside the brambles, the leafy arms that thrust out to ensnare him, the flying bugs that he promised himself he'd catch one night and burn to death in one of his killing jars.

When he was just opposite the house, at the furthest reach of the lawn, where the party spread out before him like a picture postcard, flat as a photograph but full of promises, he stopped and rested. His face was grimy with dirt where he had rubbed at it; his hair was tangled. An angry welt, crisscrossed with red scratches, rose on his neck. He gulped for air and heard a wind that wasn't there, rushing in his ears. He had to hurry or the sky was going to fall, to squoosh him dead as a bug under a sneaker, and the ground was going to surge up and crunch him flat as one of the pancakes that the Sarah person used to make.

He settled on his knees and peered out through the interstices of a bush, glimpsing truncated images, legs and arms unattached, trunks without heads and heads that floated like balloons in the nighttime sky. He wanted to mush it all together like play dough between his hands, squeezing it through his fingers, and roll the various colors

out on the kitchen table, cutting them all into different
pieces.

Maggie was trying, really trying, to have a good time.
But there was so much to do penance for, so many ghosts
to placate with pain, that, despite her promises to Klein,
she knew that happiness would scratch at her soul and
make her feel guilty.

Yet parties had always given her pleasure before; she
had always been the princess at the ball. But now it
seemed she was out of sync. Besides, though she tried not
to show it, she was wounded by Miranda Simon asking,
her hand, condescending, patting Maggie's arm, how do
you really feel? And wounded also by Joanne Dubois's
suspicious stare of pencil-thin raised eyebrows and pursed
red mouth. And wounded yet again by the Wardens'
glances that as much as spelled out: She's mad. All of them
touched her tonight with their disapproval, their suspi-
cions, their disbelief.

"This is fun," Matt Orenstein said, nuzzling her hair.

She slipped closer to him and put her arms around his
bulky waist, feeling safe for the moment, more substantial
and not liable to blow away on the next breeze. But Matt
saw someone he knew and rumbled off, leaving her bereft,
her smile tacked in place. She thought, there is no reason
that I should feel like such a stranger. It was, after all, the
way it had been before. The women were all beautifully
dressed with hair streaked and tossed and impeccably cut;
their husbands or attachments all stood around with their
hands loosely tucked into pants pockets and were all
indignantly vocal about politics, the state of the nation,
taxes and the Dow Jones. And all of them were peaked
with sexual longing, narrowing their already narrow eyes
at the hint of possibilities.

Yet they weren't really her friends, Maggie realized, for

they had abandoned her, even Matt. She had committed an act of bad taste by losing her daughters, by breaking down.

Lee came from the back of the house and went around by the buffet table. Maggie waved at her, but Lee didn't see her, so Maggie walked along the lawn until she caught up with her, sitting alone at one of the tables.

"Lee," she said, "I have someone I want you to meet."

"No thanks, if you mean what I think you do." She smiled languidly, her cheeks flushed, her pupils so dark they were black. Her tongue darted out, and she licked her bottom lip, full and swollen.

She looks like a woman who's just made love, Maggie thought with shock, and glancing from that satisfied image, she saw a face in the brush, all wrinkled and hacked by lines. Maggie blinked. Far below, Lee was saying something she didn't hear. It was Jeb's face now cameoed in the bush, smooth as polished stone.

She clenched her fists and said to herself: I will stop imagining things, making them up, seeing what isn't there, as though there is a third eye in the center of my forehead.

She looked away and saw Maria Rogers arriving late, as usual. Maria was a tall, overripe blonde who had once been a Rockette before she married the senior and most elderly partner in the second largest Wall Street firm. Maria, who was invigorating with her sheen of ingenuousness, drove everyone to stiffen his muscles, but Maggie liked her enormously and smiled hopefully as she got up to welcome her.

Maggie could just imagine herself saying to Maria, I keep seeing my little boy when he isn't there, when he can't be there, or where I see him, when I know he is someplace else, and Maria answering, of course you do, honey, why not. Maria believed in Santa Claus, the Easter

Bunny, witches, ghosts, spirits, things that go bump in the night, and as she had once explained to Maggie in a wild and eventually drunken hour in the Oyster Bar, in reincarnation, because she just *knew* that she'd once been Cleopatra.

Yes, Maria was just what Maggie needed then.

Half of the Mommy person appeared for an instant, and he turned, parting the scratchy bush to watch her. And then he saw her stop and say something to that Lee person, which made him go still as glass.

She was sitting at a little table, alone, looking up. The Mommy person touched her arm, and he wanted to scream at her, *don't*. Her head shot up as though she heard him. They stared at one another across all that space, but then she ran off. A fat, dumpy man like a sack of flower in his white suit, came and took her place.

Jeb broke cover, running bent over to the nearest empty table, his arms and legs pumping like pistons. He dove under the cloth, coming to a dead halt, and scrunched up, the post behind his back, his legs jackknifed to his chest.

This was almost as good as his secret place, but he couldn't stay for long, only until he caught his breath. He picked at the prickly things snared in his pajama legs, then bent low and peeped out under the edge of the tablecloth. Almost near enough to touch was the next table, the one with *her* and the doughy man who rose, leaving, just as Jeb crept underneath, her leg and foot with its silver shoe swinging past his nose.

He didn't make a sound. The silky ankle, the glittering shoe with all the stars on it, the black full dress so close it brushed his cheek, as he took the matches from his pocket. He struck one, and as it flared, he set a corner of the cardboard burning. The small flame swelled, and he held it to the hem of the dress that dangled just above the ground. Then, as it rippled up the blackness, he touched the flame to the part above the swinging foot, caught in a half arc, and on to the other side so that in a flash the entire hem was burning. The table exploded over him, going up and up as Lee screamed and seemed to leap into the sky like one of those flying sparkly things. As she turned and turned, a ball of fire revolving on the lawn, the flames devouring her sleeves so that she had wings—burning, fiery wings like an angel of death—Jeb ran for the woods. He raced through the brush, bumped off trees, fell and rolled, dirt up his nose, eyes tearing from pain, the music of her shrieking all around him, filling up the spaces in the night and carrying him along in a cloud so that he thought he, too, was flying.

15

Maggie tried not to think of Lee burning, but the smell of charred meat clung to her clothes, her hair. She didn't seem able to wash it away, that cloying sweetness. Wearily, she dried herself and looked out the bathroom window, thinking she could see in the darkness the large, irregular burn in the lawn—black, obscene, like a shameful birthmark. And then the image that had been sitting ghostlike in her mind, of Lee on fire, of the cartwheels of flame, came; and the screaming echoed in her ears, just as Tracy's and Kathy's had. Quickly, she turned away. She knew she'd be haunted by the burning, that it would flare in her dreams until the whole inside of her skull would be smoldering.

The fire department ambulance that David called had rushed Lee to a special burn unit in a Stamford hospital. Her condition had seemed worse than it really was, though there would be scars on her calves and thighs, probably on her arms, but her face had only been slightly touched, so no problem there, Jamie had said on his return. Maggie had phoned him at once and he rode behind the ambulance, seeing that Lee was turned over to a team of experts on arrival. The ambulance attendant had told Jamie who had told David, and Maggie couldn't help hearing, that Lee had been conscious all the way, emitting little shrieks of pain, though they had shot her full of Demerol for relief.

It wasn't my fault, Maggie told herself, though no one had said that it was. There was no way any of them, David included, could blame her. But David had said nothing, rigid with shock after the ambulance pulled out, lights flashing, gravel scattering up along the side of the road, sirens shrilling.

It was David who had saved Lee. The others stood frozen or fleeing in panic away from the flames. But David had thrown his jacket around her, and rolled her on the ground, beating the fire out with his bare hands. He was slightly burned, the hairs singed right up to his elbows.

David stood by the side of the bed, his hands and arms wrapped in loose gauze bandages that Jamie—on his return from Stamford—had applied over the ointment to cover the burns. He looked like a mummy, his arms spread wide, naked but for the bandages and pajama bottoms. Maggie thought, watching him from the doorway, that he was drunk. He swayed slightly, and his mouth was slack, his eyes unfocused.

"I thought I saw Jeb—" she started to say, not knowing she was going to say anything until the words had left her mouth.

"Don't start with me, Maggie," he slurred, his voice bottomless. There seemed nothing more left inside him, all the gauges shoved to empty, but she couldn't let it alone. In all their years together he'd never been drunk.

"First in the bushes," she persisted, "and then, it happened so quickly. Everybody . . ." She faltered. "But I did think—"

"Shut up!" he yelled, lashing out, crashing into the bed as he stumbled toward her. She pulled back, bumped into the chair in the corner and fell heavily into it. "Don't think any more, bitch!"

He stopped and clumsily rubbed the bandaged hand

across his face, blinking himself back from the abyss. "Let's go to bed," he said thickly. "Sleep."

As if sleeping brought peace. Sleep, she could have told him, brought worse things up from the darkness, regurgitated demons, foul beasts whose breath blew hot on her skin and smelled of meat cooking, human flesh on fire. And she didn't sleep, though he did. She sat in the chair, her body prickly with cold under the sheer nightgown, and listened to David's rumbling, angry snorts of breath, his thrashing as he tried to turn away from the pain. She listened, waiting for the sun to come up, for the long night to end.

But the night went on and on, and she remembered how Klein had told her that Jeb felt guilty. How he had said that Jeb felt guilty because he lived and his sisters had died, and even if he couldn't express it, even if he had buried it deep in his subconscious, the guilt was there like water at the bottom of a well.

Had he really set the fire that killed them? And if so how could he have done the same to Lee?

Did he?

Why would he?

Lee gave him a red balloon. No, Lee gave him lollipops.

Maggie was afraid to sleep, the fear sitting in her bones. But she was almost as afraid of staying awake. The tattered end of the night seemed alive with demons, and David, twisted in the sheets, his hair all matted with sweat, might have been tortured by them, rolling about the bed, groaning aloud.

Jeb's face in the bushes. Jeb on the lawn.

Maggie couldn't stop remembering. She got up from the chair and quietly left the bedroom, left David to his nightmares, and went down the hall where she paused outside Jeb's door, the tiny glow of the night-light just visible through the opening, and stroked the wood with the palm of her healing hand.

The house made its night sounds like an old woman troubled with aches and pains, and Maggie hesitated, listening. But there was nothing to hear but the familiar creaking, no voice telling her what to do, whether or not to push the door and go in and look at her sleeping son—something she had been avoiding all these hours—or go back to her chair from where she could chart the changing light as it filled up the window from gray to pale yellow.

I saw him. I know I saw him, never mind what David says.

But she was equally as afraid to find Jeb smudged with dirt, to see the scratches that the bushes must have mapped across his skin.

Finally, because not knowing was worse than knowing, she entered the room. There, between the two windows, was the bed, and sprawled out on the top of the covers, as though his arms and legs were staked to the mattress, was Jeb. From the distance Maggie couldn't see him clearly. She moved closer, holding her breath.

He looked like an angel, his small hands half closed, the blond hair falling in an untidy wave over his forehead, his pink lips slightly parted. But a bruised angel, for the hands furled like flowers were sooty with dirt, and along the downy cheeks were thin, red lines. There was a button missing on his pajama top, and the right knee of the bottoms was ripped.

Maggie gasped with pain, a huge fist having slammed her right under her heart. Her stomach churned; bile flooded her mouth. And still, behind the pain, a singled thought reared: *Now David will have to believe me.*

She ran from the room, not quietly this time, not even conscious of bumping into the door frame, of pushing the door aside so that it banged back against the dresser, ran to David. He was lying on his back, and in the dying light looked more than ever like a larger version of his son. Maggie shook him forcibly by the arm, pushed and pulled at him, slapped the side of his head that lolled back and forth on the pillow.

"Wake up, David, for God's sake, wake up!"

The Mommy person was there, or had been there just a minute before. The Mommy person making funny noises like she was going to cry, like she hurt something awful. He didn't like waking up to the Mommy person like that. But before he could cry out she was gone, running down the hall and yelling for the Daddy person.

Something was wrong, terribly wrong. The room was adrift with shadows that swung along the curtains, crept over the covers that had been tossed back and lay half on the floor, rocked in the chair with the runners hitting the wood. There wasn't that blackness that sometimes happened when the night-light needs a new bulb, but rather a menacing grayness.

Jeb leaped out of the bed. He couldn't stay in this room not one minute longer, not to wait for the shadows to wind their long fingers around his neck and choke the breath out of him. And he couldn't follow after the Mommy person, back to her bedroom where he heard her screaming the Daddy person's name, yelling that he should wake up.

There was only one place to go, and he had to return, had to get back. It was too dangerous to stay out any longer.

The mirror. He had to reach the mirror.

His feet flew as though they had wings, and the hall carpet whispered under his toes. Then he was at the stairs and soaring down them, barely touching each step. The mirror. He had to reach the mirror. The grayness was turning back into night, into blackness.

Just as he touched the wall at the foot of the stairs and went around the corner, he began the humming, and the humming raced through him like a fire out of control. A river formed from the bottom of the steps along the downstairs hall right to the mirror, and he rode on it, floating, though he could barely see because the darkness was so heavy now. He reached the glass, his outstretched hands slapping it. And the glass should have been cold, should have felt like nothing but glass, but it was warm and welcoming.

As he went in to meet that other, entered that truly secret place, the other joined him, bone merging with bone, flesh with flesh, all the molecules meeting, then separating, as the two little boys fused on the edge and parted.

"You know, Maggie, you're crazy, really crazy," David was mumbling, still half drunk, not, Maggie knew, aware of what he was saying. But it didn't matter. He could call her anything he liked, think anything he wanted about her, because now she had proof. Oh, dear God, she *knew*. Which was why she wasn't listening to David's angry voice, castigating her for waking him. She tugged at him to keep him moving, out the bedroom and into the hall. The darkness framed in the window at the other end was just paling, and everything was underexposed, without color, the edges shifting.

"Just look at him, David, and you'll know he's been outside, that he was in the bushes. You'll know I did see him!"

They stumbled closer to Jeb's room, David still muttering under his breath, a sour smell rising off him of sweat and sleep and too much liquor.

"Now, now," Maggie said, her hand on the jamb of Jeb's

room when she heard a noise and turned. Rising up the steps was a small shape, indistinct in the grainy light.

"Jeb?" she called out. The shape rose to the level of the hall and Maggie fled toward him, David behind her. "Jeb, where were you?" But he didn't answer, just looked up at her. David hit the light switch on the wall, and the harsh glow spilled over all of them caught immobile—mother, father, child. And the child's face was tilted up at the parents, and it was clean, unblemished. There was no button missing from his pajama top, no rip on the knee. And when he held out his hands they were still clean from his bath.

Don't wander off from Mommy . . .
Stay where Mommy can see . . .
Mother is watching you, Margaret, just remember, Mother knows whatever you do.

Maggie was lying out on the lawn at the back of the house, the porch and steps just a few feet away so that she could run inside to Rebecca if anything happened. Dear God, who'd run to Rebecca who never smiled, who tasted words as though they were stones caught between her teeth, who thinks I'm mad as a hatter. Well, aren't I? Seeing Jeb, always seeing Jeb, thinking he set fire to Lee, burned her up, like his sisters.

Maggie lay on the lawn, courting sleep like a hungry lover and trying to tan away the pasty, greenish tinge of her skin, cover the rings of exhaustion, bring some color to her face so that when she passed the mirror she wouldn't see an old woman staring.

The face in the brush, the old, anciently old face on a coin, in a painting stripped down to canvas, colorless.

If she could just sleep, drown in unconsciousness, as if it were a warm sea, then she wouldn't have to think about last night, about Lee burning, the flames shooting skyward, the air heavy with the stench. And then she wouldn't have to think about Jeb. Jeb there and not there. Jeb with dirty hands and scratches on his face; Jeb without either.

Surprisingly David, slightly drunk though he still was, and surly from being awakened, wasn't angry. He had just stared for a moment as though someone had thrown ice water in his face, and then lifted Jeb up and took him back to his bed.

David had thought it was a trick of light, that unable to see clearly in the dimness, she saw what she feared she might see. That's how he explained it to her, and Maggie was too frightened to argue. She was frightened of both seeing what she saw and of not having seen it at all.

When David had said good-night to her and gently patted her arm, telling her to sleep, she knew all his uncertainties had fled, and he surely thought her mad, unequivocally so, without any reservations now.

Maggie sat up. Her heart was pounding. She went inside and ran cold water from the tap, and shaking out a Valium from the small bottle taken off the window ledge, she thought, if I take all of them I can sleep, sleep, forever, sleep away the dreams, the screaming. Klein was wrong after all, the screaming never did stop.

It was almost time to leave for Greenwood and Klein, waiting like a spider in his parlor. The phone on the wall rang. She waited for Rebecca to answer on the extension upstairs, but she didn't. Finally, Maggie lifted the receiver, thinking, there is no one in the world I want to speak to; the world has been sluiced clean of people whom I can trust. But she was wrong. It was Jamie.

"What's happening?" he asked.

"No one burned alive today, if that's what you mean," she replied, saying to herself, well bad taste and laughter are two solutions I haven't tried to keep from losing my grip, slight as it is. "How are you?"

"Lonely. Missing you, Maggie. Worrying."

"Don't worry about me. I'm fine." Liar. She juggled the vial of Valium and heard the reassuring rattle the small tablets made.

"It's Wednesday, day after tomorrow. You know, Wednesday, when all the doctors in America retire to the golf course and contemplate the medical implications of little white balls."

"I can't see you playing golf."

"That's my problem. I don't. Which is a terrible handicap."

"Oh Jamie, that's an awful pun." He could—miracle of miracles—make her laugh.

"Wait 'til you hear the rest. I'm the worst punster east of the Mississippi. Which reminds me, it being Wednesday the day after tomorrow, can I see you?"

As he talked on she watched the dark splotch of lawn undulating, the outlines loose and shimmering. And she thought of making love with Jamie in his cabin just at the edge of the lake, the trees right down to the water, wrapping them in a leafy embrace, scraping the wood, the glass, as he trailed fingers over her legs, her arms, breasts, nipples rising at his touch. His mouth on hers. That was another kind of burning. And a drowning, waters rising over her head, so she suffocated when he came inside her, reverberating his groan of pleasure with her own. Yes, she had made love with Jamie, and that fact still startled her.

So much had run over that memory, bypassed it like a speeding train. Sarah's death, Lee's burning.

He was saying something. "What?" she asked.

"Do you want to see me again? I asked if you wanted to see me."

He had watched her all those years ago, seen her, and she hadn't been aware of him, had, must have, passed him by many times if he remembered so vividly that he could recall the color of the bathing suit she wore the year she was fifteen.

Would it all have been different if she'd turned at a precise moment and seen him there on Elm before the Rialto movie theater (now shuttered closed), or in O'Reilly's, or on the raft when she pulled herself out of the water? Would she be Maggie now, Maggie here, if they had fallen in love, she and Jamie, and she had become his wife, given birth to his children, filled up the corners of his world, as he would have hers?

She knew then, that she did want to see him, did want to make love with him again. She didn't know why— Defiance? Lust?—and she wasn't even certain why she had in the first place. It wasn't the kind of thing she did, unlike so many of her friends—ex-friends, she thought. She believed in fidelity, monogamy, and had never looked at another man since she had met David so many years before. But Jamie... Jamie's my friend, she realized with surprise, and said solemnly, "You're my friend Jamie."

Jamie would listen, not like Klein to catch her out. He'd listen without the need to define, to make judgments or, like David, in order to unsettle her, watching to see her trip, expecting her to sprawl on the gravel and skin her soul.

"Wednesday," she said shyly, "I'd like that."

The day had changed. She put the Valium away high up in a cupboard behind the bags of flour, sugar, the box of salt. She was bouyant with purpose. I'll tell Klein about Jeb. No, she thought, I will tell Klein and let him ask Jeb himself. And having decided that, she went looking for her son.

She was halfway around the house when she saw him in the distance, down at the end of the dirt lane just where a copse of birch trees clawed the sides of the road like skeletal fingers.

He was so small that for a moment she thought she was mistaken. Straining to see, the trees dancing before her vision, she realized suddenly that he wasn't alone. There was another child with him.

Crossing the curve of the front lawn, she went after them, calling because there was something out of kilter, something not quite right with the two little boys, something undefined and nebulous about their slight, tiny figures that made her anxious.

Who was he, the other one?

There weren't any houses near enough to Four Oaks for such a young child to just wander over unannounced. And he couldn't be more than Jeb's age, being the same height, the same stock build. She hollered out to them but neither one turned, and as fast as she moved, the distance between them, between her and the boys, stayed the same. She knew eventually they'd reach the end of the road, marked by the mailbox, and surely wouldn't go any further, not out into traffic, though even there the traffic was slight. Because of the murderous curve a mile on down toward Route Nine, no one drove this stretch extra fast. No, they were safe out there. It wasn't that.

Then why was she sweating?

What scratched at her about the two little figures so determined, marching along like tin soldiers, left foot up, right foot down, arms swinging in unison?

Their bright plaid shirts sparkled with color as they darted in and out of the patches of sunlight that dropped through the trees. How strange that the plaids were alike. Maggie stopped and shielded her eyes so that she could see better, more precisely. Yes, the plaids were identical, and the jeans, and she was almost certain, though she couldn't see them absolutely, the scuffed and dirty sneakers. She tried to take it all in as she ran behind them.

Two little blond-haired boys in plaid shirts marching off... to where? Where were they going?

A dark cloud sailed past the sun, and the light settled

pale and ashy. She slowed to catch her breath, to wipe away the sweat trickling down her forehead with the sleeve of her blouse. And then, looking up, it was as though the light, which went yellow and buttery once more, was playing a trick. Where there had been two there was now only one.

Jeb was facing back toward her, toward the house behind her, and trudging down the road, swirls of dust sprouting from underneath his sneakers. She went to meet him, as though swimming underwater.

"Where were you going?" she asked when he was close enough so that she didn't have to shout to be heard.

"Nowhere," he said truculently and went right by her. She might have been a tree or a rock to be avoided by navigation.

"Who were you with? Who's that little boy? Does he live around here?"

"Nobody," he said, ahead of her now.

"That other little boy? Who is he?" She hurried after Jeb, but he stayed just a hair's breath beyond her outstretched hand and her fingers grasped at air. She hadn't thought he could move so fast without seeming to rush.

"Nobody."

"What do you mean, nobody? Where did he come from?" They reached the edge of the grass, to their right the burned-out spot, a cancer in the green. Jeb had started to march across the lawn with heavy steps, too heavy for a six-year-old, when she grabbed the edge of his shirt, stopping him. He froze in his tracks and she had to turn him around by the shoulders.

"Who was that other little boy, Jeb?" she asked once again.

"There wasn't nobody," he said, his bottom lip jutting out, a usual precursor to tears. In the full light, the planes of his face were bone flat, and his features slid like paint dissolving, leaving his round, dark eyes staring hard as nuggets of anthracite.

She shrilled, "There was too, somebody. I saw him. He was just your size, and he was wearing a plaid shirt just like you're wearing. Jeans too. I saw the both of you at the end of the road. And I yelled to you, but you didn't answer."

"Nooooo . . ." The sound was a whinny, so thin, ready, and high-pitched that it sent needles slivering through her. Her hands flew away from his shoulders, and set free, he ran, circling around to the far side of the house.

Maggie went after him. For a moment she thought he was in two places, veering off into the stand of trees that shrouded the flank of the side lawn and yet bearing right and heading for the back porch and the kitchen door. Was she seeing things, or had the other little boy returned, come back when she wasn't looking, making his way through the woods where he could have possibly passed unseen?

She didn't go after him, that other fleeing image, coming aground, the air punched out of her. But because holding onto sanity was a habit now, she decreed that it was all a mistake there on the road, the shimmering, unreliable light of the sun making her see—forcing her to see—two little boys instead of one.

Later, Klein, dismissing her confusion at having seen what wasn't there to see, said, "Maggie, in your mind Jeb is always connected with fire."

She hadn't brought Jeb after all. When she found him drinking orange juice in the kitchen—just one small boy getting his face all sticky—he clung to Rebecca and begged for more of *Alice.* so she had left him sitting out on the front porch, Rebecca with half glasses perched on her nose, bent over the book, and Jeb, so intent, his eyes never leaving her face, as though expecting revelation.

Maggie rocked back and forth, her hands hooking her elbows. "Why don't you ever believe me?" She had found a cassette of Mozart concertos in the back of the glove compartment and could now still hear the flute, that thin, almost invisible whistle, humming in her ears. "You keep saying fire, fire. . . ."

Flames leaped and died before her eyes.

". . . and it's all the other things too," she continued doggedly. "There he is one minute, and gone the next. Like two different children."

Klein pounced, his leather chair wheezing beneath him. "Two children that you saw at the end of the road. Don't you understand, Maggie, you think something, fear something, and then, poof," he waved his hands in the air, "you conjure it up. Actually see it." He almost purred with contentment.

"Like Rhea," she said suddenly. Rhea, the waif, the teenager who'd had the next room to Maggie at Greenwood, was only survivor of a four-car collision, fifteen dead in the biggest smash-up even on the Connecticut Turnpike, all sixteen and seventeen-year-olds on their way to a graduation dance. The road had been blanketed in blood, as though the sky had spit wide and rained blood witnesses had said. And Rhea walked out of it with not a scratch, rose from the middle of all those broken bodies without a rip in her pink tulle dress. But she never stopped seeeing them, the others. The dance went on in Rhea's head. In Rhea's head the music continually played, the dancers swirled. The prom night never ended.

"No, not like Rhea," Klein said, not caring for comparisons, and suspecting too that Rhea would drift forever in the arms of her phantom partner. Maggie, his star patient, had to put aside her ghosts, though even he did see that the fates were conspiring against her. It was bad luck, her friend having an accident involving fire. Klein would have been happier if Lee had slipped in the tub.

"Would you speak to Jeb?" she asked. Would Jeb say no to Klein?

"Of course. I've offered to before this, you know. But what is it you expect? You've talked with him, so has his father. He denies doing any of the things you've accused him of. I can't make the child plead guilty to acts he never committed, Maggie. And you wouldn't want that. It's your responsibility." He bit down hard on his pipe stem. "You must stop blaming Jeb for everything."

Blaming Jeb, she thought, driving away from Greenwood while Mr. Miller, ninety-two and senile, waved her off, fluttering her white handkerchief, as if Greenwood were her home and she was saying good-bye to a guest. *Klein thinks I blame Jeb for living too.* For the first time she was angry, angry at Klein and at herself. She wasn't so frightened that she didn't know nonsense when she heard it. She didn't blame Jeb for being alive when his sisters died—even though he might, just might, have accidentally started that fire—but she did *know* and know without questioning, that he had stabbed her in the closet, that he had been playing with matches, that she had seen him outside the window—

—on the lawn . . .

—at the top of the stairs . . .

—down the road . . .

—in the bushes . . .

Lee, poor Lee. Like innocent Melissa, Lee had wandered into their lives with the best intentions, and look what had happened to her. Even if it wasn't Maggie's fault, she felt obscurely guilty.

She turned off the air conditioning and rolled down the window. The day had gone bad; the sky was quilted now in grimy clouds that spread out overhead like dirty laundry. She switched on the radio heading off the turnpike into Brighton.

"This is WADS, New Haven. Temperature dropping down to seventy-two, and a duster buster is in the making. Scattered showers all through southern New England. Batten down the hatches, folks, because the winds are going to reach gale force. Small craft warnings in effect all along the Sound. And now, remember the Chipmonks? Well, here they are from 1968 with—"

The Brighton streets were almost deserted. People were fastening their shutters, rolling up awnings, taking in lawn furniture, metal chairs folded flat. On the front lawn of a large white house, porches like barnacles fastened to its sides, a mute, sorrowful ceramic fawn with soulful eyes, surrounded by dwarfs in peaked hats, charted her passage. She watched it for a second in the rearview mirror. It said, *the rains again, beware of water.*

Fire and water . . .

. . . the world will end. . . .

Maybe her mind had gone out, a ship to sea, having slipped its moorings. She could ride around again—something she had stopped doing since the fat man fell at her in warning—drive in the rain. Heavy drops were spitting at the windshield now. She turned the radio off and heard the wipers hissing like snakes. The wind began its currying along the car as she drove into the square and parked at a meter in front of Lee's bookstore. When she got out the gusts were already strong enough to whip the skirt between her legs.

There was no one in the bookstore but a bored clerk who glanced up at the tinkling of the bell, then looked down to the book he was reading. Maggie went straight to the desk where he sat and said, "I'm a friend of Miss McCann's. My name is Mrs. Brace."

He watched her with a bored look from behind horn rims that magnified his eyes. "Is it a particular book you want?" His shoulders hunched, he wasn't giving anything away.

"No, no," Maggie said, "not a book. I plan to go down to the hospital to see her in the next day or so and I thought I'd bring her some things." She went on endlessly explaining since the owlish stare unnerved her. "You know, toothbrush, robe, slippers. That sort of thing."

"This isn't a department store. We sell books," he said, surveying his domain where all the books waited unread except for the one he was now impatiently tapping his finger on.

"I know that," Maggie said, suddenly annoyed. "I just need the key to her house so I can pick up what she might need."

"Well, I don't know about that," he said, suspiciously tugging at his bottom lip.

The wind was knocking on the front windows. "I won't be able to get her things if I can't get into her house. Will I," Maggie asked, all her nerve ends sizzling.

He finally agreed that made sense, though Maggie could tell, as she reluctantly handed over the keys with its cardboard tag—*Lee front door house*—that he did so only to get rid of her.

Outside, the air had gone black. Fat drops of rain machine-gunned the sidewalk, and the few pedestrians who were still out scurried for cover. By the time Maggie reached the car door her blouse was stuck to her back. Inside, with the windows fogged, the rain pelting away at the roof, she felt trapped. She was entombed, caught and held so tightly, unable to see out except momentarily as she cleared the glass with her hand. The water flooded the windshield in rivers. The street at the other side elongated and ran, dribbled off like a reflection in a fun house mirror.

The car shook on its springs as the wind slammed furiously against it. She hit the ignition. The engine coughed asthmatically; the wipers swished away. Shifting into drive, she opened the defroster, frigid air flowing up at her. Carefully, she inched away from the curb, off down the south side of the square, the grass churning under the torrents of water, the treetops whipping about, frenzied.

Jeb. Jeb alone with Rebecca. Four Oaks. Suddenly, she remembered the last storm, the night of Sarah's death.

Jebbie sees monsters.

How did she know that?

Water surged over the tires as she sped right onto Grove, the only car moving, all the others pulled in, waiting out the storm. Phantom cars, abandoned, prehistoric remains left in the silt. She lumbered by them, their windows fogged too, so that they appeared uninhabited, as if no one was lost inside as she was in the Dodge.

Hurry...

Hurry...

Jeb. Jeb. The wipers sang his name. The defroster whimpered. Jeb.

And Maggie thought, tears filling her eyes, blurring her vision even further so that the road home was a treacherous obstacle course, studded with nightmares, *if I lose him I will die.*

But where would she lose him and why?

16

By the time Maggie reached Four Oaks, the flash summer storm had abated. The rain had stopped. The water left shimmering in pools at the edges of the road, was already evaporating. The world was clean, renewed, and Jeb was smiling radiantly at her when she walked into the house. He was coloring in a big, oversized *Star Wars* book at the kitchen table, his crayons neatly laid out in a line.

"Where's Rebecca?" she asked uneasily. Just because someone isn't in your field of vision doesn't mean they're dead, she told herself, seeing in her mind's eye Rebecca stretched out somewhere—Sarah's bed—death silvering her limbs.

"Washing the clothes," he said, his head already bent over the page, the crayon in his right hand moving slowly, as he colored neatly within the outlines.

She realized then that she heard the whine of the machine in the basement just beneath her feet as she looked over Jeb's shoulder. R2D2 grew a green skin like mold as she watched.

A pot steamed on the stove. Maggie went over and picked up the lid. Spaghetti sauce bubbled away inside. Bright red and bubbling. The acrid smell of burning. She lowered the heat. Her stomach was acidy, unsettled. Her head ached. She found a bottle of aspirin in the spice rack and shook three pills into her palm, gulping them down

with a glass of water. The washer stopped. Pause. Hum.
The dryer started. She went to the basement door, opened
it, and peered down through a shaft of darkness into the
pale light below.

"Rebecca?" she called, and started down the steps.

The dryer thumped loudly, the sound slapping along the
cement walls. It was cold and damp in the cellar, like the
earth itself. A musty smell rose in a cloud as she descended.

Ahead was the furnace room, its door cracked, the
somnolent boiler hulking unseen, waiting for winter. Maggie
thought of the winter, of being in Four Oaks when the
snows came, closed in, the drifts pillowing the house,
obscuring the road. The three of them together, Rebecca
and Jeb and her. . . . Where was David?

She tried to imagine David just then, conjure up his
face like a moon rising, but there was only blankness, like
an outline from Jeb's coloring book no features, no skin
tone, just emptiness.

"Mrs. Brace?"

Maggie jumped. There, just below, her head level with
Maggie's stomach, was Rebecca, the half glasses sitting
like a headband over her hair, the lenses glittering with a
pasty glow from the forty watt bulb in the ceiling.

"Rebecca, I didn't see you," Maggie said, gripping the
railing, one foot up, one down, trapped—fogged in, the
only person left in the world, all the dead up from their
graves. Her brain whirled, the headache hammered away
on her skull. Goose bumps prickled her arms.

"Is everything all right, Mrs. Brace?" Rebecca asked. In
a sweater the color of used dishwater and a tailored skirt,
she looked more like a school teacher than someone who
should be in the cellar doing the laundry. More like one of
the nurses in Greenwood, watching, always on the alert
for a deviation that would send them all spinning away,

screaming, behind locked doors with their little Judas holes. Steel doors.

Had David hired someone to spy on her?

There was something heavy and inert in the dryer, banging at the sides with each revolution.

Maggie breathed deeply and asked, "Did anyone call?"

"No, no one." Rebecca's bloodless lips pursed into a thin line. The two women stared at one another. "I'm making spaghetti for dinner," Rebecca said. "The little boy"—doesn't she remember his name, Maggie wondered—"likes spaghetti."

"Yes, I know I saw it on the stove cooking. I turned down the heat. It was sticking a bit."

"Oh," she sniffed, disapprovingly.

To the right, at the side of the short slope of stairs that led up and out to the back—heavy doors at a slant above them—the window was sooty, filmed with grime. Though the sun had come out, the light didn't penetrate.

The hair prickled on the back of Maggie's neck just as Jeb above her began to sing a song she remembered from her own childhood. Where had he ever heard it?

"The worms crawl in, the worms crawl out, into their tummies and out their mouths . . ."

"Jebbie!" she screamed up the steps.

Rebecca didn't move. As still and incomplete as one of the ruined Etruscan statues that Maggie recalled from the south wing of the Metropolitan. Her face was blank, her arms stiffened in stone. It was just possible to detect the slight rise and fall of narrow breasts, lungs filling, emptying, heart thumping. No, it was her own heart thundering.

Rebecca watched her strangely. And why not, Maggie thought—I'm as strange as one of those phantoms in their barred rooms, Greenwood's security ward, where the cantatas of screams and slaps of rubber soles on hard floors and swish of freshly starched uniforms sang through the

sanitarium, promising, this is what will happen to you
if . . .

"Jebbie!" she called again. His singsong voice was silent
now.

"Whaaaat?" It seemed too far away to be just in the
kitchen above.

"Why don't you go lie down until dinner, Mrs. Brace."
Rebecca suggested, her dry lips barely moving. Has anyone ever kissed those lips, Maggie wondered irrelevantly.

"Lie down?" she echoed stupidly, thoughts sluggish as
heavy machinery in her head.

"A nap, Mrs. Brace. You don't seem right."

Maggie came unglued then, bolting back up the stairs,
running from Rebecca, the guardian of the dryer and
washing machine.

"Jeb," she cried, bursting into the kitchen. But he
wasn't there. The chair was angled out from the table, the
crayons not neatly aligned now but scattered across the
coloring book and on the floor. The picture opposite the
one he had neatly colored was a riot of steaks and slashes,
as though it had been done by a different child. "Jeb!" she
called, going after him. Where is he now, she wondered,
yet knew with a certainty that was verified as she found
him before the mirror. Mouth to mouth, eyes stuck together, his nose flattened as though chiseled away.

The two little boys were tightly gripping one another,
holding on for dear life, as she came up behind him, them,
and said, "Jebbie, what are you doing?"

"Just talking to himself, Mommy," he answered dreami-
ly, his voice a bare whisp of smoke clouding the glass,
blurring the image in the mirror like the vapor on the
windshield so that she hadn't been able to see out.

A wave of terror seized her as she saw herself with eyes
so magnified the pupils swelled to black, diluted with
fright, the cords in her neck bulging and beneath the faint

honey tan the bones heavy as rock, skin dropping away, flesh melting. She was staring at her own skeleton emerging—bony arms, naked phalanges, the gold wedding ring dangling on the knuckle, sliding down with a clang as she raised the two hands to a mouth in which teeth were big as piano keys, locked in a perpetual grin.

She closed eyelids she no longer had and tried to reassure herself with the feel of flesh, willing muscles and skin to be there when she looked at herself again. The vertebrae in her neck creaked as though rusty when she bent her head, thinking, if I'm dead and this is a dream, all a dream, then how can my heart be beating? There was a high storm in her chest, naked of organs, ribs burnished white. Femurs and tibias were polished stancheons holding her upright.

"Mommy, why are you crying?"

Her eyes snapped wide, and Jeb was right, there were tears in tiny riverlets tracing down her cheeks.

No skeleton grimaced back at her. Jeb, his face still plastered like wet cement to his image, stared up at her, smiling. His teeth clunked against the mirror. "Are you unhappy, Mommy?" he asked.

"No, sweetness," she said, ineffectually wiping at tears. She couldn't stop the tears, the crying was an act outside her volition, some other woman's emotion squeezing the ducts.

"Then why are you crying?" he asked, breaking away at last from himself. A weight as oppressive as a coffin lid rose from her chest as he turned and hugged her legs.

Because I hallucinate; because I'm an emotional alcoholic with DTs, an addict in the throes of withdrawal. "Why don't you go finish your picture, and then Rebecca will get dinner ready," she said instead, prying him away from her.

"Aren't you going to eat with me? Is Daddy?" he asked, swinging on her hand. She kept her eyes on him, refusing to look up in the mirror, at either of them in the glass, reflected back, God knows how, she thought. I mustn't tell Klein. Only the worst of the Greenwood sick ever saw themselves so far after death that nothing of their living bodies remained.

"No, Jebbie, Mommy's feeling a little cheesy. You know, like I'm coming down with the flu. And Daddy's staying in town for the night." She patted his hair, ran her fingers down to his neck and felt the warmth, his skin so hot— burning—that she drew back. The pulse just under his chin had throbbed alarmingly, as though he was at high speed. "I better go up to bed and rest," she said, thinking again of the bottle of Valium. Little yellow pills, glowing in the dark of the cupboard.

Ah, Maggie, my love. . . .

She didn't know why, but she conjured up Jamie's voice, Jamie's face, the feel of Jamie's belly sliding along hers, his tongue licking at her breasts.

Before she went upstairs, Jeb pushed off to the kitchen— her eyes never left him until through the doorway she saw him sitting at the table. She went into the study and took an unopened bottle of Cutty Sark from the liquor cabinet.

At the top of the stairs she realized she didn't have a glass, and she went into Jeb's bathroom with his Mickey Mouse towels neatly folded over the bar, his plastic ducks marooned on their sides in the empty tub, and took his Yogi Bear mug. She didn't want to go to her room, hers and David's, as if she was about to commit a sin so egregious that it was only possible in the anonymity of the guest room. Yet it was only when she was naked under the sheets, the first shot already sliding down her throat, warming her insides, that she remembered that this once had been her room, this bed, simple and narrow, hers as a child's.

As night furrowed in through the slits in the blinds, the

top of the dresser filled up with her old rock collection, an ancient bird's nest, her jewelry box (key hidden underneath), hairbrush, and pink comb. The desk was littered with pencils, erasers, crayons, water colors, little jars of poster paints, and notebooks in which she had once written her thoughts, bits of poetry, observations. And in the chair on which her mother never allowed her to leave her clothes—*hang up everything neatly, Margaret*—sat her doll, Susie, blond hair, ruffled white blouse, short red velvety skirt, and on tiny feet were ice skates, the blades gleaming.

"Hello, Susie," she said, drinking away, the level of the scotch sinking in the bottle.

"How's tricks, Maggie?" Susie asked, just at that moment when Maggie passed into sleep, but not before she slurred in answer . . . .

". . . backwards and forwards, Susie."

Sirens were going off in her head, fire engines speeding to the scene, ambulances, police cars. Yet her head was concrete, heavy as a cornerstone, which she carried in two hands, afraid it would fall from her neck, crash to the ground and shatter into fragments. She could see all her memories, all her thoughts, ground into the carpet underfoot, and carefully she moved, lumbering, into the bathroom, into the shower. The icy water shocked her eyelids; the tiled wall spun in tumbling patterns.

Maggie threw up all over the shower, streams of red vomit splashing on her feet. She threw up until her insides stopped heaving in turbulent waves, and then, still dripping with water, returned to her bed. Drifting off to sleep once more, she realized that this time she was in her own bed, the bed she shared with David, and he wasn't there.

Again she woke up, hours? days? later, and rolling on her side, she saw a silver tray on the night table. A steaming pot of coffee, a flower-patterned bone china cup and saucer, a delicate pink linen napkin. She drank two cups of coffee before she saw that she was still naked. A rank smell came off her body and her hair, hanging limply like seaweed, was matted.

This time she took a hot shower, washed her hair, and scrubbed her skin until it glowed.

"How are you feeling Mrs. Brace?" Rebecca asked when she came down to the kitchen in a robe, hair wound turbanlike in a towel.

She handed Rebecca the tray and, ignoring the question, said, "The coffee was wonderful."

The lips tensed in a smile. "It's a Moroccan blend that I'm particularly fond of."

"Where's Jeb?" Maggie asked.

"Outside playing." Maggie glanced through the kitchen window but there was no Jeb. "Mr. Brace asked that you call him in the office when you got up," Rebecca said. Her eyebrows arched and danced along her forehead like two caterpillars. Maggie stared her down until Rebecca, defeated, silently left the room. Maggie called Jamie and asked, "What day is it?"

"You've been drinking," he said, laughing. "What do you mean what day is it? It's Wednesday and I was just about to call you. I'll pick you up at the end of your road about one-thirty. Okay?"

"I have been drinking," she said, "and it's been a class A, world championship drunk. Apparently I misplaced all of Tuesday."

"Good for you," he said, "Tuesday was an awful day. Temperatures in the low nineties, four murders in Stamford alone, a new uprising in Central America, and ah, yes, a threatened teamster strike. Nope, Maggie, you didn't miss a thing being zonked out on Tuesday."

"I'm serious, Jamie," she said, annoyed with him. He didn't seem funny just then, with the headache creeping up her cheek bones again. Cradling the phone against her shoulder, she groped for the aspirins and shook out a handful, dropping them in the sink. She shook out three more and crunched them in her mouth, having read somewhere that chewing makes them work faster.

He was breathing at the other end of the wire like an obscene caller, but he didn't speak. They listened to one another's silences. "You can get drunk, Maggie," he said finally; "it's not a capital offense."

"If you make love to me, will I stop hurting?" she cried suddenly, tears in her eyes, splashing her words, thinking: I'm not hung over, I'm still drunk. What am I saying?

"I'll see you later, then we'll talk, all right?" But he didn't hang up the phone. She could feel him there alive at the other end, holding her in place.

Jeb drifted by the window, dragging a broken kite on the ground. "Okay," she said, drying her eyes with a dish towel. And then, quickly, "I'm sorry, Jamie." She hung up the phone before he could say anything more and went to the back door, calling out to Jeb.

He came up on the porch, the kite bumping along the two short steps and stood staring up at her through the screen. "Are you still sick?" he asked in the chilling wooden voice which so disconcerted her.

"Sick?"

"Rebecca said you were sick."

Rebecca would, Maggie thought. And David. She'd have to call David who had probably called Klein, who, knowing she never drank more than wine or beer or the social cocktail, would be scrambling for meaning. I can't even get drunk anymore, once in ten, fifteen years, without there being a psychoanalytical reason for it.

Well there is, Maggie, the other voice in her head said. *Repression, more commonly known as running away, or being scared of . . . scared of what?*

Nothing, everything.

And now you're going off with Jamie because scotch didn't work.

Jeb's face was flat as a coin, the ridges barely perceptible with the light behind him. Face in the bush, she thought, seeing Lee's cartwheels of flame.

I have to take Lee's things over to the hospital, she remembered.

"Mommy has to go out for the afternoon, but I'll be back by dinner time. What do you say if tonight we work on that model airplane Daddy brought you last week?"

She heard her voice coming from a long way off, echoing down a tunnel, and she wasn't surprised that he didn't respond, just turned, the kite jouncing, fluttering up for a moment on a wisp of air, and ran off across the lawn.

I won't think about Jeb right now, she said to herself, going upstairs to get ready for Jamie.

I don't like the smell of her. It's his fault, the Doctor person, making her drink that awful tasting stuff in the bottle, making her sleep all the time, be sick, smell bad.

He was so angry, his little face puffed up and red, that he crawled into his secret place and jiggled a baby frog in a killing jar, shaking it hard. The frog crashed from side to side, frantic with fear. At last his arm got tired of all the shaking, and he droped a burning match into the jar, but it fizzled and went out. Which made him angrier.

He thought of the sisters in their graves and dug a hole right in the middle of where he usually sat, dug a big, deep hole under the baby quilt and buried the frog, killing jar and all, the frog alive, right in the ground. He can talk to the sisters, he thought, imagining lines like electrical cords running through the dirt, connecting the whole earth and all the dead, still as rocks. Which made him feel somewhat better.

He had just finished immolating the frog in its glass

coffin when he saw the Mommy person leave the house and walk down the dirt road, tottering slightly on the funny shoes she wore. He lost sight of her in the distance but *knew* the Doctor person was waiting down there to take her away in his toy car and the sky was going to fall right down. It just had to happen.

Jamie was skipping stones along the glassy surface of the lake. Inside, Maggie was sleeping, the drugged sleep of the terminally ill, the dead, having slipped away in his arms, gone limp and heavy, her hair spread out in a weave along the pillow of the cot upon which they had made love. He had lain with her in his arms and watched her face go slack, the mouth with bruised lips slightly agape and her breath settling into short hums that puffed up at him, and thought that happiness was a huge stone on his heart, which like Sisyphus he pushed away only to have it return and overwhelm him. He wasn't accustomed to being happy; it didn't fit into his scheme of things, and he no more knew what to do about it than about the woman sleeping now curled like a baby under a khaki blanket bought from the army and navy store down on Route Eleven.

Plop, plop, eddies formed, tiny whirlpools that spread out in fine waves. Lake Wenoche had been, his father once told him, a valley. Long, long ago, before any of them were born, before their parents and grandparents and their grandparents before them were born, there had been an indentation in the earth's crust where the hills sloped downward into a wide, flat field. And on that field a man had built a house, a barn, and began to farm. Then the rains came, and with the rampaging rains beating against the earth, flailing the farmers's field, springs burst forth from the ground, as if the water beneath was frantic to push its way upward to meet the rain pouring down, and a lake formed. Floods cascaded across the field, overwhelmed the house, the barn, the old stone wall the farmer had built, and eventually claimed everything—the farmer, his wife, his children, his livestock. And now they were all down there, so deep that no one could penetrate that darkness, waiting like incubi to startle a man in his sleep and sit upon his chest with the weight of all that water, strangling the air out of his lungs, claiming him in the coils of nightmare forever.

Jamie didn't of course, believe his father's story, told, he remembered, on nights when it rained so heavily that the air was thick with a pounding noise—God's fist upon the ground. But still, when the lake was low, far out in the middle, if you looked carefully, it was just possible to make out the white gleaming of an old stone wall.

Beware of getting what you want in life, he recalled some prophet, saint or wise man saying, because you'll never be satisfied, you'll only want something more. Which was true. He had wanted Maggie, first to look at her, to talk to her, to touch her, to make love with her, and now, that wasn't enough. He wanted to make love with her always, to leave her in the morning and return to her at night; to spend all the nights of his life with her in his old fourposter, her limbs sprawled out next to his so that even sleeping he could move against her.

Old sod, you've become a real romantic. Plop, plop, stones perfectly skimmed the surface, sinking downward through the holes in the roof of that ghostly farmhouse where the man and woman and children sat entombed. Long ago, as a boy, he had seen Maggie, and that seeing had forced open a door, and now, years later, he discovered himself in a strange room from which he could not escape. And didn't want to.

Across the lake and to the right he could just barely make out the public beach and, bobbing in the water, the raft, the size of a postage stamp. "Hey, you, listen," he sang out, "listen all you ships at sea, I'm in loveeeeeee." His voice like the stones, skipped, bounced and tap danced over the lake surface.

"Why are you yelling?" Maggie asked. She stood framed in the window, her face and torso shrouded in the blanket that she'd wrapped about her.

"Because I want the whole world to know," he cried, laughing, turning toward her, the leftover stones trickling through his splayed fingers.

"You're impossible!" she said, disappearing.

He went back into the cabin, which was just one big room with an exposed kitchen at the far end, a small bathroom hidden off the back, and scraps of Salvation Army rejects for furniture—a cot, a ladder-back chair pushed up to a wobbly wood table with cigarette burns and circles overlaid by circles from the bottoms of endless glasses and coffee mugs, a rocker with an interweave of vines painted on its seat beneath a red cushion, and a bookcase with its ravaged paperbacks. And a telephone, of course. A doctor always had a telephone. Jamie thought, there is nowhere in the world that I can go where the sick, the maimed, the dying can't find me. I have given my life over to others, handed it out like a premium at McDonald's, and possibly more to this woman than to all the patients I have ever treated or ever will.

"Maggie, I want you to marry me," he blurted out.

Surprise skittered over her features. She clutched the blanket to her breasts, knuckles white from the pressure, and said, "What are you saying? There's David . . . and Jeb . . ."

" . . . and divorce," he interrupted. "Half of America is divorced, why not you and David?"

"Because I can't. I'll never leave David. It would mean" —she faltered—"it would just be impossible, that's all."

She said it so softly that he wasn't sure at first that he had heard her, but then realized he hadn't wanted to.

"I love you, Maggie." He couldn't think of adjectives to embellish the simple statement, so he left it, three words so abused by their familiarity that they were, he understood, almost meaningless. Everybody loved everything. How could he make her comprehend that his saying it, his feeling it, was a revelation?

"It's late; I better be getting home," she said, fumbling for her clothes, suddenly shy, a faint blush over her cheeks. She pulled on the white linen pants and tugged the green shirt over her head.

"No, don't go yet. There's time." He knelt before her. His chest was bare, and he took her hand and placed it over his heart. "Have dinner with me, please."

"David—"

He stopped her by putting his fingers on her lips, feeling the wetness. "Maybe he stayed late in town. Why don't you call up and find out? If he's coming home, okay, I'll drive you right back."

She stared at him, her eyes the color of moss, their soft green light seeming to make promises; and barely, almost imperceptibly, Maggie nodded her head, whispering between his fingers, "All right."

But first they made love again, this time softly, sweetly, in slow, indolent strokes, the passion muted, but the love making them vibrate like tuning forks, until Jamie thought he'd snap from the pleasure of it.

"Your father had to fly to Chicago unexpectedly, and your mother's decided to have dinner out with a friend," Rebecca explained to Jeb, as she put the neatly cut wedges of tuna salad sandwich on a plate in front of him. He poked at one experimentally, lifted the top layer of Wonder Bread, sniffed at the mayonnaise and tomato, then, finally took a bite. Rebecca, satisfied, returned to the kitchen cabinets she was relining with sheets of shelf paper. Jeb munched away and read his Pooh book. He was able to read very well, much better than most six-year-olds, and he knew the book almost by heart. He closed the book in disgust and gazed at the fading light outlined by the screen door.

Sometimes, if nobody was around, like his mother or father, and he was left alone with Rebecca, he was lonely. He had been lonely with Sarah too, though now he didn't like to think about her much, dead just as Tracy and Kathy were, but still something worse, something that ticked away in his head, just past the point where he could reach. He didn't try too hard, afraid it would explode in his head and send all the squooshy pieces of brain splattering around the inside of his skull. Sarah gave him the shivers in the night before he finally went to sleep, though when he talked to the other himself about it, he knew it was okay, that some things like morning coming after night, *had to be* or there was big trouble. The thing about Sarah was one of those *had to be* things, but, no matter how many times he told himself that and himself told him back, Jeb got the shivers, tiny goose bumps covering his arms even under the pajama top.

"There're strawberries for dessert," Rebecca said, eyeing him over her shoulder.

"I'm not supposed to eat them," he told her sadly, "they give me a rash."

"All right," she said, and taking a cigarette from a pack in her pocket, lit it, puffed, and put it down on the edge of the sink. "Time to get ready for your bath then."

He stared at the thin curl of smoke, mesmerized, and said, "It's early."

"I'll read to you for a while when you're done." A compromise.

"Okay," he agreed as the cigarette went up to her mouth and down again.

"Put your plate in the dishwasher," she said, pointing as if he didn't know where it was. "And finish off your milk."

Because he was an obedient little boy, Jeb complied, though he was thinking how much of what he did he was told to do by other people. Maybe being grown-up meant not listening.

The house was seined with shadows that crept out of corners and along the hall down which he was pulled as though on roller skates, the hall sloping away under his feet. He looked down at his Keds, laced loose, the left lace dangling. His feet were moving of their own accord. Stop feet, he said, but they kept going. They could have belonged to another little boy, but one just like . . . him.

"Jeb! Don't dawdle!" Rebecca called out from the kitchen, her voice as insinuating as the smoke that puffed from her mouth, the dragon's mouth.

But standing before the mirror he didn't hear Rebecca, he only heard the humming. The surface was satiny smooth under his palms as he stared into the dark eyes so like his own, exactly like his own, and he felt himself begin to slide, growing sleepy.

And then he was plodding up the stairs, feet now heavy lead weights, reluctant to leave the ground. Where was the Mommy person? He was worried and nobody else understood, certainly not he, himself, that this was a case of *had to be*.

"Where is she?" he asked after the bath in which he had sat, stubbornly not soaping himself. Dried, dressed, and in bed, he listened as the Rebecca person read, the book open in her hands, her voice a droning.

Rebecca knew whom he meant. "I told, you, out with a friend."

Friend . . . friend . . . friend. . . .

After their chapter, after the light that Rebecca read by, the one on the bedside table, was out, he lay awake and thought, *friend*. . . .

That Melissa person was a friend.

That Lee person was a friend.

A friend was a bad thing like the water in the bathtub, which, if he wasn't careful, would soak inside him and make him go all soft and yucky like the sponge in the kitchen sink.

He listened to Rebecca downstairs, her sounds faint and far away, then he heard her come back up the stairs again, and saw through the narrowed slits of half-shuttered eyes that she had stopped in his doorway for just a minute. Then she went up into her room. The TV popped on. Laughter. Music.

Jeb waited while his heart beat slowly, steadily. He put his hand over his chest and smiled at the unremitting thump, thump. Then he got out of bed and dressed himself again. He had to put on clean jeans and T-shirt, and a fresh pair of socks taken, rolled up, from the dresser drawer.

He moved without making noise, as though he were weightless, as though he were a ghost sliding down the stairs. He stopped before the mirror where he smiled, running the reel of words through his head, and then, before the humming could start, ran quickly into the kitchen.

The knives gleamed in darkness in the drawer under the counter, their shiny, glittering blades clean and sharp. He took the largest one he could find, slid the edge along his finger, feeling the pain of it that was no pain at all, as a red line the width of a hair sprang up across the pad of his thumb.

Outside it was dark, darker than the inside of the closet without the bare bulb glowing. No moon, the stars hovering behind clouds that slipped and faltered. Methodically, he made his way to the end of the dirt road and put one foot out on the macadam, glancing right and left into silence. Far away he heard an owl hooting and further than that the swish, swish of tires out on Route Nine. The night was stuffed full with silence and night noises that swayed and tossed.

He crawled into the brush behind the mailbox, flag up, and made himself a burrow of old leaves to sit cross-legged upon, and went still as an animal waiting for its prey.

It didn't take long.

Jamie had to let go of Maggie's hand as he down-shifted to make the turn into the Four Oaks' access road. He was feeling good about himself, satisfied in a way that had nothing to do with sex. The TR was filled with yet another smell of her, honey and lemons, and he had kept saying all the way from the restaurant, I love you. And each time he said it, she laughed, but there was nothing derisive in her laughter. It was a happy sound, ruffled with pleasure.

"Think about it, about us, Maggie," he said as he pulled up just short of where the lawn began, black as a pond with shifting depths.

She leaned into him, kissing his cheek, holding onto him for a second before pulling away, saying, "I don't know. Change is hard for me. And options. It's been a long time since I could make choices for myself. So much has happened, Jamie. If I could go back again to the beginning—" she stopped, her face splintered by shadows that the dash light splayed up. "I'll call you. Let me think."

"Maggie—"

But she was gone. He watched her run across the grass, into the house, where for an instant he could see her in the open doorway, before darkness was slammed shut on him once more.

He put the TR into reverse and turned it around, heading back down the dirt road, going slowly. Just at the end something darted out from the brush. He hit the brakes, and there in the shaft of light the high beams threw he saw Jeb, his right arm outstretched, smiling at him.

"Hey," he said through the rolled-down window, "what are you doing out here this time of night?" But Jeb didn't answer. He stood still as a tree planted firmly in the road, the smile like a layer of paint across his mouth.

A tickle of apprehension hit Jamie between the shoulder blades, but he got out of the car, leaving the engine running, and approached the little boy. "Jeb, you should be home. In bed, sleeping." The boy didn't speak. Jamie inched toward him, thinking, he's six, yeah, that's right six, so why are you scared. "Com'on, I'll take you back to the house. Your Mom's going to be worried when she finds you gone."

The arm stuck straight out like an iron bar. Jamie would have thought Jeb was sleepwalking except that he was dressed in jeans and a T-shirt and not in pajamas. "Is something wrong, kid?"

They eyed one another across three feet of dirt and rocks. All the saliva dried up in Jamie's mouth, and he could hear his blood thundering through his veins. He had the feeling that this wasn't a little boy, that this was something awful and terrible and had been spewed up by the night, by the woods on either side of the road. Even now, the trees seemed to be inching toward him. He could almost feel the scrape of branches against his back, the leafy arms bending, creeping at his shanks. The thickness of his fear swamped his thought, sucked him down, and he lashed out at himself. Stop it, you idiot. He's only a kid. And then, pushing himself forward, he closed the distance, stretched out his own hand for the hand beckoning him down a long road more lonely than this one, darker, and heavier with dread. He was being drawn down a path he had never traveled before; he saw that in the boy's eyes, but it was too late now. He knew it was too late, but he couldn't stop himself. His fingers reached for the baby fingers, curled into the little boy hand cold as winter, and all his bones went loose as feathers, and he could feel his bladder giving way, the warm spill of urine down his pants legs, as the hair on the back of his neck went rigid from fear. Jeb's left hand—hidden behind his back Jamie saw far too late—came forward. The knife, swift as a snake springing, launched itself right into the soft midsection above his belt.

He gazed down stupidly just as the boy dropped his hand from the hilt, just a second before he let go of the freezing little fingers and saw that the knife was buried right in his guts, and thought, there isn't so much blood.

17

The heat was unremitting during the last weeks of
August, the sun heavy in the sky day after day, and Maggie
thought that at last she too was incinerating. She was
constantly feverish, burning up, and though the heat was
coming from her insides as much as from the sun, there
seemed no relief. Often now she slept until late afternoon,
and when she wasn't sleeping she'd sit on the porch and
stare off into space. Trying not to think, to escape her
memories, she managed to forget many things. Sometimes, for example, she'd reach for the phone to call Jamie
and even begin dialing before she remembered he'd been
found lying dead on the dirt road. Sometimes, when she
remembered that, she'd imagine he was still there, sprawled
in the dust, rocks cutting into his cheek, the knife jutting
out of his belly like a strange appendage.

It was the postman who found him, a Mr. Savage who
"never in my twenty-one years of driving this route came
across anything like this. No siree, I ain't never stumbled
over a corpse before when all I intended was to leave some
letters in the box." Savage had driven up in his official
black Ford—U.S. Mail neatly stenciled on the side—and
seen the TR in the middle of the road, door ajar, and lying
before it looking "just like a bag of mail," Jamie's body.

Mr. Savage had left his Ford blocking the road and run
down to Four Oaks where he banged on the front door, his

face flushed with terror. Rebecca let him in to use the telephone to call the Brighton police.

Maggie had still been sleeping, though it was after ten. Jeb had been watching cartoons on television in the study. But they all had gone into the kitchen to watch Mr. Savage propped up against the counter, his face all red and sweaty, though it was a chilly morning, using the phone.

Maggie knew when he said, "One of those little bitty foreign cars, don't recall the make," but went anyway down the long, long length of the drive, her silk robe flapping about her ankles to Rebecca's—

"—Mrs. Brace, please wait. Don't—"

And Mr. Savage's, "Hey, lady," as he ran after her, his short legs pumping, his breath wheezing out from under the salt and pepper mustache that abutted his mouth. "Hey, lady, don't go down there."

She went without thinking, thoughts slammed to a dead stop in her brain, having to see for herself, having to have that image which Mr. Savage had described on the phone spread out before her. Nothing would make it real unless she saw for herself, though later, even that memory, sometimes fading like an old tintype or going to sepia and browning along the edges, or sometimes so vivid on the inside of her eyelids that it might be there all over again, was a bad dream. Jamie might still be waiting dead in the road, his arms twisted under him, legs pushed up, hands locked in place on the hilt of the knife. Or Jamie still might be in the examining room of that office on Dumont Street, stitching up cuts, thumping chests, straining to catch arrhythmic heart beats, taking temperatures.

She waited with Mr. Savage as the sun rushed toward noon. They heard the sirens coming from a long way off, shrieking decibels of pain, screaming Maggie's pain, which was like little crystals detonating in the blood.

Maggie never took her eyes from Jamie's body—his

corpse—lying there at her feet, in such an unnatural position that her first thought was, Jamie, get up, you can't be comfortable.

This is one death too many, one death I can't emcompass, she said to herself, as Chief Kessel lumbered out of the police car, his shirt already stained with half-moons of sweat, and hunched down, fingers on the side of Jamie's neck searching for a pulse. He looked up at her and said, as though she had asked him for verification, "Yeah, he's dead."

The final statement from which there was no turning back or going forward either. The period. The last sentence of a story.

Dead. Four letters strung together, she thought, that drain all the light out of the sky, and it did seem as though Kessel in that moment of saying, "dead," took the day with him, put it in his pocket buttoning the flap. A gray haze settled like dust over the road.

Afterwards, they said she had fainted or started to faint, folding up as though someone had snapped her spine shut. Savage caught her and held her and finally took her to the side of the road behind the TR so that when she came to she wouldn't be looking at Jamie dead.

"The way I figure it," Kessel said later, sitting once again in the study of Four Oaks, this time holding a glass of iced tea that Rebecca had thrust at him without asking if he wanted any, "is that somebody stopped him lookin' for a ride. You know, a drifter. This part of the country is filled with no-goods in the summer. Addicts; the worst. There was a rock festival over by Ridgefield, so it could of been one of them. We got an all-points out for suspicious characters, for crazies. Whoever did it never even went through his pockets, though. Senseless," he said, shaking his head, rolling the glass back and forth between his palms. "Senseless."

Maggie had told him she'd heard the TR drive off. Rebecca, up in her room that overlooked the side lawn of Four Oaks, heard the same thing, though she didn't see the car when she glanced out the window, couldn't have anyway. But she heard it. Heard Maggie coming in the door, heard her on the stairs. Not that Kessel ever thought . . . he dribbled off into silence, his little eyes dark with suspicion.

"He took me out for dinner," Maggie had said first to Kessel then to David who returned to Brighton hours later by way of Hartford and a rented car, flying in on the first plane he could get out of Chicago. "Just dinner."

Kessel talked about drifters, about strangers, about crazy dope addicts and rock freaks, about nuts who always go after doctors looking for pills, for morphine, yet all the time he followed Maggie with his eyes, never letting her stray from the frame he snapped over and over like a mug shot while he drank his iced tea. His eyes still followed her while he smoked a Benson & Hedges, pinching it between his fingers as though smoking it was the last thing he wanted to do—which was true since he was trying to wind down with Smoke Enders and normally smoked Lucky Strikes—and explained to David, "It hadda be a nut."

But that didn't stop him from searching Four Oaks, which he had sense enough to do before David arrived. He went through the house along with two deputies who didn't seem much older than teenagers. One, with hair fluttering his collar, might have been that kind of rock groupie whom Kessel said he detested for their foul ways. They searched from stem to stern, turning over cushions, opening drawers, bending low to browse beneath beds and chairs and sofas, but paying particular attention, Maggie would recall, to her room, to her clothes, to the cellar where they looked in the washing machine, the dryer, the dirty laundry hamper.

But they knew she had nothing to do with Jamie's dying, his death, they said.

"I heard that car drive off and right away I heard Mrs. Brace coming up the steps," Rebecca had told them.

But they searched anyway.

Looking for blood, Maggie thought and watched them in her bedroom hold up the white pants and green shirt that she had worn and tossed over the chair.

"A no-good," Kessel had said to David whose face was stubbled with a five o'clock shadow, whose suit needed a pressing, and whose hair was mussed as he treaded his hands through it restlessly.

And that was the end of it for Kessel, who grumpily hauled in every suspicious character he landed in his net, ruthlessly interrogated him, but tossed each one back, not one of them weighty enough to pin a murder on. As for David, that was the end also. He said to Maggie, he was sorry because he understood that Jamie had become a friend, that they shared a similar past, "and you don't need someone else dying on you." A statement so unfeeling, so egregious, that after Maggie told Klein David had said it, Klein, in a rage that was both uncharacteristic and unprofessional, tracked David down in his office high up over Madison Avenue and demanded to see him the next morning at nine. David refused. He told Klein on the phone that he neither had the time anymore, nor the inclination, that tragedy stalked Maggie as though she had magnets attached to her spine, and the only thing he could do was keep a level head and hold emotions at bay.

With a rare burst of metaphor, he said, "Unlike Orpheus, I don't intend to look back." And then, "Maggie's a diviner, she points toward death."

Klein lost his temper and yelled into the phone, "That's the biggest bunch of bullshit I ever heard!"

David hung up on him and sat in his light-filled office with his head in his hands, feeling as though he was walking across quicksand. He was afraid to stay at Four Oaks and just as afraid to leave. He didn't believe anymore than Klein held the key to Maggie's well-being, that there was even the possibility left that she could eventually float back to the shores of sanity. Too much had happened, and it was true that too many people had died, and that all those deaths—which he had never for a moment truly blamed Maggie for—were still somehow her responsibility. As if her madness were catching. But, of course, he didn't believe that either. Just that she was a jinx, and, more important, he didn't want a life any longer that read like a bad novel or the latest edition of the *National Enquirer*.

The mental coin he had tossed weeks before while trapped in a Saturday traffic jam in Brighton was tossed again, went up and came down and rolled into a crack between the floor boards, because David didn't want Lee either. He had extinguished his need for her just as surely as he had beaten out the flame and would tell her so tomorrow when she left the hospital.

The only question left was, what did he do now?

For the rest of that day he sat in his office, all his calls on hold, two meetings postponed to a later, unspecified time, his staff of junior lawyers impatiently stalled outside his door, and asked himself—what now?

Among the many things Maggie didn't do after Jamie's death was go see Lee in the hospital, bring her robe, slippers, hairbrush, all those personal belongings she had intended to pick up from Lee's house. The young man from the store went instead, using the key Lee carried on a silver chain with a seashore medallion and had had with her the night of the fire. Maggie even forgot she had a key—*Lee front door house*—and when Lee came out to Four Oaks after her release, Maggie had to spend some time finding it.

Lee, sitting on the front porch of Four Oaks, waited while Maggie searched. Her arms and legs were judiciously hidden—sleeves to her wrists, pants legs to her ankles, and she seemed as enveloped as a Bedouin. She covered her eyes with the darkest of dark glasses and thought, as she looked across the lawn, that the fire was still burning, scurrying along her bones.

David had come to see her in the hospital at first every day, then every other day, then only occasionally, and finally not at all. She watched his attention dwindle and was helpless, as her body mended, to stop the drying up of his love. Her mouth was filled with sand; her eyes felt gritty, but it took her until her first day home to ask, "What's the matter with you, with us?"

He said, mixing a drink in her kitchen and sitting on a high stool facing her, "I don't know." He shrugged and unbuttoned his collar. "Maybe it's just. . ." But he didn't finish, just shrugged again and watched her watching him.

She wanted to hurt him, so she asked, "Was Maggie having an affair with Jamie Evers?"

David brows arched in surprise. "You know," he said, "I never thought of it."

"Don't you care?" she asked, angry at his half-hearted response.

He shrugged again and replied, "Not much. Everything's been washed out of me. If Maggie was screwing her pet doctor, it doesn't matter now."

"What does? Anything? Or are you so anesthetized that you don't have any feelings left?"

He put down the glass and lit a cigarette. "I don't want

to feel anymore. There's been too much pain. The only way to deal with it is not to care."

"For Christ's sake, David," she snapped at him, "you're talking like an idiot."

"Shut up, Lee." But there was no fervor in his voice. She thought she was witnessing a movie in her own kitchen, a screen thrown up, film unwinding, and for a moment could feel again the terrible pain of her burns, that searing of her flesh that had to be damped down with narcotics. Only this time the pain was inside rather than out, and there was no narcotic strong enough to mask it.

"And what about me, David? What about us? Are you going to leave Maggie now that you don't love her anymore?"

"I never said I didn't love Maggie. I'll always love Maggie. How could I not? It's just that if I want to survive," he leaned forward on crossed arms, his breath whistling against her, stale and smelling of smoke, of more than the one drink he was now finishing, "if I want Jeb to survive, I *can't* care anymore."

A knot was forming in Lee's stomach. She thought, I am standing on a road watching two cars bear down on one another, and I'm helpless to stop the collision, but if I have any sense left, I will turn my back. She knew she should leave it alone, knew she shouldn't push David, but she was worn out, achy and tired, and irrationally she thought that words from David, promises from David, could make all that vanish.

"What about us, David? You still haven't answered me."

He pushed the empty glass across the bar toward her and got off the stool. "There is no us left, Lee, not anymore."

"What are you talking about?" she asked, knowing full well just what he was saying, having known he was going to say it before he said it. She had pushed him into it like a fool who has to have her worst fears confirmed.

"I love you just as I love Maggie, and I'll love you forever, just as I will love Maggie. And I can't explain how I can love two women. It makes no sense, but there it is. I've stopped hassling myself about it. I love you both, and I've got to stop caring about the both of you. There's a plague in my life right now, that's all I know. And I want it to stop!" For the first time he raised his voice, and grabbing the glass, he heaved it across the kitchen. It shattered on the wall above the stove. In the stillness that followed he took in great gulps of air. Lee waited unable to move, to shift an inch either way, the burns on her legs throbbing. Then he said, "There's nothing left of us, Lee, not today, not tomorrow. I'm sorry."

But to Lee there was one thing left, one fragment, one act yet to perform.

Now, as she sat in the wicker chair, watching Maggie hand over the front door key, she cut off Maggie's hesitant words of apology, of concern, and said right into Maggie's smiling face, "Do you know that David and I have been having a love affair? It's been going on for over a year, all the time you were in Greenwood and since you've been home."

Maggie's smile died, as though Lee had fired a gun at her point blank and the bullet, shattering bone, had lodged in her brain.

Lee thought, satisfied, she doesn't look so beautiful now. Picking up the keys that had dropped from Maggie's outstretched hand, she lifted herself up, feeling better than she had in a long time.

Somehow David's betrayal was the worst of it. Maggie thought, the absolute most terrible thing that can happen is to lose a child, and I've lost two of them. And, again, the death of someone you care about—even at this point she couldn't say to herself that she loved Jamie—is devas-

tating; and that has occurred also. So why is this simple
fact of adultery, of a love affair, so brutalizing? What has
David done that I didn't also do with Jamie?

School was beginning two days after Labor Day, and
Maggie drove Jeb into town, to the elementary wing of the
consolidated school, a complex of buildings that rambled
haphazardly for a block, and registered him for the first
grade.

"Don't want to go," he said, dragging at her side,
clutching her skirt in his fist. He scuffled his sneakers on
the polished gymnasium floor.

"Why not show Mommy where your classroom was last
year," she said, trying to encourage him. All her sinuses
were clogged. Her thoughts seemed wrapped in bandages. She saw again the white gleam of gauze beneath
the wide sleeves of Lee's shirt. "And look, see, over there
by that table, is your new teacher. Her name is Mrs.
Moran. Let's go meet her."

"No!" he howled and broke away. "I don't want to go to
school."

David had said that Jeb liked school, that he had done
extremely well—if one could judge by finger painting and
block building and his ability to read so well—but then
David lied. She thought, I'll always think of David lying,
always hear the opposite when he says something to me.
Distrust was, she knew, the price she had to pay.

Dejectedly, she followed Jeb out to the parking lot
where she found him sitting in the front seat of the
Dodge, staring intently through the windshield, as though
the Marx Brothers were on the other side cavorting in
horseplay.

"It's okay, sweetness," she said, getting in beside him.
"It will work out. You'll see. School's fun. Lots of interesting things to learn. And friends. I bet you'll have more
friends than anybody else."

He said, firmly, "I have a friend," as though she was stupid for not understanding that.

She knew he meant the little boy in the mirror and gently replied, "Everybody needs real friends, Jebbie, not imaginary ones. Other little boys and girls just like you to play catch with, or hide and seek."

He beat his clenched fist against his legs, but didn't answer her. She thought, driving off, let him alone, he'll be fine once school begins, but she really just didn't want to think about Jeb then. She put him on hold, letting her love for him lap around her, soothing away the fear.

But she couldn't put David out of her mind, David and Lee, David making love with Lee while she, Maggie, was battling against the walls of Greenwood skinning her knuckles, slamming upon her own interior walls, trying to contain the beast and yet bring it out into the light of the day where it would shimmer and fade.

There were too many ghosts now, all the old Davids dancing about when they tucked themselves in bed for the night, each of them careful to remain on his own side of the mattress. David coming for her that first time, up to the apartment on East Eighty-Third Street, talking with her father before the fireplace, a highball in a crystal glass upon the mantel, the sweet smell of warmth and of pine logs burning. It was snowing outside, and the flakes drifted down soft as confetti falling. She wore a beaver coat and high boots and her head was bare, and when they got into the taxi he leaned over and kissed the wetness on her hair. There was David when Tracy was born, with his arms full of orchids, blossoms cascading over him, a cigar unlit in the corner of his mouth. There was David. And there was David. . . .

Maggie didn't, though, tell him what Lee had said. She wouldn't confront him in the downy hours of the night. She surveyed the ghosts instead, read romance novels, listened to Haydn on the stereo, and said to Klein, "Everything is calm now. I think I've come to terms at last."

She knew that Jamie was never going to answer the phone.

And Sarah wasn't in the kitchen making supper.

She found the baby books for Tracy and Kathy and relived each moment of their short lives, then closed the pink satin covers and put the books away again.

It was a week of calm if not serenity, a week muffled in cotton batting, all the hard edges muted. Maggie saw that week as being the rest of her life, of getting up in the morning and having her coffee on the front porch, of driving into Brighton to buy fresh meat, fish, vegetables, and flowers. The house, like a funeral parlor, was filled with flowers. She saw herself forever giving instructions to Rebecca on what to make for dinner, of losing herself in the saccharine story of boy meets girl only to lose her and then find her once more, or forgetting herself in other people's imaginary tales, just as Jeb lost himself in the game of the mirror. And of sleeping heavily, buried in the watery depths of an ocean, so deep that even dreams didn't intrude.

It never occurred to her that David would leave her.

"I have to talk to you, Maggie," he said, the night of a Labor Day that had been hot with the ferocity of dying summer.

They were on the front porch, Rebecca off for the weekend, Jeb asleep in his bed. The night air, cool now and smelling tartly of fall, clicked with unseen life. The moon cast a silvery, icy coating across the lawn. Maggie was wrapped in a long sweater, her bare feet curled up under her in the corner of the wicker loveseat. David sat too far away for her to see him clearly in the dim light that oozed from the house.

"What about?" she asked.

Then he told her. "I'm going to London," he said. "I'm leaving at the end of the next week, and I'm taking Jeb with me. Rosen has found us a house in Hempstead and someone to run it. I'll be taking over the London office."

Maggie sat up, her feet on the cold planks of the porch. "I don't understand," she said.

He lit a cigarette, the glowing tip burning a hole in the night, and said, "I want a divorce, Maggie. It's over for us. Nothing's left but Jeb, and I'm taking him away before something happens to him too."

"And Lee?" she asked.

"Lee? What about her?"

"She told me that you and she—"

David interrupted. "I'm sorry about Lee, Maggie. I wish I could explain that to you, or wipe it out somehow, but it happened. Now that's over too. Lee won't be coming to England with us."

Maggie was suddenly nauseated, sick to her stomach. The last section of her life was breaking away, flowing out to sea, and she was helpless to stop it. But she tried, whispering, "David, no, you can't do this to me."

"God, Maggie, I don't want to, but I don't have a choice any more. I have to get away, from you, from the past, from—" Abruptly, he stood up and began pacing the porch. "I have to get away from everything."

"No, David, no. I won't let you do this to me, to Jeb!"

Her voice rose, drifting upward into the porch ceiling, rising up to the ledge of Jeb's window where, lying awake in his bed, curled like a question mark on his side, he listened to his mother, to his father, and his heart was a wooden block in his chest. He had never been so scared in his life, hearing as he couldn't help doing, his world coming apart down below on the porch. Mommy and Daddy leaving one another, Daddy taking him somewhere, to that place, London, that he had never heard of, out of Four Oaks, away from the mirror, away from himself. . . .

He bolted out of his bed, galvanized by fear that rivered through him, and flung himself from the room, rushing on bare feet down the steps to the mirror where he leveled himself upon himself and cried, tears creating smudged, wet spots on the glass.

Mommy is going away again. . . . No, this time I'm going away with Daddy, and Mommy isn't going to be there, in that other place, in—

Hmmmmm.

—yes, the sky was coming down, soaring through space, clouds sinking into fog, the moon and the stars and the sun all flying toward the ground, which was beginning to churn, the beast within angry, grumbling, struggling, hurling rocks.

The humming grew to a roar.

He knew it was going to happen, the Daddy person this time, betraying him. He thought the Mommy person was going to do it, but he'd stopped her. He'd stuck a knife into the Doctor person, and that stopped her from going away again. This time it was the Daddy, and if he didn't do something quickly, there was going to be a smash-up and he'd be pressed just as flat as a piece of paper between the pages of a book.

He flew back up the steps and crawled into the still warm bed.

He waited, sitting up, his back against the headboard, the pillow clutched to his stomach, knowing he couldn't leave Four Oaks, certain he needed to stay here, in this old house with its creaky, whiney ways. He thought of himself as having been born here, of coming truly to life here, and if he left, would the other go too, or would he be trapped, forever a prisoner?

The earth was in spasm, and crouching there in the

bed, he was surprised the others didn't feel it, didn't have to hold on as he had to do now to the headboard, to the small spires of wood. And still the sky was descending, cascading through time and space. He thought of the bugs in the killing jars, thought of the beetles squashed to death between his fingers, and felt the grip on his chest and spine as the voices below rose, fell, attacked his skin, inched in through his pores until suddenly there was silence. For an instant the earth seemed to settle, the sky slowing its rocketing descent, and Jeb heard first the Mommy person come up the stairs and then the Daddy, the roaring whirlpool of the night eddying about the house. He wouldn't have been surprised to look out the window and find the house sailing through the sky like one of those stars that flashed and sparked and plummeted to the ground.

The Mommy person and the Daddy person went into different rooms. *She* went to where they always slept together in that big bed, and *he* went down the hall to the little room that looked out over the back porch.

And Jeb waited, all the whooshing of the disintegrating world in his ears.

He knew about choosing and he knew didn't have any choice. It was a *had to be* thing.

He squinted into the darkness that was heavier now, as if all the light too was being squeezed away, and then crept from the bed again and went down to the kitchen.

The knives in the drawer whispered up at him, each one pleading, take me, take me, each one seeming to leap forward like darting minnows in the pool in the woods, until his hand grasped the long, triangular-bladed knife he'd seen them chop vegetables with. It fit neatly against his palm, his fingers curling over the wooden shaft, and he remembered how it was out on the road, that Doctor person moving in slow motion through the glare of the headlights, the knife—much like this one—rising, rising, in a satisfying swing that made his stomach tingle as it rose and then shot into flesh as easily as cutting into butter.

He licked his lips and padded out of the kitchen, the mirror beyond him, the mirror with its sheen of gray film. Upstairs in the hallway he listened to their sleeping sounds, holding off the sky by an act of will he wasn't conscious of, and went past the Mommy person's door, to the end where the Daddy person dreamed away, dreaming awful things that Jeb could almost pull from his drowsing mind right through the door where he stood waiting with the knife, his other hand around the knob.

Slowly, slowly, he turned the knob, and opened the door.

The room throbbed with moonlight, white, chilled light that caressed the window and splayed out over the floor with its small brown rug, and onto the bed, lapping in waves, onto the face of the Daddy turned upward, the Daddy person on his back, his mouth slack, tiny whistles of breath escaping through parted lips. Jeb saw how the sheets journeyed up and down in the watery gleaming and went forward.

David stirred in sleep, the edges of a dream burning away, the corners curling, the long, straight wall up which he was climbing slipping beneath his feet so that he was all at once sliding backwards, the air singing in his ears, as he felt the coldness of the knife, of death falling down to him as he was rising up to meet it. He came awake suddenly, wide awake, his eyes opening just as the knife reached the sheets, cut through the flowered percale. . . .

Yelling, "Jeb! Jeb! What the hell are you doing!" He rolled away, and the knife slashed through the sheets into the fleshy part of David's upper left arm, right through muscles and fatty tissue, and plunked against the bone. He could hear it strike the long, thin humerus, as his blood spewed out of the wound. And then the knife was withdrawn, and Jeb came slashing at him again.

"Jesus!" he was screaming, "Jesus, Jeb, are you crazy! What are you doing? Jeb!"

In a final burst of energy like that which had taken him along the wall in his dream, he jerked away, right out of the bed to the floor and came up on his haunches, straight up, dizziness assailing him. He shook his head trying to clear his vision. Warm blood jetisoned down his arm. And then he lunged across the bed at his son, whose eyes in the moonlight were on fire, and whose skin was so chalky he was a specter there on the other side.

"My God," David said with awe in his voice, "you're trying to kill me!"

Jeb ran, dropping the knife in the bed, running so fast that when David blinked he was no longer there, like a nightmare unseated from sleep with the first flush of morning. Only the blood remained and the pain as he called out, shaking so badly that he stumbled, falling across the mattress. "Maggie, Maggie, help me, Maggie."

Maggie, asleep in her own dreaming tide, thought that she heard David calling, David's voice painfully throbbing.

"Maggie, oh, please, God, Maggie! Help!"

Inch by inch she threaded her way out of sleep, and opening her eyes, she thought: I do hear David calling.

Maggieeeee

Mommeeeee

It was Tracy screaming, begging her to save them—

Mommeeeee

Kathy shrieking for help—

No! No! She sat up and listened.

"*Maggie!*"

It was David down in the second guest room, not the room that had been hers, the other one, sterile and unused.

"David?" she called back and opened the door. The hall was empty, the runner a dark stream stretched end to end like a current of blood. "David?" she called down to the gaping door of the guest room through which, even at this distance, she could see the thin blade of moonlight. "Are you all right, David?"

"Maggie, help me!"

Don't go! her mind screeched at her. Don't go. If you do, something terrible will happen. If you do, nothing will ever be the same.

Frightening thoughts whistled through her mind. She took one step into the hall and couldn't move. It wasn't possible to go ahead, nor to return to her bed, to sleep.

David groaned. The sound escaped through the door and bounced along the hall to where Maggie stood rooted. She didn't want to move, but suddenly came unstuck and ran. This time she was going to get inside the bedroom, beat out the flames flaring along her daughters' limbs. This time, she told herself, I'll save them.

"David!" she called, "Wait, David, I'm coming!"

He was half in the bed, his legs on the floor, his hands clenching the sheet. Blood was everywhere. She had to go around to the far side of the bed and, braced against the wall, lever him up so that he sprawled on his stomach. Carefully she turned him over, then lifted his legs, straightening them out along the crumpled blanket. Her hands came away sticky with blood, and she left markings over him, over her nightgown, her own body.

"What happened? You're hurt. I'll get help." Words jumbled together, running into one another. She could barely breathe her heart thumped so rapidly, her rib cage vibrating. She was freezing even in the warm bath of blood.

"I'll get help," she cried, holding onto his unwounded arm, afraid to move, to go out into the hall again.

He whispered, and she had to bend close to his mouth to hear him say, "Jeb stabbed me."

Maggie drew back as though he had struck her, reeling away from the foul smell of his breath, of what he was saying.

"No!" she cried out and fell back to the wall. "He didn't! You were dreaming."

"This isn't a dream, Maggie," he said, power edging into his voice as if someone had switched the electricity back on. "It was Jeb. He stabbed me. Look around, the knife is here somewhere."

"No!" she cried again, "it's . . . it's . . . it's not Jeb. Somebody else. There's somebody else in the house, I'm going to call the police."

She inched along the wall, feeling for the door, which eventually loomed up under her fingers. "Just lie still. I'll be right back," she said, and forced herself to turn around, to face the rest of the house waiting for her there in darkness.

She didn't want to step out, to leave the room. As terrible as it was to remain with David and all that blood, to have to hear him say it again—*Jeb stabbed me*—she wanted to stay.

Silence oozed through all the crannies in the old house, as though every corner was alive with unseen terrors, a silence that she couldn't penetrate even as she descended the stairs that this night didn't make a sound.

She would not think about what David had said, not now, not ever. This was one horror she was incapable of grasping, that she had to secret away in the back of a drawer, or in a deep well too far down in the earth for anyone to find it.

Jeb couldn't have stabbed David, yet she knew that he had.

She held onto the wall with one hand and the railing

with the other, stretched across the steps, each tread rising up to meet her bare foot as she went down, down.

As she reached the lower hall, she heard the humming. She knew where to look, right to the front of the house where the mirror hung on the far wall.

"Jeb?" she called and fumbled for the light switch just at the edge of the wall.

There was a blur of movement, as though she wasn't focusing properly. And a scramble of little boy arms and legs went crashing through the front door which gaped wide, then banged back on her. The humming went also, into the night.

Maggie ran, flying, her feet barely touching the floor. She was out on the porch, the wood cold, as though rimed with an early frost.

The grass was wet as she left the porch and careened across the lawn dizzily, trying to snatch the ghostly glimmer with her fingertips. But the light was so bad, the only glow slipping through one window, through the screen, and then the crescent moon that slid backwards and forwards behind the tufted clouds.

One moment she thought she saw him, but immediately he was gone, and she couldn't call out; the cry strangled in her throat, impeding her breathing. Around at the back, just at the steps, she imagined she saw him again, but again she was wrong. He was there and he wasn't, every way she turned. First to the right and in a moment on the left. A montage of little boys in pajamas danced in her vision.

I should go back, she thought, and call for an ambulance, seeing David cut and so grievously bleeding. But she couldn't leave Jeb here in the night. His secret place, she remembered suddenly, and ran to look there. But bending low she stared into darkness so total she might have closed her eyes.

All at once she heard a thud and knew he had run back into the house. She took off again, tripping on her nightgown, falling flat and getting up to her knees, all in one motion.

The mirror, she thought, he's going back to the mirror. And she forced herself upright, pushing herself to run faster, gaining the front door and the hall just as he did the mirror.

Yes, there was something, somebody, some *monstrosity* in front of the mirror. A person with too many arms and legs.

She saw Jeb before the mirror, Jeb with his pajamas streaked with blood, Jeb with his blond hair standing up in rough ridges on his head.

She saw Jeb without any blood on him, not even a speck, Jeb with his face all clean and unmarked by smudges of blood.

She saw two Jebs, two little boys with round cheeks and upturned noses, full pink lips. Only for a second one of the faces wasn't so innocent, all furrowed with anger, skin tight as parchment over bones. But then that face smoothed out until it matched the other.

There were two little boys in identical pajamas; two little boys exactly the same, standing before the mirror. *Two little boys who were mirror images of one another.*

And they both opened their mouths at the same moment, tiny white teeth barely visible behind two pairs of soft baby lips.

"Mommy! Mommy!" rang out at her, echoed and slapped the walls. "Mommy!" they cried, the two voices merging.

She moved down the hall to the boys, the mirror, her temperature having plunged so that she felt frozen, a block of ice sliding along, numb, without feeling. Her throat had closed, locking in the scream that pounded on her insides, and she wished in that moment, wished frantically, that she could spiral back down again into madness. She no longer wanted sanity like an aching lover. But she was stranded, and all her visions were real. She wasn't imagining, lost in the whorls of her own mind.

There *were* two little Jebs, two little boys, and she understood with the sharp edge of terror that she had been right all along. She thought her brain would burst with the impossible knowing. And soaring down the hall, she wanted violently, wanted more than anything now, to have been wrong.

Her arms were thrust before her like those of a sleep walker, pushing away nightmares, while the two little boys with the same expression gazed up at her, screams flying like bats from their mouths. Then she was upon them, right at the mirror, the mirror in which she saw herself in motion.

And there was only Maggie.

There wasn't even one little Jeb reflected in the glass.

For one long unbreaking moment, her eyes wide, she stared at herself staring back, trapped there on the other side, and began to howl with an inhuman sound. She keened and shrilled and, whirling about, flailed her arms right and left at the two little figures. She struck first one, then the other, her hands coming away bloody. The screaming reverberated in her mouth, in her head. She was filled with screaming as her hands grasped hold of one little pair of shoulders, leaving bloody tracks. And she flung that child—her vision so clouded it was impossible to see—flung him, it, they, them. The madness came alive then in her, a rabid dog, lashing out, biting, savage jaws snapping. And one child struck the other, the thud of one small body with bones as delicate as a bird's, ricocheting off the other, smearing the blood across both faces and hands and pajamas.

There were two little boys, the same down to the last molecule, and now both of them were imprinted with blood, David's blood, and some of their own, as Maggie mercilessly threw them about. She didn't know, couldn't tell any longer, which one was which, which came from inside the mirror and which belonged out.

Dementedly, she clawed at them, catching one child, shaking him like a rag doll, and screaming, "Tell me! Who are you?" And he didn't answer, couldn't tell her, as she threw him against the hard slick surface of the mirror. The tremors from the impact raced up her arms.

The two children whirled about her like dervishes, and she slapped at them, hitting one a glancing blow to the head, slapping one so hard in the face that blood flew, arced, from his nose. She flailed at one—or was it the other? There was no way of knowing now.

One boy came within her reach, and she grasped a right arm, and then snared another one, two different arms, and spun both children about her as they kicked at her legs, howling with rage and with fear.

She heard them shrieking, heard her own ragged cries, heard the humming so loud that the house shook with it. And heard over that David crying her name.

David was at the bottom of the stairs, holding onto the railing, blood streaming in riverlets down onto the runner.

Maggie looked up wildly, and her eyes locked with those of her husband's, only David's eyes had sunk far down into bone. His face was limned with terror and knowing, but before she could run to him she lost her footing and fell in a tangle of little boy limbs.

Blows from four little fists rained down at her head. Fighting them off, she caught the legs of one Jeb and climbed to her knees, clawing her way along the small body. She rose to her feet, and with all the strength she had left in her—her screams in waves pitching through the house—she lifted him in her arms and threw that one, that single child, as hard as she could, at the mirror.

The glass splintered in long, deep grooves like the earth splitting open. Small cracks danced off the larger ones. Shards fell to the carpet, and there, suddenly, was a screeching, contorted little boy, with a Jeb face, embroidered by stitches, by black streams. And a little boy, a Jeb body in pajamas, two buttons opened at the top, on the other side, beneath the cracks that ran rampant through his skin. There was one little boy smeared with blood behind the rippling veins flying to the edges of the mirror, right to the frame where the snake lifted up his scaly head and hissed.

One little Jeb beat at the mirror from the inside, diamondlike pieces scattering in a shower over her feet. His mouth, opened wide, shrilled soundless screams against the humming that slowly was ebbing away, growing softer.

Maggie cried louder, turning away from the gargoyle in the glass who was coming apart in triangular sections as the humming diminished and died.

She spun away from her son's face, Jebbie's face slashed by lines, by tears, pulsing with anger, to the other Jebbie, waiting outside of the mirror's sphere of vision, away from the possibility of his own reflection.

And she wasn't sure. Which Jebbie had been sucked into the void, disintegrated in the shattered glass? Which one was it who remained outside, still as death now watching her? *Which one?* Him or the other?

She frantically looked to David to tell her, but he had sunk to the steps where he sprawled. Only his eyes were gaping, two terrible dark pits, and his mouth had dropped open as blood trickled across his lips. "Maggie," she thought she heard him whisper, "forgive me."

The terror and the pain were all too much for Maggie, the unending darkness trying to snare her, pulling at the edges of the ragged nightgown, crawling with insidious fingers up her legs. One last time she cried aloud as she fell to the floor and drew the Jebbie who remained against her breasts, feeling the thud of his heart near to her own. And she thought, I don't have any choice, there's only one left. She said to herself, this is Jebbie, and I've saved him. And clutching him to her she started the long crawl to David because she had to save him, too.

The one little Jeb, his cheek against her cheek, didn't speak, letting her hold onto him, docile as she dragged him with her across the floor. And then slowly, very slowly, he lifted up his left hand and stroked her hair, smiling secretly.

"Mommy," he said sweetly, his breath so cold on her skin that she stopped, "you broke the mirror. Now you'll have seven years bad luck."

ABOUT THE AUTHOR

DIANA HENSTELL grew up in Forest City, Pennsylvania. She has two children—Joshua and Abigail—a German shepherd, Casey, and two cats—Shadow and Rosebud. They all live in New York City. Before becoming a writer, she worked as an editor in publishing.

The captivating new bestseller by the author of
A WOMAN OF SUBSTANCE

VOICE
OF THE
HEART
by Barbara Taylor Bradford

Katherine Tempest, actress, star, ravishing paradox. Her greatest role was her own life, supported by the best of friends and lovers—until she betrayed them all.

Victor Mason, film idol and producer, gambled his career and fortune on the unknown actress who would soon make his nightmares come true.

Lady Francesca Cunningham, English aristocrat and biographer, gave her trust and loyalty unwisely, and far too soon.

Nicholas Latimer, bestselling novelist, was immune to Katherine's dangerous allure—until he fell passionately in love. . . .

Four destinies inextricably intertwined; twenty-three years of blind ambition, incestuous friendship and reckless love that swept them from the playgrounds and palaces of Europe to New York's glittering towers, from the hectic crossroads of Hollywood and Vine to the silent VOICE OF THE HEART.

Buy VOICE OF THE HEART, on sale March 1, 1984, wherever Bantam paperbacks are sold, or use this handy coupon below for ordering:

DON'T MISS
THESE CURRENT
Bantam Bestsellers

RELAX!

SIT DOWN

and Catch Up On Your Reading!

SPECIAL
MONEY SAVING
OFFER

Now you can have an up-to-date listing of Bantam's hundreds of titles plus take advantage of our unique and exciting bonus book offer. A special offer which gives you the opportunity to purchase a Bantam book for only 50¢. Here's how!

By ordering any five books at the regular price per order, you can also choose any other single book listed (up to a $4.95 value) for just 50¢. Some restrictions do apply, but for further details why not send for Bantam's listing of titles today!

Just send us your name and address plus 50¢ to defray the postage and handling costs.